CHRISTINA's SAGA:

From Norway to Dakota Territory

Wayne P. Anderson

Published by Compass Flower Press
an imprint of AKA-Publishing
Columbia, Missouri
AKA-Publishing.com

Second Edition 2015

ISBN: 978-1-942168-13-3

CHRISTINA's SAGA:

From Norway to Dakota Territory

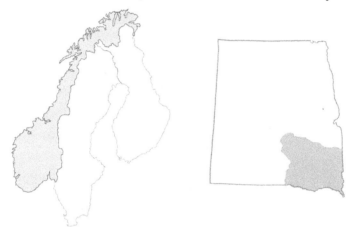

Wayne P. Anderson

CONTENTS

This book is dedicated to my Scandinavian
grandparents, both maternal and paternal,
who risked the dangers of the unknown
to find a better life in America.

PREFACE

I grew up in an extended family noted for not letting the bare facts stand in the way of telling a good story as long as the spirit rang true to our heritage and the conditions of the time. Many of those tales centered on my maternal grandmother, Christina, who emigrated in 1880 from Norway alone at age nineteen and homesteaded in South Dakota. In that same spirit I have woven those stories together imagining how this family matriarch might have coped in both sites.

Christina's story is based on many sources. First my parents told me a few stories that included how her fisherman father died. Then my older cousins, who had met her, gave me more incidents from her life in Norway, such as the bear assaulting her cow through the roof of the cottage.

Cousin Clayton Carlson in Watertown, South Dakota, introduced me to the editor who gathered the stories of the Hamlin County settlers into a book that also included maps of the homesteads so I could find who lived next to Christina and could read their stories and imagine their lives. My sister-in-law Jacqueline Erickson provided a helpful family tree.

At one time I collected books about pioneer women which gave me insights into the problems of homesteading, such as the isolation that can result in cabin fever, what we now know as a reaction to sensory deprivation. I learned about a Lapp wolf hunter in a book written in the 1880s that I can no longer locate in my university library. Christina's meeting with him is pure fiction. The ski trip to Russia to trade, however, was told to me by my cousin Marvin Anderson. My older sister

Gladys Larson remembered our grandmother and told me Christina didn't like to talk much about her past but preferred to dwell on the good life she had achieved here in America.

Finally I interviewed my mother's cousin who was 104 years old at the time. Although she didn't tell me much that was entirely new, it was still an important part of this interesting experience of reaching far back in time to learn about my heritage.

CHRISTINA's SAGA:
BOOK ONE
NORWAY

NORWAY

CHAPTER ONE

THE ISLAND

Summer 1870

The man plodded up the rocky slope toward the graveyard, his eyes down concentrating on his feet. A bouquet of pansies and forget-me-nots hung loosely in his left hand. Sweat filmed his brow and his face was flushed from the midsummer heat. He scratched his full red beard and mopped the sweat off his forehead with a handkerchief from the pocket of his stiff blue Sunday trousers.

Her blond pigtails flying, a small girl raced around the corner of the church and skidded to a stop in front of him. "Come on, Pa, don't be so slow. I've already been to Ma's grave." She grabbed his hand and pulled with the eager impatience of a ten-year-old. Anders increased his pace to keep up with his skipping daughter.

"I'm never in a hurry to get to the graveyard, Christina. We'll all spend plenty of time here soon enough." Under his breath he muttered, "If a good blow and the fishes don't get us first, that is."

Christina dropped his hand and moved down the row of tombstones. Anders stood watching, marveling at how her feet danced as she flitted from one stone to another. She stopped abruptly in front of one of the headstones and asked, "Where are the men buried? These are mostly women and children's graves."

Anders handed her the flowers and sat down on the low rock wall that bordered the cemetery. He patted the sun warmed stone next to him and put his arm around the girl's shoulders when she climbed up next to him. Clearing his throat, he began, "The Sea is cruel to us fishermen. We don't get a living from her without a fight and sometimes we lose. The bodies of most of the men aren't here because they're buried on the bottom of the sea."

"I don't understand," she said, looking up at him from eyes blue as the ocean with sunlight dancing across it.

His face clouded. "Too many storms and no way to know when one will come at us. All over the world people have heard of the brave Norwegian seamen. After a man has learned to sail the waters around Norway, the rest of the seas are no threat."

Christina watched him carefully, not sure why he sounded angry.

Anders went on, "When one of our boats is swamped by waves, we're as good as dead when we hit the cold water."

A shadow of fear crossed her young face. "Why do you keep going out then?"

"So it goes. We have to eat. Fishing is a dangerous way to earn a living, but at least when you die it's quick. Starvation is slow and much more miserable."

The two sat watching the white puffs of clouds in the sky over the tranquil sea. An occasional whitecap forecast a coming change in the weather. Anders went on, "It's not so many years ago the potato crop failed. We couldn't find where the fish were, and many starved right here in Vardo and all of the Finnmark area."

"But, Pa, the ocean is so big, there must have been fish."

"Sometimes the sea doesn't choose to share her fruit. We couldn't find any herring or cod. It was like the sea had gone dead." Father and daughter sat in silence thinking of the hard times.

An idea occurred to Christina. "Weren't there even any mackerel?"

2

"You know we don't eat mackerel, child, but there weren't even any of them."

From her earliest years Christina remembered her dad's friend Ivar saying, "Mackerel are the devil's fish; they're cannibals. They eat the bodies of them that die at sea. Eat a damn mackerel you might well be eating a friend." She shuddered at the thought.

In her imagination Christina could see the whole Norwegian Sea as a giant mackerel intent on eating fishermen. From that moment on Christina thought of the ocean as a live being that changed unpredictably from friendly food giver to eater of bodies.

Summer 1875

"Christina! Stop reading that book." There was irritation in Anders' voice. "I've told you, young woman, without everyone pulling their side of the net there isn't going to be enough to eat. If you don't get off your behind and go find some seaweed to feed Bossy, there won't be any milk."

Christina looked up from her book at her father, his large frame filling the doorway, an ominous scowl on his face. Anders Gunnerson's reddish beard was laced with white, and deep creases surrounded his blue eyes from squinting into the sun. He wore a cracked, stained oilcloth coat pulled over his heavy knit wool sweater. Even in the summer warm clothes were needed on fishing trips.

The smile Christina gave to her father softened her plain features. She had inherited her mother's sallow complexion and prominent front teeth giving her face a severe look in repose. "Pa, I'm fifteen years old. I know enough not to forget to feed the cow."

The tension around his eyes relaxed and his voice was gentler as he said, "Take me seriously, young lady. Your brother

Olaf is already down at the boat. Trina's doing the shopping and cooking. It's not good for you to be reading all the time. Books are for the rich and lazy. You must remember we are working people. The Bible is all a women needs to read."

She flashed him a look of surprise. It wasn't usual for Anders to spend much time on the Bible. Seeing the change in her expression, Anders changed his approach. "With so little light in here you'll ruin your eyes." Anders hadn't said this much to Christina in a long time. He believed that too much attention wasn't good for children. In spite of his reserve there were times when he found it hard not to show concern about her welfare. Looking slightly embarrassed by what was for him a verbal and emotional outburst, he bent to get out the low doorway and quickly moved away from the cave-like stone dwelling.

When he was younger he and his bride, Ingeborg, had talked optimistically of one day owning a house made of wood with decorated walls. When Christina was three, her mother had died from childbirth complicated by pneumonia. After that, Anders lost interest in building the wood house and knew it was never to be.

Christina sat on a stool next to one of the small windows that let in pale ribbons of weak light. She brushed the unruly

strands of blond hair out of her eyes, stabbing futilely at them with a hairpin. Sighing, she stood up and went to fetch the pail to carry seaweed. She found the large wooden bucket hiding in a corner of the section of the house given over to the cow. Throwing a heavy blue sweater over her shoulders, she opened the door stooping to avoid hitting her head.

Tossing her head to shake out the story she had been reading, she set off across the island. Leaving an uncompleted story dancing around in her head interfered with her concentration when she was doing chores. Not wanting to upset her father by doing a poor job, she made it a practice to avoid daydreaming when working. If that were the price to pay for making her father happy, then that was the price she would pay.

The sunlight had the thin watery quality that failed to warm her and forecast the coming of still colder weather. On the path to the water she moved quickly, her strides, long and masculine. She liked to keep the time spent getting somewhere as short as possible.

The chilled, moisture-laden air of the bay was carried past her by a light breeze that penetrated her clothing. She shivered, drawing the sweater more tightly around her, and muttered a mild oath, "Uff dah." Christina hated the cold, wet air of the island. She thought for the thousandth time, "Why do we have to live so far north? This island is only fit for Lapps." In the books she borrowed she read of lands with sunshine and warmth the year around. From her father's description even southern Norway would be better than this.

When she reached the cove with the best selection of seaweed, she slowed her pace. Picking her way along the boulder-strewn beach required concentration until she reached a place where she could walk along the water.

The seaweed would be boiled and fed to their cow. The islanders agreed it wasn't very good fodder, but if Bossy were hungry enough she would eat it. Food for the cow was always hard to come by, and at times seaweed was the best they could do. During the winter they eked out her diet with bark chips.

Most animals liked Christina, and Bossy was no exception. She even gave more milk when Christina did the milking. That kind of favoritism was all right with Christina's older brother and sister, Olaf and Petrina, who didn't particularly like taking care of animals.

As Christina piled the wet seaweed in the bucket, she thought of Petrina, who was two years older and a constant source of irritation. Christina muttered her feelings, "Why do I have to have a sister whose brain has dissolved into mush. She's so pie-eyed over Lars Nilsen that she doesn't do her fair share of the housework. She stands around holding the broom, staring into space, with a silly smile on her face. Try to talk to her about something and she finds some way to start babbling about Lars."

Her sister's beauty also annoyed Christina, who was considered plain even by her father. When she was little she had read the story of the ugly duckling and dreamed about growing into a swan. At fifteen the swan had yet to appear. She stopped hoping.

The bucket full, she turned back to the cottage. The island they lived on wasn't much more than a big hunk of rock covered with heather and shrubs. A few stunted trees clung to low hills in the middle of the island. Christina stopped to catch her breath on the rise overlooking the big island across the channel only a half-hour boat trip away. On a clear day she could see all the way to the mainland where real trees grew on the lower slopes of the towering cliffs that rose from the water's edge.

Even living on the mainland would be an improvement over the island. But that was Norway's problem, so many people to feed and so little land to grow food. Without the sea and her fish there would be no Norwegians, only Lapps living off their reindeer. The Lapps she had seen were queer little people who talked a funny language. Why would anyone in their right mind choose, actually choose, to live in the wilderness this far north? The Lapps truly seemed to like ice and snow. She had heard stories of how, when moved to warmer places, they couldn't wait to get back to their beloved snow.

With the overflowing pail of seaweed on her arm Christina set off down the path around the cove which overlooked the fishing boats. Putting the pail down and shielding her eyes with her hands, she stared out to sea. Her father's two-man summer boat was out on the water. The twenty-foot-long boat had been built years ago by Arne Vollen in his boat shop on the mainland. It was made like the boats her Viking ancestors had used with overlapping, thin, flexible planks that left the boat free to absorb the battering of the rough waves that constantly beset it.

Twelve of the larger winter boats had been pulled up on the beach where they waited to be refurbished for the long fishing trips the men made during the winter months. Wooden sheds lined the waterfront where the boats were stored during the worst of the winter weather.

Christina yearned for the excitement of going out fishing with the men. In the summer she watched them go in their small open boats, coming home every night; in the winter she watched them go in larger boats, carrying crews of from four to six men to fishing grounds they had been using for hundreds of years. It wasn't fair that Olaf got to go and she was stuck with the dull routine on the island.

Christina took a deep breath, inhaling the pervasive smell of fish. It permeated the air indoors or out. The very soil of the island seemed to reek of fish. To Christina it was a familiar, comforting odor. It meant there would be enough to eat for a while. The smell emanated from a number of sources, but a large part rose off the great stacks of drying cod hung on wooden scaffolding rising higher than the houses. From the stories her father told her, Christina knew that her Viking ancestors would have taken cod dried in the same way on their voyages of discovery and pillage.

She started back toward the low, stone house with the thatched roof. Their cottage stood back from the other buildings of the village, closer to the hills. The rest of the houses on the island huddled together, stark and unprotected from the weather defiantly clinging to the barren land through the worst that the elements could throw at them. Here and there an aspen or birch had been carefully tended, but they did nothing to lessen the impact of the weather.

The Letter

When Christina reached home, Petrina was standing in the kitchen. Turning to Christina she said, "I didn't find much except some cheese and a few potatoes. Always there seems to be so little."

"You're flushed," Christina commented, hanging up her sweater. "Your cheeks are that funny red color they get when you see that Lars Nilsen."

Petrina put a hand to her flaming cheek and turned a darker shade of red. "A letter just came from his mother," she said holding up an envelope. "He gave it to me to read."

Christina had a premonition. She saw the room empty and herself standing in the kitchen all alone. A chill rippled through her body. Her voice sharp and angry, she said, "Why does he want you to think about that awful place for? America is so far away."

"It's only a letter with news about his family," Petrina protested. "Here, let me read it to you." She unfolded it carefully and began.

Dear Son, and brother Lars,

All continues well with us in America. We often recall with gladness the day we left the chill cliffs of Norway. We are thankful that the Lord guided us to this land of liberty and freedom. Here we are enjoying all the privileges to which men are rightfully entitled without interference by the government or the church. We encourage you to take advantage of the opportunities here in America. There is much good land still here for the taking. Wages are high and prices are low.

The fear of being alone swept over Christina. She interrupted her sister, "Will he go? What will you do?"

"He hasn't asked and I don't think he knows, but I think we will marry next summer. Then I will leave with him. I am sure his mother will send the money for passage to America."

Christina fought the temptation to ask if she could go, too. She didn't like Lars. He was arrogant and bossy. Besides, her father and Olaf would need her even more if Petrina left. Her sister continued to read the rest of the letter, but Christina heard no more. She was too preoccupied with thinking what her life would be like without Petrina. She absentmindedly stuffed the seaweed into the heavy black kettle. She threw some wood on the embers and stared at the steam rising from the surface of the water.

She walked over to Bossy's stall and stood by her, resting her face against the cow's soft neck. Christina felt closer to the cow than she did to the rest of her family. They never seemed to listen to her. Keeping silent about worries and concerns was the family way. At least Bossy would listen, watching solemnly with gentle brown eyes that seemed to understand.

"Petrina is going to leave us," she murmured to the cow. "Then it'll be just you and me. I wish I could go with her and take you along. But Pa couldn't manage. Who would take care of him?"

Christina put her arms around the cow's neck and sighed. At least there was one friend who understood.

CHAPTER TWO

ANDERS

Ivar Johansen was sitting with his back leaning against an overturned boat, his gnarled hands working steadily mending a net. Ivar was one of only a handful of old fishermen in the village. His blue eyes encircled by crow's feet skimmed the crest of the white waves of his beard. Looking up, he saw Anders walking down the path toward the boat landing. Anders was slowing down, his step not as lively as Ivar remembered it. Perhaps if Anders' luck held, he would become a rarity like himself, an old fisherman.

As Anders drew closer Ivar called out, "Mornin,' Anders. You seen the latest letter in the Morgenbladet from one of those immigrants to America?"

Reaching into the back pocket of his baggy pants, he dragged out a creased and worn paper and handed it to Anders. "Arne brought it back from his trip last week to Tromso. It's a couple of months old now. Take a look at the letter on the back page. It's just like we been saying. Going to America is going from the edge of hell into hell itself."

Anders sat down on a rock and unfolded the paper carefully to avoid damaging it any further. He adjusted his arm length, looking for the range where the print was readable. The story was labeled simply, "A letter from America."

Before I came to America I read letters from Norwegians who moved here promising good land and a good life. Now that I am here I see how we were misled by these letters. It is important that I tell you that those letters are very wrong and filled with lies. It is sinful of those writers to mislead so many good Norwegians. We have traveled widely in America and have not seen the good things that those writers described.

As we traveled through the country we had high hopes that we, too, should be happy, but we have been very disappointed. Almost all the Norwegian immigrants we meet with here look sick with sallow faces and emaciated bodies. The ague and other pestilential fevers are so widespread that we are never safe from them, and daily we meet many who suffer from poor health. Our own little Nils succumbed to the fever.

The air here is not like home. It is heavy and depressing and people walk around bowed like slaves. The summers are so hot that the sweat pours from your body as you work.

Daily wages are much lower now than they used to be. Money is scarce, and you can get practically nothing but trade in kind unless you know the language and travel to distant markets. When Norwegians have to work for Americans, they are at first much too weak to stand their work. You work strenuously from morning till noon without rest. Then when you have gobbled down your food, you have to start work again. I am reminded of how hard we had to work in Norway when there was the rush to save the dry hay from the rain!

I do not advise any of my relatives to come to

America. If you could see the conditions of the Norwegians in America at present, you would certainly be frightened. One cannot imagine anything more misleading than the tempting and deceptive letters that reach Norway, for these letters have not only taken away people's relatives, but they have almost taken away their lives.

If God grants us good health and we can make enough money, our greatest wish is to come back to our good old Norway. America will always be unhealthful, and no Norseman is ever going to be happy here.

Anders smiled with satisfaction. Ivar continued weaving the strands of the net. "We were right to stay in Norway," Anders said. "America sounds even worse than we thought it might be." Ivar only grunted his eyes fixed on the cords of the net. Anders started leafing through the rest of the paper. His thoughts wandered to Petrina and her desire to marry Lars Nilsen. Lars was a good man and a hard worker. He would make her a good husband.

Ivar glanced up and saw that Anders was deep in thought. He put down his needle and stood up to shake out the ache in his shoulders. "I'm getting old and decrepit," he said. "It's hell to get old, my friend."

Ivar had been complaining about getting old for twenty years. "You bet," Anders said nodding. "But probably better than being eaten by the mackerel."

"Ya, sure," Ivar chuckled. He reached out and took the paper from Anders' hands and paged back to the letter. "Sounds pretty bad in America, but it won't keep some from going. Your daughter's intended, now, with his family in America, he's likely to want to join them. That means your Petrina's gonna have to go with him."

Anders picked up a stone, threw it in the water and stared at the widening circles it created. His only reply was, "They get married, they go where they want. I ain't stopping her." But, to himself he thought, "My lovely Petrina, gone from Norway." Anders would be sad to lose her. He had always known, ever since she was a beautiful child that someone would take her as a wife. At seventeen she was ready to set up her own home.

A Strong Minded Woman

His mind shifted to his younger daughter. Getting someone to marry Christina wouldn't be so easy. She wasn't pretty and had that stubborn streak. Christina's square face and high cheekbones came from the Finnish side. On her mother it had been attractive; on Christina it was plain. Homely, really. Also, she was much too independent minded even for a Norwegian woman.

Anders always thought the strong will of Scandinavian women was partly due to so many of their men dying young. The strong will had been true of Norse women, going back at least to the time when the men were Viking rovers. Women needed to know how to make a living, to take care of the cattle or the shop, as well as raise the children. There wasn't much place in the north country for a woman who couldn't depend upon her own resources.

But, with Christina, it was more than an independent attitude. She was too much like her mother. She had what the Finns called *sisu*. The good part was the courage and perseverance; the bad part was the stubbornness and willfulness that led them to do things their own way even when it was wrong headed.

Ivar interrupted Anders' train of thought. "The Nilsen boy is getting pretty close to your Petrina. When's the wedding?"

Anders replied, "Soon, soon." What he really wanted to say was, "Too soon, much too soon." But he couldn't bring himself to show the emotion. It just wasn't his way.

"Your daughter Christina will stay home to take care of the place then?" Ivar asked.

"Ya," Anders answered with a deep sigh.

Anders thoughts drifted inside his head, "If she didn't get married it would be good to have her stay at home and take care of Olaf and me. But, maybe I could find one of the widows who would marry me; then Christina would be in the way. I can't have two women under the same roof—it only means bad tempers and backbiting, especially if one of them has Finnish blood. There's so much to consider when you're the father of three children and no wife to talk to."

Anders returned from his mental journey and said, "We leave tomorrow for our trip to Russia. Olaf and I are taking the furs he trapped this winter to trade."

"Watch those Russians carefully," Ivar scowled. "A Russki will steal you blind if he gets a chance. Or more likely he'll tell you jokes while his wife steals you blind."

"They are poor people, too," Anders said. "Life is even harder for them than for us. I watch carefully when I am with them. At least they are safer to be with than the Finns who go crazy when they drink. A Finn with a knife in his belt and a drink in his stomach is truly a dangerous person to be around. A drunk Russian just wants to listen to sad music and cry."

Anders stood up and stretched. He grunted a good day to Ivar and headed for Hans Stammerud's shop. Hans, an unmarried man, ran a shop which supplied fishermen and their wives with basics that they couldn't make for themselves. He squeezed a Kroner like no one else Anders knew. All he ever talked of was making money.

Hans was a thin, twenty-six-year-old who had trouble making out who his customers were unless they spoke to him. The thick glasses only helped when he got up close to people. Anders shook his head and thought, "It would have been impossible to make a fisherman out of this poor material."

As Anders entered the shop, he called out, "Good day, Mr. Stammerud." Hans looked up from his account book and put down his pen. He gave one of his thin smiles to Anders. "Ah, Mr. Gunnerson, what brings you to my poor shop?"

"I'm going to Russia to trade some furs. What might we bring back that might make a profit for both you and me?" As his eyes adjusted to the dim light of the shop, he could make out floats, weights, line, rain gear, cloth for women's dresses and on the counter one of the new coal oil lamps.

With a pen Hans thoughtfully scratched his head, his scalp shining through the thinning brown hair. Finally he said, "The Russians are making some nice cotton cloth now with good colors. I think the women here might like to make some summer clothes from it. Bring me back some bolts and I'll see that you do good."

"So you think you can sell the cloth?" Anders asked. He couldn't see the women of the island wearing bright colors. Dark solid colors were more to their taste.

"Ya," The storekeeper answered, pushing his glasses up higher on his thin nose.

"Okay," Anders said, convinced if he couldn't make money, Hans wouldn't make the deal.

Their business concluded, Hans asked, "How is Christina then?"

"She does well," Anders replied. "She is still growing and at fifteen is big enough to keep. I guess I won't throw her back."

Hans smiled at the bad joke. "She is very strong, isn't she, and quite good at reading and writing?"

"More than is good for a girl. She could better spend her time in other ways." Anders turned and picked up the coal lamp and examined it. "If all goes well we'll be back in two weeks. I will drop the supplies off with you."

A worried look crossed Hans' face. "You'll take Christina with you?" he asked. "That's a long dangerous trip."

"Olaf and I will take care of her. It'll be good for her to see more of the world than what we have here on the island and over at Vardo. She'll be safe." He put down the lamp. He'd have to consider if he could really afford a luxury like that. Careful not to knock anything over in the crowded shop, he left as Hans bent back over his account book.

As he walked to his cottage, Anders thought, "How very curious it is. Hans shows an unusual interest in Christina. Maybe it won't be so hard to get her married after all. But to a tradesman? Oh, well, beggars can't be choosers."

CHAPTER THREE

THE LAPPS

It took them most of the day to load the twenty-foot fishing boat with their furs for trading and the equipment they would need on the trail. It was a mystery to Christina how Anders made the small boat go where he wanted. She had made few trips of any length in it. Her father believed that the dangers of the sea were for men and that only a son needed to be taught the skills of a sailor.

They carefully set the sled, skis and the bundles of furs in the middle of the boat. Christina would sleep at the bow and the men in the stern.

The first day out the wind was contrary and played games with the boat. Christina watched it fill the sails and send the boat leaping over the waves. Her father smiled. Abruptly the wind disappeared, the sails went slack and they began to drift aimlessly. Her father swore. The pattern was repeated. It took the better part of two days before they nosed into the inlet from which they would start across land. Anders told his children, "When I've made this trip before, it's taken me anywhere from three to six days. Now that we don't have to depend on the wind, I figure, if the weather holds good, we've got an easy three-day ski trip to Russia."

As the boat approached the shore, Christina stared up at the sheer wall of the bluff facing them. "Pa, there's no way up."

Anders was annoyed; the fitful winds had not improved

18

his patience. "Don't talk foolish. We wouldn't be here if there wasn't a way up."

Olaf waited until Anders was preoccupied with bringing the boat into the shore and whispered to Christina, "There a good path just out of sight. Look over to the left," he said, pointing. "See where there's a break in the cliff."

Christina squinted and stared at the rock wall. She could see parts of a thin dark line zigzagging up the cliff. "Over there by that tree?"

Olaf nodded. "The path's as crooked as fish guts and it's a hard climb, but you can make it."

They pulled the prow of their boat up on the rocks next to a small waterfall, took their supplies and trading goods out and stacked them close to the bottom of the trail. Once empty, the boat was pulled up to the supplies and turned over as protection from the frigid sea breeze. At bedtime Christina found a cozy spot between several bales of Olaf's furs which kept off the bitter cold descending with the night on the cove.

Christina was so excited she had trouble sleeping. Waking early she crawled out from under the boat, stretched and looked around for her brother and father. Olaf was kneeling, rewrapping a bundle of furs in a bale to carry on his back. "Where's Pa?" she asked.

Olaf laughed. "You know Pa. He left an hour ago up the trail by moonlight with the first load." Christina dug out a dried herring and began to chew on it as she stretched her muscles to get the sleep out of them.

When she turned around, Olaf had his head down concentrating on sharpening his skinning knife. The steel made a light grating sound as he drew it across the stone hone. "You shouldn't be up already," Olaf said. "It's going to be a long day. Pa wanted you to get as much sleep as possible."

"I can't. I'm too excited." She readjusted her clothes, which were wrinkled from being slept in. "I want to see everything."

"Well, there's not much to see, lots of snow, maybe some Lapps, if we're lucky, and a rundown Russian village."

After tying the bundles on their backs they began trudging up the zigzag path to the top of the fjord. About an hour into her first trip Christina could feel her legs turning to jelly. "I can't go on," she moaned to her brother. "This trail is never going to reach the top."

"Let's stop for breath," he said. They slipped their loads to the ground and sat on them breathing deeply. Olaf examined Christina's pack. "We loaded too much. I'll repack the load and we'll leave part of our stuff here to be picked up later. No use wearing ourselves out on the first trip."

It took the three of them most of the day to make enough trips to carry the sleds, skis, supplies and furs to the top. Christina's knees shook from the exertion, and her back felt as if little people were skating over it with sharp skates. That night she slipped into a state of profound unconsciousness, and Anders had to shake her twice next morning before she was ready to crawl out from under her covers.

For Olaf it had been a very good year trapping. There were bundles of fox, wolverine, and lynx skins to be traded. Anders carefully packed the furs onto two sleds lashing the bundles to the wooden frames with netting cord.

Like a captain planning a campaign, Anders addressed his crew. "Olaf and I will pull the large sled. Christina, you take the small one. It is fifty or sixty miles to the village; and if the weather is good, we can be there by late on the third day. If a storm comes, we'll wait it out in the tent." He pointed at his daughter. "You lead." Orders given, they started across the vast expanse of snow.

Even pulling the weight of two sleds and traveling on skis, the trio covered the ground swiftly. They stopped infrequently for rest and ate dried fish for lunch while moving. Light was beginning to fade when Christina pulled to a halt. She stood with her head down catching her breath for a few moments, then turned, expecting to see Olaf and Anders close behind. To her surprise her father and Olaf had dropped some distance back.

She shielded her eyes with her hand and gazed around at the unfamiliar flat, snow covered landscape. Something moved on the horizon but she couldn't make out what it was. She stood still, watching the spot while she waited for Anders and Olaf to catch up.

The figure in the distance grew and took form. It was a reindeer pulling a sleigh. But, what was leading it? Maybe it was one of those gnomes that she had seen drawings of in her book of fairy tales.

She heard the swish of skis behind her and turned as her father and Olaf pulled up behind her. She pointed at the distant figures. "Look, a gnome leading a reindeer."

Her father grunted. "Looks like we'll soon be meeting the Lapps. They'll be on their way to the summer grazing grounds on one of the islands."

As the Lapp approached they could see that he was dressed in skins dyed blue and trimmed with embroidered red cloth. Behind him many sleighs appeared, each pulled by a single reindeer.

When the Lapp finally reached them, Christian was surprised to see that he was very short. His head came only to her chin. She whispered to Olaf, "It's his legs. He's got almost no legs below his knees."

Olaf whispered back, "It's not that he's so short; it's that his bowed legs make him look that way. If you hammered his legs straight he'd be as tall as you."

Christina continued to stare at the Lapp. "His feet, they're huge."

"No, they're regular size; it's his shoes." Olaf answered. "They use reindeer skin filled with grass to keep their feet warm.'

The Lapp spoke to Anders in Finnish. Christina listened in amazement as her father answered haltingly. Her father frequently surprised her. He never bragged or talked much about what he had done. To learn anything she had to observe it directly or hear about it from others. It would be so much simpler if they could just talk to each other more.

All at once the vast herd of reindeer flowed around them. As they passed around her, she could see that they were already shedding their winter coats. The long white belly hair was patchy and gray as it was falling out and their brown sides looked moth eaten. She was surprised to see that even the females had antlers. The animals were moving swiftly with their warm bodies giving off a heavy odor.

As interesting as the reindeer were, Christina was more fascinated with the Lapps' dark blue costumes with the embroidered red trim. They were even more beautiful than the colorful native costumes of Vardo. It struck her as strange that some of the children had blond hair and blue eyes and could easily have passed as Norse. She must ask Pa about this later.

After talking with the leader, Anders told his children, "The headman speaks Finnish. He is pleased to learn that Olaf's load of skins for trading contains so many predators. He said he loses many reindeer to those animals every year. Last year he lost almost half of the calves to bad weather and the wild animals."

Christina asked, "Can we stay overnight with them?"

The headman grinned at her and spoke to Anders.

"He guessed what you wanted by your expression," Anders told her before turning back to the Lapp and continuing the exchange. Finally, he turned back to his children. "He says we are welcome to stay here tonight and invites us to come to his tent when we finish setting up ours." Anders motioned Christina and Olaf to follow him.

They pulled their sleds a hundred yards up wind from the herd, set up their tent and stowed their belongings. Knowing that the Lapps were likely to serve food that his children wouldn't like, Anders had them eat a light supper of dried fish and hard bread. The sun was long gone and the moon well out before they set off for the headman's tent.

Before they entered, Anders took Christina and Olaf aside and spoke to them quietly. "Don't be shocked at how dirty things are here. The Lapps never wash either themselves or their clothes. It will stink of sweat so bad inside you'll find it hard to stay. Don't show any distaste. We wouldn't want to offend our host."

Anders held the tent flap aside for them to enter. The warmth and smell hit Christina like the inside of an uncleaned barn in the heat of high summer. She gagged and felt her dinner of dried herring rise in her throat. Holding her breath she forced it back down. "I'm glad Trina isn't along," she whispered to Olaf. "We'd have something else smelling up the air."

A stooped old lady was stirring something in a pot hanging over the fire in the middle of the tent. The headman noted her interest in the old woman and said something to Anders. Her father translated the leader's explanation. "He says his mother is very old. She'll make this trip to the summer grazing grounds, but he is afraid that when they return she'll be too weak to make it over the mountains. When they go, they'll leave her in the tent to die. Her body will freeze, and when they return on their next spring trek, they will bury her."

Christina shivered, suddenly cold. To be left alone to freeze was a terrible thing to do to his mother.

Olaf saw her shudder and leaned over to whisper, "Ivar says that he's seen them get rid of the old people another way. He says they strapped an old man to a sleigh when he was still alive. They pushed the sleigh down the snow covered precipice into the fjord. Ivar said it shot way out over the water and fell with a big splash. They all stood around congratulating each other like they had done a good thing."

"Olaf, that's awful." In her disgust at the idea she took a deep breath, frowning from the sudden intake of foul odor. When she got her stomach under control again, she said, "Oh, Olaf, you made that up."

"No, that's the truth. The old people expect this to happen. Old Lapps don't even complain when their time comes. Ivar said that sometimes when an old woman is near death, they give her a cold bath to help her die faster."

Anders, who had caught the last part of Olaf's whispered comment, glared at them. They immediately hushed.

Some of the foods were an unpleasant surprise to Christina. First there was reindeer meat. That was tasty enough. Next, they brought out cheese made from reindeer milk. Despite being used to strong Norwegian cheese, she could only eat a sliver. She almost became ill when they offered her reindeer blood to drink. Her father and Olaf drank it, but she could see her father understood her distaste and was grateful he didn't encourage her to show good manners by drinking it anyway.

24

As they broke camp the next morning the headman gave them a present of a large hunk of reindeer meat. It would be a pleasant change from the dried fish they had brought.

When their sleds were loaded, they pulled the harness on over their shoulders. As they started to leave the camp, the headman said to Anders, "You may meet our wolf hunter camped out on the fell. His name in Norwegian is Wolfman. Since you are Norwegians, he'll be very cautious around you until he knows you're not one of the dangerous ones."

"Why should a Lapp be afraid of us?" Anders asked.

"Norwegians are greedy and take much of our good land. Norwegians have killed Lapps who have tried to keep their reindeer on old grazing grounds that you now say is yours. Wolfman knows that the day of the Lapp will soon be ended. You will move us to the villages, and we'll live in houses like you and no longer follow the reindeer. When that happens, Wolfman says our brains won't work right any more."

Wolfman

The trio left the camp and continued their trek across the flat snow covered land. Shortly before the sun set, the Gunnersons saw a tent. Anders, in the lead, called over his shoulder to the others, "Probably the tent of the wolf hunter."

As they came closer, they could see a Lapp watching their approach. Close up, Christina saw the weathered face of a man probably in his late forties. Wolf skins were stretched out at the side of the tent to dry, a wolverine and fox skin among them. He answered her father's greeting in heavily accented Norwegian.

Once he found they had the blessing of the headman, he invited them to set up their camp near his for the night. After pitching their tent they went over to where he squatted next to a small fire. He studied them for a few moments. Christina could feel his mind reaching out and entering hers. At first the weirdness of a foreign presence in her brain frightened her, but he quickly withdrew and was just a small, older man sitting by a fire. Whatever he had found in their minds must have reassured him, and he motioned for them to sit down.

At first Wolfman was cautious about talking. Christina finally got him to start by asking, "The headman told us that one day all Lapps will live in villages, but their brains will stop working. What did he mean?"

Wolfman thought a long time. She began to wonder if he was going to answer her question. Finally, with a sigh he said, "When a Lapp goes into a room, his brains go round and round—they stop working. The only way to make a Lapp's brain work is if the wind's blowing in his nose. He can't think quickly between four walls. I have been to your towns; there I am nobody. When I get back on the fells and cold wind blows across my face, I can think like a Lapp again."

As he talked Christina got used to his accent and was hardly aware of the strange intonations. She encouraged him to go on. "Your headman says you lose many reindeer to the wolves."

"Always we worry about the wolves. If we didn't kill them, soon there would be so many that none of our reindeer would be safe. Even if we keep watchers on skis circling the herd, the wolves sneak by in the darkness and cut out a bunch to drive away and kill. If we didn't kill wolves, we'd soon have no reindeer left and we'd starve."

"And you are the one who hunts the wolves?" Christina asked.

"God is good to us. He always sees that some Lapps are born to hunt the wolves. The Lapps know who we are when we are young. They watch the children to see who moves very quickly and runs the fastest. It is said we are born running. When they find one of us, they give us to a hunter so he can teach us how to kill wolves."

Once he started talking, Wolfman was enjoying sharing his experiences and ideas with these strangers. He continued, "When I was a young man, I thought of the wolves as my enemy because they killed my reindeer. When I killed a wolf, I told him his crimes."

He stood and turned away from the fire and stared at a spot twenty feet from the fire as if holding the eyes of a wolf. Then in a loud voice he said, "'You have killed my draft reindeer, you devil, you Satan of Hell. Now you long tooth of a cursed race, you shall no longer eat my reindeer.' Then I would strike him dead." He jabbed the air with an imaginary spear. He turned and took his seat by the fire.

That he should talk to the wolf as to another human seemed strange to Christina. "You told the wolf why you were going to kill him?"

"Only when I was a young man. Then I hated wolves. Now I am just an old hunter, and I know the wolf only does what he must. He will not kill more than he needs for himself and his cubs. The reindeer have increased so much that they roam over the fells the whole winter and in the forest belts in the valleys in the summer. The wolves get as many as they want. But, I must still kill him or we will not have enough reindeer for ourselves. The wolf breeds when he is well fed and soon there would be too many of them."

Smoke from fire changed directions and drifted toward Christina. With her eyes smarting she got up and moved. This gave Olaf an opportunity to compare methods of trapping. He used steel traps and killed the animals he caught with an old smoothbore muzzle loading gun. As Christina sat down on the other side of the fire, he leaned forward to get Wolfman's attention. "How did you kill the wolves we see around your tent?"

"I use many ways. I sometimes use a spear. When I was young, I would run them down on my skis and kill them with the shaft of my ski pole, but that was very hard work and brought blood to my mouth. I could hardly find strength to return to my tent. Now I find the best way to kill a wolf is with poison."

Olaf was startled by the answer. "You poison them? How?"

"When a wolf has killed a reindeer, if he hides it away, I know he will come back to eat it later on. I take away the torn up animal, and in its place I scatter pieces of meat in all directions where the body has lain. I study the snow to see how many wolves there were, and then I put out that many pieces of meat. The poison is in the meat.

"Sometimes the best way to kill the wolves is to put the poison in a whole reindeer body. If the wolves come and eat it, then you get rid of them all at one time."

Christina, who had lost the floor to Olaf, watched as he changed where he was sitting to get closer to Wolfman. He was fascinated by the older man's knowledge. "What poison do you use?"

"Strychnine. When you use poison, you must be careful that there are no sores or cracks in your hands. It would be dangerous if the poison gets into wounds. You must not even get the smell in your nose. And when you are preparing the meat, you must take care that no poison falls on your clothes, or on any things that other animals might eat. The meat you use must be half frozen. You dig a little hole with your knife and put in the poison."

Christina saw that she was not going to get the rest of her questions answered because Olaf had Wolfman's full attention. Olaf asked, "Have you ever been attacked by a wolf?"

Wolfman nodded and said, "I have killed wolves with my hands. When the wolf seizes hold of your arm, you must thrust your hand into the wolf's jaws, right down his throat and squeeze the lowest part of his gullet. Then the wolf cannot bite. With the other hand, you must strike with your knife. If the wolf gets a grip on a foot or the middle of the arm, he bites through to the bone."

Wolfman paused. He peeled off his reindeer skin shirt. Christina held her breath as the gamey smell in the tent moved up to stinking and stared at the arms the hunter held out for their inspection. Jagged, white scars rippled both arms where they had been gnashed by wolves. She was surprised to see how much lighter his skin was where it had not been exposed to the weather.

Wolfman continued. "I've not always been lucky in my battles with the wolves. Sometimes they've bitten me so badly I nearly died. The hunter who was my teacher died when he was bitten. He held out his left arm for further inspection. "When the wolf chewed on this arm," he said tapping the jagged scars on his left forearm with a gnarled finger, "I was sick for a month. I had to lie in my tent and be fed by others as if I were a baby. When the wolf bit this arm," he held the right arm up, "I could do nothing for the whole winter."

Wolfman was satisfied that Christina was impressed. He slipped his shirt back on over his head. "The scars of a wolf bite last as long as a man lives."

Olaf began asking about other predators, but Christina had trouble following the conversation. Her eyes were heavy and kept closing and her head nodded forward. Anders noticed and said, "You're falling asleep, girl. It's time for you to go back to the tent and go to bed."

It was dark when they hit the trail the next morning. Starlight against the snow was their only light. As they finished loading the sleds, Olaf said to his sister, "You look well rested. Would you pull on the big sled with Pa for awhile? I didn't get to bed until late, and I can hardly move. Wolfman had so many stories I just couldn't leave."

Pulling the small sled, Olaf walked alongside of Anders and Christina. After they were on the trail awhile, some of his energy came back and he started to talk to Christina. "You missed some good stories last night. Wolfman asked us to stay another day, but Pa wanted to move on to take advantage of the full moon."

"What kind of stories?" .

"One was funny. The Lapps tell stories about a people they call the Savolacs. They think the Savolacs are pretty dumb. It was even worse than the stories those crazy Swedes tell about us."

Olaf had her attention. She liked a good story. "Who are the Savolacs?"

"Pa and I aren't sure, but they aren't Scandinavians. We think maybe it's some group in Russia. The story was about three Savolacs who went hunting for a bear. They found a den and decided to send one of them in with a rope to tie up the hibernating bear. They put a rope around the man going into the cave so they could pull him out if he had any trouble. Being a Savolac he does a clumsy job of tying up the bear. This makes the bear angry so he rises up and tears the man's head off. The two Savolacs outside wait a long time but finally decide something must have gone wrong and pull their friend out. When they see him without a head, one of them asks the other one if he had a head when he went in. After thinking for a long time the second one says, "Yes, I know he must've had a head; I remember that he had a beard.""

"Oh, no one is that dumb," Christina protested.

"Well, when I said that to Pa, he said, 'Son, you just haven't met the Russians yet.'"

The Russians

The Russian village was not as neatly kept up as those in Norway, and to Christina the buildings looked shoddy as if the workmen had not learned their jobs well or just didn't care. A Scandinavian would never have settled for such conditions.

The people also appeared to be made of cruder material than the Norwegians or Finns. Maybe God hadn't been as careful when he put them together. The men were shorter than her father, but taller than the Lapps. They had dark hair and beards and looked very fierce. She wondered if they frightened Olaf and her father also.

She said to Olaf, "They seem like animals. Are we safe here?"

"Don't be a baby. They know we're Vikings. The Russians respect us as great warriors and know we're not to be trifled with."

Christina stared at him—he was talking nonsense. "We're not warriors."

"The Russians have fought Scandinavians before. Even the Swedes beat them, and everybody knows we are better soldiers than the Swedes."

The Russians all seemed so strange—even stranger than the Lapps. They darted from one building to another, hardly looking at the Gunnersons. She could understand the Lapps staring at them, but to avoid looking at strangers didn't make sense to her. Did they really fear Olaf and Anders?

They were given a room in one of the houses in the village to sleep in and store their goods. As they unloaded their effects into the corners of the room, Anders said, "I don't trust these Russians. They'll steal anything that isn't watched. They're cowards and won't take anything from you directly, but they'll sneak it away when you are not looking." Christina knew enough history to know that Vikings had felt it acceptable to take things from other people as long as they killed them first, but they never stole anything.

Staying close to her father, Christina kept her mouth shut and listened closely. She was surprised to hear him talk to the Russians in that awful sounding language of theirs. After he finished trading a small fur for honey, they took it back to the room. When they were alone, she asked, "Pa, how do you know Russian?"

Anders stopped wrapping the honey jars in straw and sat on the edge of the bed in the room. "I have fished and traded with them for years, so I know some trade talk and some fishing talk. It is not much, but I can get by."

Since he was giving her his full attention, she continued, "The people in the village seem so unhappy. They never smile. Everybody seems afraid. Is something wrong?"

Anders moved to get a more comfortable spot on the bed. He paused pondering her question before speaking. "Their leaders are worse than ours. As bad as the Swedish king is, he doesn't demand what the Russian Czar demands of his people. The powerful in our country always have the upper hand, but they don't sit on us. Here the people are little better than slaves, not free men like the Norse who can come and go as they wish."

They were interrupted by a knock on the door. Two men with full black beards and heavy fur coats were standing there. Looking serious, Anders stepped forward to shake hands. He gestured toward Christina and they nodded in her direction. After a brief exchange Anders pointed to the furs and the two men began sorting through them. While they worked, Anders turned back to Christina.

"These are the buyers I hoped we would find. They travel around the country buying furs. They'll give me credit at the trading post they run here in the village. We'll be able to pick up all the supplies we need and get back to Norway."

Having examined the furs, the men began dickering about the price. Christina saw another side of her father she hadn't known before. The Russians were emotional traders, waving their arms, shouting, and occasionally laughing. After one exchange when her father shouted at them and pointed to the door, she saw tears in one of the men's eyes. She could imagine him saying, "If we pay you that price, my children will go hungry, my wife will have no clothes. You are being unreasonable."

After an hour the deal was struck, and they shook hands. The Russian who had looked as if he had been ready to cry before the dealing was done brought out a bottle of vodka from the pocket of his bearskin coat. From another pocket he dug out three small glasses. Carefully filling the glasses, he handed one to each of the men. They raised the glasses, shouted something she couldn't make out and drank down the vodka. It took four more toasts to finish the bottle. When the toasting and shouting were finished, all three men were happy. The Russians hugged her father, hugged her, hugged each other and floated out the door.

When Olaf came back, Anders lay snoring on the bed. "You missed so much," Christina told him. "The Russian traders came, and Pa acted just like a Russian. He shouted. He hugged the traders, and they cried. Then they all got drunk on vodka."

Olaf looked confused. "Slow down. Tell me one thing at a time." It took her the rest of the evening to tell him all the remarkable events of the afternoon.

The next day was spent picking out supplies at the trading post. The following morning they loaded the sleighs with honey, beeswax for candles, vodka, a bolt of white fabric for Petrina's wedding dress, some bolts of gaily-colored cloth, and some bags of salt and sugar.

Christina was disappointed when they didn't see the Lapps on their way back to the fjord where they had left their boat. With the help of the Northern Lights they were able to travel late into the evening making the land portion of their journey in only two days. The boat trip back to the island was uneventful. Christina was brimming with stories of her adventures to share with Trina, her neighbor, Mrs. Peterson, and Ivar.

The only one who wasn't pleased by her exciting trip was Hans Stammerud. He was concerned that Anders would take his daughter into such a dangerous situation. He made this clear when Anders came over with his bolts of cloth as payment for his debts. When they were finishing up their business and the accounts had been entered into the book, he said to Anders, "A young girl shouldn't be exposed like that to dirty Lapps, wild wolves and thieving Russians. Have you no shame?"

Anders held his tongue. He had mixed feelings about Hans' reaction. He didn't like younger men talking to him that way, but he did appreciate that at least one young man was concerned about his Christina. When he told Christina about it, she replied, "What a blubberhead Hans is. What does he think I am made of, sugar?"

CHAPTER FOUR

THE BEAR

Spring 1877

Petrina searched all the places in the small cottage where food might be kept. "It's not here." She frowned, trying to think of another place to look. "I was sure we had one more jar with honey in it."

Christina looked up from her reading with anger in her voice. "I wish Pa had gotten more honey and less vodka. The honey was so nice. I tasted some of the vodka. It was awful."

"Pa says he needs the vodka," Petrina replied. "He says it eases the pain of living and restores his spirits."

Agitated, Christina put down her book and went to stare out the window. After a moment she turned back to her sister. "When we came back from Russia, I thought we had so much. It went so fast. I think Pa traded some of the honey for vodka. I don't care if it does make him feel good; I think it's awful. Besides, he always gives some of the vodka to Ivar and the others. That honey was meant for us."

"You don't understand Pa. Life hasn't turned out as he'd hoped. He has so little now. You should appreciate that he's able to be happy once in a while. We still have the cloth you brought back to make my wedding dress and linens for our hope chests. We'll do fine. With God's help everything will turn out for the best."

It wasn't just honey they couldn't find in the house. Food was scarce too. Fishing had been poor all year. To add to the problem there had been only a few potatoes per hill last summer. As yet no one was really starving but fish were getting harder to find, and most families could see the bottom of the potato barrel. The fishing boats had to go farther to find fewer herring and cod. Olaf and Anders had gone out in the big boats a week ago with most of the other men of the village, leaving Christina and Petrina alone.

With only household tasks to do Christina was painfully bored. She paced, she fidgeted, she sang, nothing seemed to break the dreary tedium. She couldn't understand how Petrina could tolerate the isolation.

At each meal Petrina carefully measured out the potatoes and a portion of dried cod, never taking more than her share. After she carefully divided the portions, she let Christina choose first. The fairness bothered Christina who really wanted more to complain about.

Christina was becoming preoccupied with food. She began writing down recipes and thinking of ways she would prepare different foods if she could find them. In her dreams she was in a room with many kinds of foods, but just as she would reach for them they would vanish.

The days were still short but the bleak gloominess of winter was gone, and even despite the sparse diet she could feel energy beginning to flow in people she met in town. After church neighbors gathered to speculate whether this time the men would come back with plenty of fish for all.

Monday morning, ten days after her father and Olaf left, Christina was abruptly awakened from a deep sleep, fully alert, her body tense. It was still dark; she sensed it was near morning but not the usual time to wake up. She lay quietly and listened. There it was again. Scratch! Scratch! Something large was working away at the thatched roof over the barn end of the house. She could hear it clearly from her bed in the room next to the cow's stall. She poked her sleeping sister. "Petrina, what was that noise?" she whispered.

There was no answer. Petrina had been known to sleep through the fierce winter storms that hit the island. Her father was fond of saying, "If Trina doesn't watch it, she'll find herself sleeping through the resurrection."

Christina poked her sharply with her elbow. "Petrina, wake up. What's that noise?" This time there was an edge of fear in her voice.

Petrina groaned and muttered, "Leave me be."

Christina struggled to make sense of the sound on the roof. It was being made by something large and persistent. The heavy tread moved across the roof and the scratching began again. This time the terrifying noise came from right over her head. Thatch from the roof rained down on her. She stared up. In the murky light she could just barely make out long sickle shaped black claws slicing through the roof. Her screams echoed in the darkness.

Petrina sat up, fully awake. She focused her bleary eyes on the roof and shook her head trying to comprehend what was happening. "It's a bear," she gasped. A black, fur clad leg probed through a hole but the roof was too firm for the bear to work a larger entry.

"I'll bet he knows it's your time of the month," Petrina whispered accusingly. "The smell of blood brought him here."

The leg withdrew and the footsteps padded across the roof, back over Bossy's stall.

Petrina grabbed her sister's arm and whispered, "What should we do?"

"Let's wait. Maybe he can't get in."

Suddenly there was a crash and an explosion of dust and thatch as the roof collapsed over the cow's stall. The terrified animal bellowed. Christina jumped out of bed and dashed the few steps to the stall. By the faint moonlight coming through the hole in the roof she saw a large shadowy object. The cow screamed in pain. Christina could make out the shape of a large black bear grasping the cow, arching Bossy's neck at a strange angle. The bear's left leg pinned the cow's head to the rock wall. Without thinking she yelled, "Stop it, you black devil! You're killing her!"

The bear glanced at Christina as if she were annoying him and growled, swatting at her with his right front paw. Christina leaped back, her eyes darting quickly around the room to find a weapon she could use to save Bossy. Petrina was still in bed paralyzed by the scene in front of her. Christina's frantic gaze turned toward the fireplace, and she saw hot embers under the kettle. Grabbing the shovel leaning on the

hearth, she scooped up embers and ashes and rushed at the bear. Petrina's screams now joined the roar of the bear as Christina threw the fire into his face.

The bear dropped his hold on the cow, twisting and batting wildly, blinded by the ashes and burning embers. The thatch, which had fallen to the floor, started to smolder. Shaking his head, the bear cleared one eye and saw the smoke rising around him. The smell of singed fur filled the room. The bear wheeled, seeking escape. He turned to the door and clawed at it. It held. Christina knew she had found the right weapon. She filled the shovel again and aimed another batch of embers at the bear's head.

Wheeling around to attack his tormentor, the bear roared his rage, but the thatch on the floor was now ablaze. He turned to the door, dug his claws into the old wood, and with a final frantic effort, ripped it from the hinges. Throwing it aside he fled into the dark followed by a trail of smoke from his smoldering fur.

The flames from the thatch danced around the fallen cow. Petrina leaped out of bed and began stamping on the embers with her bare feet, oblivious to the burns. The adrenaline pumping through Christina's body had not only given her extra speed but cleared her mind. She was thinking so quickly that everything around her was happening in slow motion.

What to do was obvious to her. "Petrina, help me with the kettle." Christina commanded. Petrina stopped her frenzied dance and stared at her sister. Christina repeated the order, "Help me with the kettle."

Petrina moved over to the fireplace and grabbed one side of the handle. The two girls lifted the steaming kettle of seaweed, set it close to the flames and tipped it over. Hissing steam and smoke filled the room as the flames died down. Christina threw a mat to Petrina, "Here, use this to beat on the fire." She said pointing to the few remaining smoldering embers.

Their eyes were teary and smarting from the smoke but fresh air was pouring in the open door and the hole in the roof.

A few minutes later gasping for breath they stopped fighting the sparks. "We got it out. Are you all right?" Christina asked.

"I think so." Petrina looked at the blackened sole of one of her feet. "My feet are going to be sore."

A pitiful cry of pain came from the direction of the stall. Petrina rushed to her side. "Oh my, Bossy is hurt bad." A quick inspection showed that Bossy was bleeding freely from wounds where the bear's claws had raked her. The front of her body was covered with blood. "We've got to get help for Bossy," Christina said. "Go get old lady Peterson; she'll know what to do."

Petrina stared at her, confused. A look of understanding came into her eyes; throwing on her shoes and a heavy black coat, she rushed out the door. Christina paced the floor for the five minutes it took for Petrina to get back with their neighbor, Emma Peterson. The old woman carefully went over Bossy. "There's nothing we can do. Her shoulder's broken. It's just a matter of time."

"We've got to save her," Christina pleaded. "We need her."

The old woman shook her head, put her hand on the distressed girl's arm and said, "Christina, there's nothing we can do. The kindest thing would be to kill her so she won't suffer anymore."

Christina stepped back as if she had been slapped, her eyes wide and dark in the dim light. "I can't," she whispered. She turned to her sister. "Petrina, you do it."

"I can't," Petrina moaned.

Bossy bellowed in pain. Her brown eyes stared hopefully at Christina begging her to do something. Christina looked at Emma Peterson's arthritic hands and bent back then at Petrina who seemed to be in a trance. Petrina was useless.

Sighing deeply, she walked slowly into the kitchen, picked up the sharp filleting knife and came back to Bossy. She murmured to the thrashing animal, "Everything is going to be all right, Bossy. I'll take care of you." As Christina stroked her velvety nose, Bossy quieted. Christina placed the tip of the knife on the jugular vein and closed her eyes. In a few minutes Bossy lay quietly in a pool of blood. Her pain was over.

As Christina cleaned up the shambles of her home, she thought, "How nice it would be to live in a land where the women don't have to be so strong. Oh, if I could just be taken care of like the women in the books who don't have to do anything but be beautiful. I want to live somewhere where someone else has to do these things, not me."

CHAPTER FIVE

PETRINA

$\mathcal{T}$rina found it hard to understand Christina. For a seventeen-year-old she could be such a child. There were times when she acted as though she were five. Then, when something happened like the bear clawing through the roof, she became like a responsible adult. Trina was impressed with Christina's presence of mind when she drove off the bear. And then to be able to cut Bossy's throat. Trina shuddered and thought to herself that it had to be done—the child can always seem to do what has to be done. Why can't she be more grown up the rest of the time?

Taking care of the house and overseeing Christina was a bother. Christina didn't respect Petrina's seniority, and she often had to appeal to her father to get Christina to behave. For example, Christina acted like a five-year-old when she was supposed to take her cod liver oil. "You must remember to take your *tran*," Petrina reminded her holding out the bottle of thick yellow oil.

Christina screwed up her face. "It tastes awful and it makes me burp up that terrible liver taste all day. I don't want to take it."

"When you were little, you took it for Ma. You know if you don't take it every day you'll get the winter sickness and die."

"If I die and go to Heaven, it will be nicer than living on this horrid island where nothing ever happens. I took it for Ma because she was nice and gave me honey to make it stay down." Christina put her hands on her hips and stamped on the floor.

"If you don't take it, maybe you won't die. Maybe it'll be worse," Petrina taunted, her eyes narrowing as she tried to think of something that would move Christina. "Maybe your eyes will go bad and you won't be able to read. Maybe your hair and your teeth will fall out, and no boy will ever marry you, and you'll have to stay here the rest of your life and cook for Pa and Olaf."

"Oh, all right, but you give it to me and I'll shut my eyes." Christina screwed her eyes tightly shut, held her nose and opened her mouth.

"You're such a baby," Petrina said as Christina struggled to swallow the oil. "Now maybe you'll have energy until at least noon."

Although they squabbled about it, both girls really believed that there was nothing that could substitute for cod liver oil to keep them healthy.

Petrina's betrothed, Lars Nilsen, came around more frequently now. When he wasn't out in the fishing boat, he was likely to be somewhere within calling distance of Petrina. He reminded Christina of a puppy the way he watched Trina, his blue eyes adoring as they followed her every move.

Lars was nine years older than Trina. He was almost twenty-eight, the oldest of three brothers and a sister. The rest of his family had left for America six years earlier. Lars had been at the point in his life where he wanted to be free from the responsibilities that his widowed mother expected him to carry as the man of the house. Their leaving had given him that freedom.

Lars and Christina were leaning against the drying racks draped with herring, absorbing the welcome sun and watching Petrina gut a catch of fish. Christina asked him, "Do you miss your mother?"

"Of course, but I miss my brothers more. I should've gone with them. But, I was the oldest and was ready to have my own place. I thought I'd be happier in Norway, but with Trina with me I think I'll be happier in America."

Petrina had finished with the fish and went inside the cottage to wash the blood off her hands. Lars made a move to follow but Christina pulled him back. "I was just a little girl when your family left. I remember your mother saying she wasn't happy here."

Lars glanced toward the cottage and then returned his attention to Christina. "No, she liked it here all right. My mother figures life will be hard wherever you live. What bothered her was the idea that Magnus, Jacob and I might die like our father in the sea. She kept having dreams, nightmares really, about our bodies lying at the bottom of the sea being eaten by fish. She thought that a farm would be a safer place for her family."

Christina knew that Lars didn't want to work on fishing boats, but he couldn't find any other work. So here he was, back on the sea which had killed his father. As he went back to the cottage to hang around Petrina, he said, "There's nothing for me here in Norway. My family is doing well in America. I want to join them and try my hand at farming. The government is giving land away to anyone who will work it. At least I won't end up food for the mackerel."

A little later Christina and Petrina were taking inventory of Petrina's hope chest. Starting when she was twelve, Petrina had been getting ready for the day she would be married. She had spent hours during the long winter nights sitting at the loom, passing the shuttle back and forth making her linens.

The sisters took the carefully folded pieces out and laid them on the bed: a dozen sheets and matching pillowcases with fluted tie ribbons, tablecloths, one large enough for a banquet table and ones for everyday use. Stacks of napkins made of shiny, smooth linen with her initials carefully embroidered on the corner were folded neatly next to the tablecloths.

Christina was jealous. She would never be as good with the loom and needle as her sister. The chest at the foot of her bed had only a few simple things in it that had been saved for her when her mother died. Looking at her sister's beautiful work, she complained, "Maybe I won't get married and no one will know that I'm such a failure. You're so beautiful and do such good work and I'm so plain and clumsy. I'll never find anyone so nice as Lars. It's so unfair."

"Oh, don't fuss so, Christina. Everybody knows Hans Stammerud wants to marry you. You know he'll be a good husband and you'll have nice babies."

Christina didn't know any such thing.

The Wedding

Petrina Gunnerson and Lars Nilsen were married in the Lutheran Church filled to overflowing with townspeople. The community's attitude toward the marriage was summed up by their neighbor Mrs. Peterson who told them, "You're strong Norse stock; you will make good babies together."

Even before Pastor Erickson had read the banns three times at the church, Petrina had talked of little else but her coming wedding. She acted as though if everything wasn't perfect at the wedding, it would damage the foundation of her marriage.

She had insisted on having a traditional wedding crown made of sprigs of myrtle wound around a wire frame. The evergreen plant was difficult to find, and she petulantly made every one around her uncomfortable until Anders finally discovered some in Vardo. He hadn't found much myrtle, but there was enough to make the ceremony legitimate. Her response when he brought it in made the effort seem worthwhile. "Oh, I'm so happy. Now it will be a real wedding, and I'll have a proper crown. I love you, Pa. You're so good to me."

Christina didn't like to see her father controlled like this by Trina, but after thinking about it she concluded that it was worth some trouble just to shut Trina up about how awful it was that she wasn't going to have a proper crown like the other brides had.

While recognizing that she felt jealous, Christina took satisfaction when she read that the Greeks believed that myrtle was sacred to Venus, the goddess of love. She didn't tell Trina this partly because she liked knowing something that Trina didn't and partly because Trina would say, "Oh, you read such nonsense. You know Pastor Erickson wouldn't approve of you saying things like that. It's sacrilegious."

Under Mrs. Peterson's direction the two girls had made a long white dress from the material brought back from Russia. Christina helped Petrina into the dress. "Oh, you look so good. You look just like someone from a fine house." A pang of resentment grabbed Christina as she looked at her own gawky, undeveloped frame.

"Let me put the crown on your head." Christina placed the crown with an attached veil carefully on Petrina's head. Petrina looked in the mirror and just as carefully readjusted it. As a final step she picked up a small, tightly trimmed bouquet with long ribbons.

As Petrina walked down the aisle, her face was radiant with satisfaction. She was about to become a woman. Anders' face was strained and tears glistened in his eyes. Christina was surprised since she knew he hadn't had any vodka to drink beforehand. She had expected that a father would be all smiles at marrying off a daughter.

Petrina received a plain gold ring from Lars. After the ceremony the wedding party moved to Oscar Forsberg's barn for the wedding feast and dance. His barn, while not very large, was the only one that had a floor sturdy enough for dancing. The barn smells lingered in the air. Manure, ammonia, old leather, hay, and damp hair all blended into a welcoming harmony.

Two older women didn't notice Christina standing behind them. The first one said, "Do you see that, Emma? That's the Devil's own brew setting out in plain sight." The Devil's brew was several bottles filled with aquavit sitting on the table with the food.

In a shocked voice the second replied, "I don't know what the world is coming to. It certainly shows a lack of breeding to put it right out there where everyone knows that drinking is going on."

"Well, it's certainly a bad start to a marriage when the couple doesn't even care if people know that they drink. I declare I never led my Nils touch it."

The last declaration amused Christina. She knew that the lady's Nils frequently had a little nip with Anders.

All the friends brought food for the pre-dance smorgasbord. There were fish in many forms: fermented trout, spiced herrings, herring in cream sauce, baked cod, pickled smelts and fish soufflé. Some of the dishes Christina had rarely tasted: mutton and cabbage, loin of pork with prunes, pig's headcheese, and stuffed cabbage. In all her life there had never been so many different foods to taste.

At the dinner the bride and groom were honored with toasts and speeches. The first was to the couple from Anders, "May your sails always fill with wind; may you never hunger."

Ivar stood and cleared his throat and raised his glass to Lars, "It's never too late to marry or to mend your ways."

The ice broken others rose to give advice, each nugget of wisdom followed by a drink.

"Nothing anybody tells you about marriage helps."

"There is so little difference between husbands you might as well keep the first."

"When you have children, let their first lesson be obedience and the second lesson will be whatever you want it to be."

47

Christina noticed that even the women who had condemned the open display of alcohol were taking small sips of the alcohol at each toast. The most shocked of the pair was already visibly flushed and sweating.

The musicians took out their instruments, two violins and an accordion. The two fiddlers had come over from Vardo and the accordionist was a local farmhand. The fiddlers were old friends who had a continuing rivalry as to who really was the better player. The audience knew that later in the evening as they became loosened up by the liquor that they would compete in some fanciful playing.

Lars and Trina danced the first round to a slow melody. Christina overheard comments that made her proud of her sister.

"As handsome a team as I've ever seen."

"Good looking couple, makes me feel young again just looking at them."

After the first dance the other guests gradually drifted onto the floor. Old and young, they all enjoyed the opportunity to break free from the grueling drudgery of their lives. Christina noted how the alcohol loosened something in people that made their voices louder. The sound level in room rose and expanded until it was pushing at the walls. At its peak the sound became a solid object into which she could find no space for her own voice. She stopped trying to talk, sat back and let the sound swirl around her.

Toward midnight the fiddlers reached the point where each wanted to flaunt his skills. Their eyes met, each nodded and the competition began. The accordionist soon quit trying to keep up and just sat back, smiled and clapped his hands to the rhythm. The bows moved faster and faster until Christina expected to see smoke rising off the violins.

The musicians showing off their skills coincided with the younger men's readiness for *dansa kronan av bruden*. It was now time for each of them to take a turn dancing vigorously with Trina trying to make the myrtle crown fall off her head.

Christina and her best friend, Hilma Tandberg, pulled back into a corner to watch. What was about to happen was of great importance to all the young unmarried girls in the village. According to tradition, the man who caught the falling crown would be the next one to marry.

"Oh my," Hilma said, putting her hand up to her face to cover her dismay at the action. "Poor Trina, they're twirling her so hard she'll be dizzy for days."

"She loves the attention. She has already been dizzy for days just planning the wedding," Christina said.

Oscar Forsberg, the poorest dancer in the village, bowed in front of Trina. As he swept her away she had to scramble to avoid his clopping feet. The myrtle crown went sailing right at Hans Stammerud's head. He threw up his hands to protect himself and caught it. Blushing, he smiled shyly.

Hilma gasped, "Oh, oh, Christina, it looks like it's going to be your turn next."

"I don't know. Hans may need more encouragement than that before he works up the nerve to ask someone to marry him." Her heart beat faster, but with anxiety rather than anticipation.

She asked herself, "Do I want to be married? No, the real question is do I want to marry Hans? Oh, it's so confusing. If no one else is available maybe it would be better to stay single?" The questions put a pall over the festivities for her, and she excused herself and made her way back to the cottage. She lay in bed listening to the sound of the last of the dancers laughing. It was some time before she dropped into a restless sleep.

On the morning of the second day Petrina came by the cottage to pick up the last of her clothes. She had on a black dress, signifying her status as a married woman.

Petrina was friendly but made no comments on how

Christina was dressed or the fact she was reading and not working on something important. The change annoyed Christina. She couldn't decide if Petrina looked older or more serene, but she did look beautiful and mature.

As Christina had expected, Petrina told her that she and Lars would be leaving for America shortly. When Petrina got ready to leave, she kissed her sister on the cheek and picked up her bundle. A moan rose in Christina's throat. She wanted to say, "Stay, please stay. Come back and be with us again."

Tears welled up in her eyes and her lip quivered. She looked away not wanting Petrina to see her display of emotion. Petrina was no longer the sister that would take care of her and argue about cod liver oil.

CHAPTER SIX

MIDSUMMER

Christina marked the passage of the months by noting which of the houses the sun set behind. In March it set behind Oscar Forsberg's barn. By April it had moved over to Mrs. Peterson's house. The next month it sank on one side of the rise north of her cottage and rose about an hour later on the other side. Finally, the sun almost stopped setting barely dipping below the horizon, twilight merging with dawn.

In the summer of 1878 it was difficult for Christina to imagine living in a place that didn't have extremes of light and dark. As the light ebbed and flowed, so did the mood of the people. During the time when darkness shrouded the world, the expressions on people's faces became stolid, mask-like, hiding all feelings. Everyone slowed down until at the depth of winter they were in a semi-vegetative state.

People stayed in their houses much of the time and moved quickly from one place to another to avoid being out in the open too long. This was out of fear of the hidden people who roamed the night-covered land. Sitting in the darkened cottage, Christina could hear them moaning, brushing against the house, or simply wailing and whining in the distance. Some of the villagers, like Mrs. Peterson who lived near spots that the hidden people were known to frequent, would leave small offerings of food to keep their good will.

Then, as light began to return, the masks on the villagers' faces softened and were melted away by the sun. Energy grew until at the height of the summer some of the islanders became so lively they hardly stopped to sleep.

Christina was one of those. During the summer she found it hard to go to bed with sunlight streaming through the windows. It would have been a shame to waste an opportunity to move about freely. She would lie down at two in the morning sleep several hours and then take a nap for an hour or two in the afternoon.

As the days lengthened she felt the building of excitement among people in the village. They acted like her father did when he was drinking. They would sit in the sun with smiles on their faces. There were even a few who sometimes laughed aloud for no apparent reason. They talked more to each other, and even strangers visiting the island found themselves regaled by the locals. With the increasing energy came a restlessness and sense of anticipation that felt like the village was moving toward an emotional climax. That climax would be midsummer night and the bonfires.

Christina's friend Hilma was bursting with vitality, a poorly capped volcano. She threw herself onto the ground, spread her arms and legs letting the sun warm her body and burst out laughing uproariously.

She stopped laughing long enough to say, "Tomorrow night let's build the biggest bonfire you've ever seen."

Christina gave the possibility serious thought before saying "We couldn't do that alone. We'll need help."

"Ask your father and Olaf. Maybe they'll help us. We'll build it so big that even people on Vardo will see it."

Later when she came back from Hilma's, Christina found her father sitting by the window, a slight smile on his face and his body totally relaxed. He had been drinking and had the bottle on the battered kitchen table in front of him. She had mixed feelings about his use of alcohol. Pastor Erickson told them repeatedly that anyone who took to drink would soon be doing the work of the devil, that liquor should never pass the lips of those who desired to live upright lives and inherit the kingdom of Heaven. She hung her lightweight coat on the peg next to the door and said, "Papa, Pastor Erickson says we shouldn't drink, that it robs us of our senses and leads us into evil ways."

Anders slapped the table for emphasis, his voice gruff, and some words ran together as he spoke, "Pastor Erickson doesn't read his Bible right. God gave us a hard world to live in. Then he recognized that he had made it too hard so he gave us grain and potatoes and taught us to turn them into alcohol so we could ease the pain."

"Papa, that isn't true, is it?"

"It's as true as what the good Pastor tells you." He pulled out the chair next to him and motioned her to sit. Christina frowned. If drinking were so bad then why was it that her father was never happier, friendlier and more willing to talk than at times like these?

"Sit, little one, and let's enjoy the sun before the long nights close in."

Christina sat silently, watching him. His hands were clumsy and when he poured more vodka into his glass some of it splashed on the table. He was drinking more than usual but saying anything about it was guaranteed to ruin his good mood. With eyes glazed, he was staring into space beyond her.

"Papa, will you help Hilma and me build the biggest bonfire ever on a high place where it can be seen all the way to Vardo?"

Anders jumped with a start. "A fire?" He nodded slowly. "Yes, a fire would be nice, but it won't be the biggest ever. I did that with my father when I was boy. But we will build the second biggest."

"Father, why does everyone build a bonfire on Midsummer Eve?"

Anders expression changed and the far away look returned to his eyes. "True, true everyone lights a fire tonight, even on the farms where no one else can see them." Anders raised the glass to his lips and took another sip. Christina could see that he was having trouble focusing on the conversation. Perhaps he was seeing something from his childhood. She wished she could read his thoughts and find out what memories flickered in his head. Maybe then she would understand this man who was her father.

"Let's build our fire over on the side toward Vardo where everybody can see it," she suggested. "If we make it big enough maybe even Jesus will see it and be happy."

The name of Jesus caught his attention. Anders scowled fiercely and stared into the clear liquid in his glass. The abstract look was gone. "It isn't for Jesus we build these fires. It's not even for St. John, the Baptist, but Pastor Erickson can't tell you that. These fires are for the old gods, the ones we had before Christianity came to this country. Those gods led us into battle and gave us a Heaven fit for warriors. Sometimes I think it would be good if we looked to the old gods instead of this fancy new God with his blood sucking priests. If Pastor Erickson and his kind were better men and not so stiff necked, there wouldn't be so many good Norwegians full of nonsense, running off to America."

"Oh, Father, don't say such things. If Reverend Erickson hears about it, he'll preach a sermon against you, maybe even condemn you to Hell."

54

"That old reprobate can't prevent us from rewarding the old gods for the light they've given us. We've got to give thanks before we sink back into the darkness." He pushed his glass aside and stood up. He swayed and stumbled toward the door. "Come on, let's go to the cliff and prepare a proper offering to the old gods."

Shortly before midnight Hilma and Christina climbed back up the hill to the tall pile of brush and dried grass. A gentle evening rain misted down, softening the daylight but not obscuring the far bank of the shallow inlet which was already illuminated by a line of bonfires. On Vardo the fires began to flare, and still farther away on the mainland here and there they could see a faint glow.

After their own fire died down, Anders sat staring silently into the glowing embers. His eyes were fixed on a place beyond where the two girls could see. Then a truly rare event for Christina, she saw a tear trickle down his cheek into his mustache.

The pinnacle of the year had come and gone. As her father had said, from now on the days would begin to contract until there was little left but long dark winter nights. Then the hidden people would reclaim their ownership of the village, scream their unintelligible sounds, and play their malevolent tricks on those who didn't take steps to placate them.

The House

Anders stooped his shoulders and bowed his head to enter the cottage. Once inside he barely glanced at Christina who was sitting at the kitchen table. Christina put down the heavy woolen sock she was darning and stood up and walked to the stove. She poured steaming black coffee into a chipped mug and handed it to her father. "Fishing bad, huh?"

"Ya, not so good." He sat down wearily at the table to sip his coffee. Christina poured herself a cup and joined him.

After drinking half the cup his spirits were revived, and he found his tongue. "Here," he said, reaching into his pocket and handing her an envelope, "someone on Vardo sent you a note." Christina carefully broke the seal on the envelope aware that Anders was watching her intently. He was as curious as she to know what it said but would never have considered opening it himself. Christina smiled and said, "It's an invitation from Linda Golseth to come over to Vardo and spend the day. She's just moved into her new house and wants to show it to me."

"Is that the Peerson girl that married the rich widower from Vardo?" he asked. Without waiting for an answer he went on, "By golly, that was quite a deal. Now I remember. Old man Golseth set it up for Linda's father to make a nice piece of money by talking her into marrying him."

"She wanted to marry him, Pa. He had a big house and lots of nice things. It'll all be hers when he dies."

"She never came around here much. How come you know her so well?"

Christina took a sip of the bitter dark coffee. "She didn't learn fast in school, Pa. The teacher had me help her with her reading. She was older than me and never did learn to read very well, but she liked to hear me talk about all the interesting places and people I read about in books."

Two invitations had been sent. The other was to Hilma, so the girls decided to go over together and sent their note of acceptance to Linda. A week later Hilma and Christina sat at the bow of a small sailboat, facing toward the aft so they could watch the wake. Ivar's brother Eric, an old sailor who ran a ferry service, sat at the tiller. A sharp wind snapped the sail taut and pushed them quickly toward Vardo. Hilma pulled her sweater closer around her to keep out the spray of water tossed up as the sturdy little boat smacked the waves. "I haven't been over for almost a year. When did you go last?"

"It's so much trouble to get over to Vardo, I don't go very often. I rode over with Pa last year, but I didn't stop to see Linda. She'd just gotten married, and I didn't want to be a bother. Besides I was nervous about all her new rich friends."

"Well, from what I've been told you don't have to be nervous about her friends over there because she ain't got any," Hilma said smugly. "Her husband's friends are all older than her and I hear their wives were very upset about him marrying such a young girl. They don't hardly speak to her. She's bored, bored, bored. The older lady that wanted to marry her husband, Peers, is very spiteful, but Peers doesn't know it because she's always such a fine lady around him."

"How awful." Christina screwed up her face in disgust.

Easing the boat close to the dock, Eric looped a length of rope over one of the wooden pilings, and the two girls jumped ashore.

"I expect to see you young ladies down here when the sun is over that steeple," he said, pointing to a church overlooking the harbor. "I'll be around here someplace, so you just give a holler when you get here."

They headed up the street that led toward the main part of town. Vardo was the largest town either of the girls had seen, and they always found it a fascinating place to visit. They held each other's hand and looked admiringly at the many houses and shops. In a small voice, as if fearful of being overheard, Christina said, "My Pa says that there's over a thousand people living here. There's so many you couldn't even get to know all their names."

"Well, some of them are so high and mighty that they wouldn't let on they knew your name even if they did. They look down their noses at poor fishermen's families."

The outside of Linda's two-story house was well cared for with new paint, well pruned plants, and a shininess to the stone stoop in front of the door that could come only from frequent scrubbing. They stood awhile on the path leading to the house both admiring it but also feeling envious of anyone who owned such a magnificent building. Finally Christina said, "It's nice that she can live like this."

In a sharp tone Hilma said, "Christina, we both know she only got it because she was beautiful not because she worked and earned it."

Christina sighed, "Well, I know. But don't be such a dog in the manger. She's got it and it's nice."

Linda appeared in the window, saw them standing outside, and rushed out to give them each a hug. She was a classic Norwegian beauty with fine features, silky blond hair and blue eyes. Many of the women had found it hard to imagine why an older man would marry such a young woman, but few of the men had any trouble understanding.

Christina pulled back from the hug; it was a bit too familiar but Linda was so excited she didn't notice. Taking them both by a hand, she led them inside. "I'm dying to see you and show you the house. I really miss all my old friends. You never seem to get over here very often. Come in. Come in."

They stepped inside a large hallway where the ceiling and walls were decorated in a series of brightly colored designs that took Christina's breath away. For a moment she stood staring, transfixed by what was the most beautiful house she had ever been in. She reached out to trace a lustrous vine woven through a pattern of showy flowers. No amount of Norwegian reserve could keep her from exclaiming, "Linda, it's lovely. I love the wood and the carvings. Everything is so beautiful that it makes my head swim."

Color tinted Linda's cheeks as she smiled happily. Christina's response was what she had been hoping for. "Let's go into the kitchen when we can have coffee and talk," she said leading the way toward the back of the house.

The kitchen was larger than the main room at home. More than coffee was laid out on the table: cheeses, little cakes with roses in the frosting and slices of bread with different meats and vegetables on them. "Linda, it's a feast," Christina exclaimed.

Christina cut a small piece of khaki colored cheese and let the sharp taste explode in her mouth. "Linda, I love this gjetost. This is wonderful. Pa says we Norwegians are the only people in the world who like it. He says if you don't get to taste it when you're little, you never learn to really like it."

Hilma made a face. She had never learned to like it, but kept her opinion to herself that the goat's milk used in making it had been wasted. She thought, "If it wasn't for its smell that heavy brown brick could have been used as a paving stone or maybe a weight to hold a net down."

Linda scooped some orange berries shaped like raspberries into cut glass bowls. "It's *moltebaer* season. Since we never had any on the island, I thought you might enjoy them. My husband says God gave them to us as a reward for living in a land that is so demanding."

Before Linda could pour the coffee into the fine china cups, Hilma picked one up and studied the bottom. She read the inscription, "Bone china from Germany. My goodness."

Christina knew that Linda was showing off her new found riches and smiled inwardly with pleasure at her friend's prosperity. For the moment the dog in the manger was shoved into the background.

The front door slammed and a moment later a tall, robust looking man entered the kitchen. "Oh, Peers, I'm glad you're home." Linda's pretty face radiated pleasure at being able to show him off. "I want you to meet my friends, Christina Gunnerson and Hilma Tandberg."

The two girls jumped to their feet, their faces blushing. It was a rare occasion for them to meet someone who was so important. Peers Golseth was a government official and imbued with considerable power. Christina noted that he wasn't as old as everyone had implied, perhaps forty. His well kept beard was still a rich brown unmarked by gray, and his eyes lacked the crow's feet of the fishermen on the island.

Peers solemnly shook their hands, motioned for them to sit and joined them at the table. Neither visitor could think of a thing to say. Peers surprised them by beginning to talk to them as if they were his equals. "It was good of you to come. I know Linda gets lonely for her friends from the island." He paused, took a small piece of bread with dried fish on it. While Linda poured his coffee he went on. "Be sure to try the *gammelost*; it's just at its peak of ripeness. It's the last of a batch my mother put up some years ago."

Neither girl was particularly fond of the strong anchovy flavored cheese. When first made, it was inedible and became so only after it had decomposed into the powdery form that was in front of them. Christina took a small amount and fought to keep from making a face as she forced herself to swallow.

Oblivious to her heroic effort, Peers went on talking. "We would like to develop some industry that would keep our better people in Norway. We are losing too many of our young men and women to America. If this emigration business keeps up, we may lose half our population." Setting his empty coffee cup down, he suggested, "Why don't we go into the living room?"

In keeping with the national custom Linda had hung carpets on the walls along with a collection of paintings by Norwegian artists. She pointed at the paintings. "Don't you just love the colors?"

Peers frowned at her statement. Having a beautiful, attentive wife was pleasant; it would have been more pleasant if she also had some understanding of paintings and music. "I selected these paintings very carefully. I'm trying to encourage our Norwegian artists by supporting their work. I think a number of them will someday be hung in the great museums of the world."

One painting of a fisherman in a boat emerging from a fog in a choppy sea made Christina shudder. Peers saw her staring at the painting. "That's one of my favorites."

Christina was so moved by the work that it was a moment before she could say, "It's so misty and dark it has the same eerie feeling of a tune played on the Hardanger fiddle. There's a sadness in both as if death were standing watch over someone. It's a very strange feeling."

Peers gave Christina a closer look. "That's very perceptive. You've studied art?"

"No, never. Where are the people in this painting going?" she asked, pointing to a painting of a family carrying bags, walking behind a cart loaded with household goods.

"That's a scene we see too much of today and will see more of tomorrow if I can't get the industry I was talking about earlier to come to Vardo. That's a family going to the boat to move to America. I know we have to send more of our people abroad. For now that's our only solution to there being so many Norwegian babies and too little food for them. We must look to the future and do something for those who stay."

The girls would like to have stayed together longer, but Christina remembered Eric's instructions to meet him when the sun reached the steeple. They didn't want to be on the water after dark. When they left, Linda hugged both warmly. This time Christina returned her friend's affection. Peers shook their hands. "Remember where we live and come again. I can see that Linda has brightened up by having you visit. She gets tired of only having us old people around."

Eric was waiting for them at the dock. Both girls were silent for some time, reflecting on what they had just seen. Finally, Christina broke the silence. "Linda got more than a fine house when she married Peers Golseth. He's a wonderful man and he cares for her so much."

"Well, it's not fair," Hilma said petulantly. "She's beautiful but not bright. Did you notice how eager Mr. Golseth was to talk with you about the paintings?"

"Talking about painting won't find me a husband, Hilma." Christina paused then changed the subject. "He was so different from Pa and Pastor Erickson about going to America. He thinks there's no other answer for our hard times, that it might be good for the country."

"Well, don't you go. I don't know what I'd do without my best friend."

The next day Christina went down to see her friend Emma Peterson, who had filled in for her missing mother through so many crises. They sat outside her cottage drinking coffee as Christina told her about the marvels of Linda's house. "I don't want to live like this always. Why should others have everything and I have so little?" She sipped her coffee and set the cup down. It was cold and bitter the way she sometimes felt inside.

"We don't understand the ways of God. We must pray for strength to accept what is given to us. Count your blessings: you have good health, a fine father and a good brother and sister."

Sometimes when she was reminded of what she had, Christina felt guilty because she wasn't more grateful. She felt no guilt today. "I know God has given me much, but I want more. I want a good wooden house, a husband of my choice, and babies. I don't want to live forever on this horrible, dreary island. I've got to find a way to make my life better."

Mrs. Peterson's expression remained impassive, hiding the pain she felt as she remembered the death of her husband and son while fishing. That brought to mind the frustrations she had felt at being trapped here on the island. She wished there was some way Christina could be helped to escape so that she could have a chance to find what she was longing for.

CHAPTER SEVEN

THE ACCIDENT

The morning was clear. The sea was a mirror of glass reflecting the blue sky and fluffy puffs of a few clouds. A slight breeze rippled its surface. The god of wind and the god of the ocean had a peace treaty. An ideal day for sailing. Pushing their boat into the water, Anders and Olaf swung over the side and busied themselves raising the small sail. The boat jumped ahead eagerly as the sail snapped taut capturing the wind.

Anders said, "Today we'll do good. I feel this is a lucky day for us." They zigzagged their way into the open water of the Norwegian Sea tacking to make the most of the fitful breeze.

Once in the open sea they picked up a heavier breeze that propelled them toward the fishing grounds. As the sun rose it warmed their faces and sent gold sparkles dancing across the sea toward them.

Olaf was content to admire the soft white of the clouds against the blue sky as he leaned back, holding

the tiller loosely with one hand. There's no finer life than that of a man on the sea, he thought.

It was two hours later that Anders found the first school of herring and they began to trail out their net. As they dropped the net into the water, the top hung from the floats as the bottom was pulled down by the lead sinkers. At the exertion from setting the net, Olaf began to laugh with pleasure. "Pa, this is the good life. Clear weather, a good school of fish to harvest and the best fisherman in Norway as partner."

Anders blushed. It wasn't right for men to give compliments, but inwardly he swelled with pride at having such a son. "Olaf, you look to your side of the net. I think we got fish that need tending to."

Olaf nodded and moved to check the setting of the net. It was time to pull the purse line to close up the bottom of the net trapping the herring. The two men's shoulders moved in synchrony as they dragged in the net, heaved it over the side and spilled the silver waterfall of herring into the bottom of the boat. The shiny fish flopped and bounced in constant motion. Some, in their last moments, attempted to leap over the side of the boat back into the water. The moving mound grew.

"Coins, Olaf, they're as good as coins," Anders exclaimed. "It's just as I told you, son. This is going to be one hell of a good day."

The two were silent as they concentrated on getting the net ready for another school. Finally Olaf shielded his eyes with his callused hand and looked across the water. In the distance the northern sky was dark. A fist-sized squall was developing. "Over there, Pa," he said pointing, "wind and rain. We better keep an eye on it."

Anders straightened and followed the direction of Olaf's gaze. He nodded. "Ya, could mean a bit of blow coming. Likely it'll pass quickly. Let's find that school of herring."

Half an hour later they circled another school with their net. As they tightened the purse line, the boat slowed, dragging under the heavy weight. This time when Olaf checked the progress of the squall, the water under it had become fierce. The wind god was annoying the ocean god who in his anger sent waves leaping in their direction. The potential force of the impending thunderstorm sent a cold chill down his back. "Pa, I think we better take the net in. It looks like violent winds coming in that squall."

His fierce eyebrows drew together in a frown as Anders glared at the clouds. "You bet. It's building up fast. Looks like could be a big one. Grab your side." They fought the weight of the fish, the veins in their necks bulged as they strained and heaved at the leaden net. "We got more fish than we thought," Anders grunted, his face cherry red from the exertion. "This is one heavy load."

They each took a deep breath and once more strained against the net, fighting the heavy load of fish. The net moved in slow motion as they heaved and pulled. Finally the load of herring fell into the bottom of the boat in another silvery shower.

Both men collapsed against the side of the boat on the verge of exhaustion. They sat limp, their muscles unresponsive, their breathing ragged from the exertion. The first gust of wind hit them, rocking the boat. "Pa, we better make a run for the island." There was an edge of panic in Olaf's voice.

As they turned, a second blast of rain driven by wind smashed violently into the boat sending it reeling like a boxer from a blow. It was on the brink of capsizing, but they fought to right it. The weight of the fish kept the boat low and gave it ballast — but only for a moment.

Again a wave slammed into them. The boat rocked, fought to the peak of the wave only to be hammered by a fierce gust of wind. The boat was tossed into the air like a child's toy. The mast snapped; the boat hit the icy water upside down.

As the boat went over Anders thought, "Damn, we'll lose all our herring." As he smashed into the raging water, the extremity of his situation hit him. The frigid hand of water reached through his clothes numbing his body. The icy blow of the water confused him. Was he sinking down or was he pushing to the surface? Which way was up? His boots turned to anchors pulling him down. Now he knew. His feet were down. He kicked with all his strength against the pull of the sea. Air, he needed air. Another kick and his head broke above the water.

Olaf, where was Olaf? He blinked the salty pain from his eyes and scanned the surface. Through the rain he could see the boat floating twenty yards away. He yelled into the storm, "Olaf, Olaf!" No one answered.

The storm shrieking at him with cold fury was now in control. Fighting his way to the boat he struggled to right it. It was too heavy. "I need Olaf. Maybe I can get on top of the boat." His fingers clawed at the curved timbers, but the sides were too slippery.

He had little strength left. His water-logged clothes were dragging him toward his death. His fingers were too stiff to get them off. The knife. His knife could help him. He reached down to his boot. His numb fingers were refusing to close. The handle, he had the handle. He wrenched it out, stabbed it into the side of the boat, took hold with both hands and held on. "Damn this fishing life," he cursed into the fury of the howling wind.

The Aftermath

Christina chose that day to visit her friend Linda Golseth at Vardo. Because of a sudden summer storm Christina and Eric waited to cross the isthmus back to the island. Eric could barely see to dock the boat when they finally got back to the island.

There was no light and no sound coming from the cottage as she walked up the path from the harbor. That's strange, she thought. She went in and hung her bonnet carefully on the peg by the door. Rubbing her hands together she checked the fire. It was out.

Christina built up the fire and put some potatoes on to boil for the evening meal. She was accustomed to the men coming home at irregular hours when they went fishing. She smiled remembering how lucky her father was feeling that morning. He had said, "I know this is going to be one of our great days. Everything is right for it. I feel it in my bones. This is our day to hit a big school." For Anders to show so much spirit was rare. On his way out he had told her. "We'll have fish enough to fill our bellies for days to come. Check the salt. With our catch we'll be able to put up a barrel."

The potatoes were done and left to stay warm on the back of the stove. She rechecked the supply of salt and picked up some needlework. After a while she put the work aside and fussed with the fire. With it burning well she paced in front of it. Maybe they ran into a big school late in the day, she reassured herself, and hadn't wanted to quit. One by one the lights in the village went out. Not even the night owls were up. Still no sign of them.

She went back to the needlework but was unable to concentrate on it. Where were they? Only pacing brought any comfort.

Her mind became a room full of trolls and ogres. Her heart was beating faster than if she had been running, her hands cold, yet wet from sweat. She wanted to scream her fears into the night. She knew what so many women in the churchyard had faced in the past.

She tried forcing herself to remember the fun they had had on the Russian trip, but the memories evaded her. This couldn't be happening. It wasn't possible that anything bad could happen to Anders and Olaf. Finally she dropped into a chair exhausted from worry. She slept fitfully.

In a dream she saw the boat tipping over and her father and brother drawn down, down in the water. Then she saw the giant mackerel turning them over and over and finally taking them into its mouth. She woke up, sweat beading her forehead, her clothes wet. Tears sprung to her eyes. "Oh, no," she thought, "they mustn't be food for the fish."

Morning came. She hurried down to the cove to find Ivar. She pounded on the door of his weather-beaten fishing shack until a sleepy-eyed Ivar came stumbling to the door. She blurted out, "Ivar, Pa and Olaf didn't come back from fishing last night."

The sleepy look disappeared from his face and was replaced with a worried one. There was concern in his voice as he said. "I have an idea where your father was going. I'll take some men and we'll go and look for him."

Christina spent the morning with Mrs. Peterson at church praying for Anders' and Olaf's safe return. In the afternoon Mrs. Peterson found work for her gutting and salting herring that one of the other men had brought back the day before. When he told them how good fishing had been, she felt tense. After he left she found it difficult to keep from breaking into tears.

That evening the men returned towing Anders' boat. Memories flooded her mind. She had seen this scene before. Her heart seemed to stop beating; her hands became icy and her insides felt hollow. She felt herself pulled down and down into a pit of despair at the bottom of which waited the giant mackerel.

Ivar came ashore in slow motion. Avoiding her eyes he tied up the boat. Finally he looked at her, his face laden with sorrow. "I sorry, Christina, it looks bad. We found the boat tipped over. There was no sign of your father or Olaf. We're sure they're drowned." He came over to her and put his arm around her shoulder. She could feel herself shaking as she fought back the tears.

Anders' friend Ingamar came over and stood next to Ivar and said, "Looks like they were caught in a sudden storm and the boat tipped over." Ingamar held out her father's fishing knife and continued, "We found this stuck in the side of the boat. He must have managed to swim back to the boat but wasn't strong enough to turn it over. He stuck his knife into the side and hung on."

The calmness of Ingamar's voice infuriated Christina. The men knew it could happen to any of them; yet they always seemed so unperturbed. How could they be so cold? What was wrong with these Norwegian men?

Another man added, "It didn't do him any good. The cold of the water and weight of his clothes, he didn't suffer long."

Christina became so angry that she momentarily forgot her grief. She screamed at the man, "You damn Norwegian fishermen. You have no feelings. Don't you see? Now I have no one."

CHAPTER EIGHT

THE SERVICE

$\mathcal{I}$t was a bleak day. Mist enclosed the island like a moist sepulcher. Christina felt that the old Norse gods were weeping with her at the loss of Anders and Olaf. She felt suspended in a faraway place, where time stood still and there were no feelings. Mrs. Peterson steered her to the church where they were joined by Ivar.

As they entered the church, Ivar was grumbling under his breath, just loud enough for Christina to hear, "I'm sorry that a good man like your father has to have the last words said for him by a pinched faced little gnome like Pastor Erickson. That man's respectable only because he has the Lutheran Church back of him. If he had to work for a living like the rest of us, he would starve to death."

Mrs. Peterson gave him a stern look and whispered, "Hush, Ivar, this is not the time for your complaints against the church and good pastor Erickson." Ivar only grunted.

Because Christina was the only surviving member of the Gunnerson family, Ivar and Old Lady Peterson joined her in the grievers' pew. The pastor opened his remarks with a short sermon on the meaning of the twenty third psalm.

When he finished he asked the congregation to bow their heads. He began, "Heavenly Father, who knows even the fall of a sparrow, accept the souls of the dead fishermen, Anders and Olaf Gunnerson, into Your house. We ask You to overlook the fact that Anders Gunnerson partook of spirits and sometimes questioned the authority of one of Your representatives on earth."

The last statement jarred Christina. She felt her face redden in a flash of anger and her stomach turned over. Mrs. Peterson placed an arthritic hand over Christina's and pressed gently. Ivar grunted again and mumbled. Christina could not catch the words clearly but it sounded like he had just condemned the Pastor to Hell.

The prayer went on and on but Christina was no longer listening. She was confused by Pastor Erickson's prayer. How could God's representative not know that her father was a good man? And why had God let him die? Why did God let so many good people die? If God was as good as Pastor Erickson claimed, why did he let so many terrible things happen? Her doubts frightened her because she was sure God could read her mind and might become angry with her. Could it be that he had let her father die because of something she had done wrong? She would never be able to understand God's ways.

Christina's mind was drawn away from her confused thoughts and back to the service by the singing of one of her father's favorite hymns. The music brought back so many flashes of scenes with her father that, from deep within, the sobs welled up and shook her body. For a moment she was embarrassed by her outburst and struggled to silence the tears. She fought to think of something else but what came to her was a picture of Anders sitting at the table laughing at something she said. Her reserves crumbled and she gave herself over to a torrent of tears.

Mrs. Peterson put an arm around her and drew her close. Ivar placed a hand on her back and make comforting sounds. Later, Christina could not remember anything about the rest of the service.

The Wake

Ivar invited the closer friends over to his house for a light meal. The mist cleared, the sun came out and the Old Norse gods stopped weeping. Christina and Ivar stood and greeted the mourners who looked appropriately sad as they stopped by to share their condolences. Each brought a dish of food to share that was placed on a long table in the front yard. It was soon covered with enough food for a feast, and the small lunch to no one's surprise, turned into a banquet.

The mourners stood in small groups around the house, making superficial conversation. Word quickly spread that Ivar had put some bottles of aquavit in the shed for anyone who needed a nip to lighten the load. Every so often one of the men would drift off to the shed and return with the look of a naughty boy keeping a secret from the adults. The women pretended they didn't know what was going on except for Mrs. Nilsen who gave her husband a sharp elbow in the ribs as he started to wander toward the shed for the third time.

With comments on the weather and fishing conditions completed, conversations moved to the mysterious ways in which God worked and how hard it was to understand life's tragedies. With the comfort of the shared food and the pleasant warmth that the liquor brought, the heavy mood slowly changed.

An older fisherman, who had made some extra trips to the shed, was sitting on the stoop in front of the house. He stood up and declared, "We're being too sad for old Anders. He's probably looking down at us thinking, "Remember, I had a good life."

Several of the women gasped at the sacrilege. The speaker gave them a hard look and went on, "You older men remember how Anders immigrated here as a young man from Tromso. He was so green that he made all the mistakes that a fisherman can make. None of us thought he would live to get married and have a family. He was tough and he was a hard worker, but he had a lot to learn." The speaker chuckled. "Anders sure made some damn fool mistakes as a fisherman because he didn't know these waters, but he learned and became a fishermen that anyone of us would have gone out with in the worst weather."

There were nods all around and sounds of agreement. Ivar shouted, "Do you remember the time Anders wrestled the Russian strong man?"

Several men laughed and the rest smiled. One of the men shouted back, "It's a good story, Ivar. Tell it again."

"Let me see, it was about seventeen years ago. I remember Christina wasn't walking yet. We had a crew out in my big boat and got mixed up with some Russian fishermen. Both boats had taken shelter from a storm in the same fjord.

"For entertainment the Russians challenged us to put forth our strongest man to wrestle theirs. They had him stand up on the prow of their boat and he looked like Goliath reborn. He was a sight to see. Well, we asked, 'Where are we going to find our David? We can't back out now. We have our reputations as Vikings to protect. But how?' Then Anders said, 'It's all right, Ivar. I think I can take him.'

"I said, 'He's as big as a bear. He'll crush you to pieces.' Anders grinned that lopsided way he had. 'Ya, then I think I must find some way to surprise him.'

"We went on the beach. Ivar and the Russian stripped to the waist. The Russian had a big belly and arms that looked like tree trunks. He laughed when Anders took off his shirt and motioned that he would crush him like an insect. You all remember how wiry Anders was as a young man?"

Thorson shouted, "Ya, and he could lift like no one I ever seen."

Ivar continued, "The Russian expected Anders would grapple with his arms like any good wrestler and make it a test of strength. Then, of course, we would have little of Anders to take back home. But Anders fooled them. He threw his whole body at the Russian's legs and knocked him to the ground, and while the giant was still confused Anders dropped his full weight on the Russian's belly knocking all of the wind out of him." Ivar laughed at the memory. Some in the audience shouted, "A true Viking!"

Ivar regained control of his voice. "The fight was over before the Russian knew it had started. His shipmates cried foul and said Anders had cheated, but we figured we had won fair and square. We Norse have always had to use our brains since we're always outnumbered. It's the Viking way."

One of the other fishermen rose unsteadily to his feet and in a somber tone said, "Let us remember the line from the Viking Havamal: 'Cattle die, kinsmen die, and so will you, but one thing that never dies is the good name of a dead man.'"

The stories continued until late in the night. Christina couldn't believe they were talking about her father. She'd thought of their life as dull and her father as just a hard working fisherman. She was hearing stories about a modern Viking, who liked a good fight, who took risks and who was a good friend to all. She was learning things about her father that she had only guessed at on the trip to Russia and during the infrequent discussions they had had, like the one on Midsummer's Eve. For the first time she felt she was getting a complete picture of what kind of a man her father really was.

When the stories finally ran out, the men, their reserve lowered by the liquor, pounded each other on the back and went home buoyed up by the knowledge that they were part of a people that produced a man such as Anders Gunnerson.

As Christina walked back to Mrs. Peterson's cottage, her sadness was decreased by her pride in being the daughter of such a well loved man.

New Hope

Following her father and brother's death Christina moved in with Mrs. Peterson. At eighteen she had no skills to support herself except housekeeping and the caring for animals. She didn't want to work as a servant to a family but didn't see that that was what she was doing for Mrs. Peterson. Mrs. Peterson couldn't provide anything more than food and shelter, and when the hard times came again, as they would, they would both go hungry.

Hans Stammerud stepped up his show of interest in Christina, but it was still so indirect and so typically Norwegian that it was hard to tell if even he knew where it might be leading. He would drop by the house and ask for her. When she came into the room, he would look very formal and always say the same thing, "Christina, would you maybe be interested in walking out with me on Saturday or maybe Sunday?"

That a prominent man in the village was showing an interest in her made Christina feel desirable. Hilma said, "Oh, it'll be such fun. You'll have lots of money and be able to have a real wooden house with pictures on the wall and everything."

Still Christina disliked the walks. If she accepted, he talked of such dull affairs. "If I make a trip to Tromso and buy some soft goods for ladies' dresses, I could mark them up and make enough money to get married. I need a wife and she could help me in the store and with the ladies' goods."

After one of their boring walks she talked with Mrs. Peterson about her feelings. They were sitting over their dinner of dried herring and potatoes when Christina said, "I wouldn't mind working in a store; my arithmetic is good enough. But to do it married to Hans? I think I could only do it if I were starving. There has got to be something else I can do. Mrs. Peterson, I've got to find another answer."

Mrs. Peterson listened patiently and waited for Christina to continue. When she didn't, the old woman suggested, "You wrote Petrina and Lars and haven't heard from them. Why don't you write again to see what they can do to help you?"

The next morning she went to work on another letter.

Dear Sister Petrina and Brother Lars,
    I hope this letter finds everything well for you and that God watches over you. With our father and Olaf dead there is little for me here. Mrs. Peterson has little to share with me. I think that Hans Stammerud is trying to get up his nerve to ask me to marry him. If he is like so many of the Norwegian bachelors, he may never find where he has his courage hidden. If he asks, I don't think I could stand to be married to him.
    I would like to come to America and live with you and maybe even get my own farm. If I stay in Norway, there will only be hard times.

She closed the letter with all the news of the area.

The answer came months later in a letter that included directions and thirty dollars U.S. money for traveling by ship from Trondheim to New York and for then going by train to Dakota Territory.

Dearest Sister Christina,
    I pray that this letter finds you well and still strong. We're still grieving over father's and Olaf's deaths. We fear for your welfare alone in Norway and wish that you would come to live with us in America. You could

work with us on our homestead or if you wish you could take your own homestead nearby. God willing you should be able to join us before the snows come. We are sending enough money for the passage to New York and for a train from New York to Brookings in the Dakota Territory.

We have no regrets in having left Reasunlund. In no circumstances would we return. It's such a wretched place that no one ought to have to live there. How our ancestors could be so ignorant of better places to live and let their fear of emigration hold them in such a poor place seems foolish to us now. You will find fertile fields for the taking, and there will be much better opportunity for you than you will ever find in Norway.

The weather is not much different than in Norway. The summers are warmer, but not much. The winter's cold and as severe as at home, but it doesn't last near as long. Every kind of grain is planted and grows well. Many people keep animals and you will enjoy the chance to keep some pigs, chickens and when you get some money perhaps even a cow or a horse.

Write us when you will be able to come, dear sister, and we'll arrange to meet your train at Brookings. We live very far from the train and you can't use a boat to travel so quickly as you do in Norway.

Your loving sister and brother-in-law,
Trina and Lars.

Christina shared the letter with Mrs. Peterson and several other friends. That was enough for word to get to Pastor Erickson about her intentions. The following Sunday he preached a sermon on emigration.

"I wish to God it were not true, that so many Norwegians have decided to leave Norway this year! America is certainly not the paradise that people dream it is. Many people want to believe that what I say is false. The letters from America confuse and fool you. The people write what they do because they're ashamed to admit they've made a mistake, and they want other Norwegians to join them.

"It's becoming increasingly evident, that peasants, in particular, who are in fairly easy circumstances in Norway who leave here will certainly some day rue they emigrated from Norway. The desire to leave has become a disease. Once they've taken it into their heads that they want to emigrate, they can't be talked out of it."

The pastor paused looked intently at the congregation. He found Christina and fixed his eyes on her as he continued. "What possible reason could I have for lying to you about conditions in America?"

Afterward Christina asked Mrs. Peterson, "Does God really care if I go or if I stay here in Norway."

"I believe that God will be wherever you are. Pastor Erickson is simply following the government policy of holding down emigration. Besides," she laughed, "if we all keep emigrating he won't have much of a congregation."

Older people confused Christina when they talked about religion. The Lutheran Church had rules to control so much of their behavior, and the elderly became upset with and gossiped about anybody who didn't pay attention to those rules. On the other hand, at times some would say things that indicated that they questioned how the church did things. She looked at Mrs. Peterson who didn't seem to see any inconsistency in disagreeing with the Pastor.

"I think, then, I won't listen to Pastor Erickson either," Christina said. "Maybe I'll go to America anyway."

CHAPTER NINE

THE CHOICE

Saturday morning, dressed in his best suit and new hat, Hans Stammerud walked up the path to Mrs. Peterson's house. His face was shiny from a new shave, and his mustache was trimmed to form a neat line over his pale thin lips. Mrs. Peterson opened the door. "Why, Mr. Stammerud, what a surprise."

Hans took off his hat and gave her a small bow. He cleared his throat and spoke rapidly in his flat nasal voice. "Mrs. Peterson, forgive me for calling so soon after Anders' and Olaf's passing, but Christina is all alone now, and I'm not getting any younger either. I would like your permission to call on her tomorrow to pursue my suit for her hand in marriage."

He had rehearsed the small speech for hours in front of his mirror at home, changing and rearranging the words until he was satisfied that they said exactly what he meant. Not too flowery or emotional, just straight to the point. He stood turning his hat in his hands waiting for her answer.

Mrs. Peterson smiled, thinking, "My, this man is uncomfortable." His formal form of address amused her. "Mr. Stammerud, we would be pleased to have you come calling on Christina Gunnerson tomorrow." She said reflecting back his formal manners.

His body relaxed, he reached out to shake her hand, and then turned and walked back down the path. Mrs. Peterson hadn't shared her feelings about Hans Stammerud as a possible husband for Christina, but that didn't stop her from thinking about it. She didn't find Hans particularly attractive; he didn't show any capacity for taking chances—everything had to be safe. Given the choice in her own youth of a man who would take no risks and live a long life and a man who would challenge the elements and maybe die young like her Karl, she would still have chosen Karl. She suspected Christina felt the same way.

Ivar had given Christina work cleaning fish when the boats came back with their catch. She stood for hours cutting off the heads, gutting fish and tying them together at the tail to hang on the drying racks.

That Saturday Christina walked wearily up the hill from Ivar's fishing shed. She couldn't wait to change out of her blood-stained dress and wash the smell off her body. As hard as she tried, the fish smell never totally left her hands. After she dressed and fixed her hair, she joined Mrs. Peterson in the kitchen for coffee and thick homemade bread spread with butter. As soon as Christina sat down, Mrs. Peterson's gray and white cat jumped into Christina's lap, purring and asking to be petted. She was never sure if it was her the cat liked or the lingering smell of fish.

"Hans Stammerud stopped by today," Mrs. Peterson said.

"Umm," Christina mumbled, wiping the crumbs of bread from the corner of her mouth. She swallowed and asked, "What did he want?"

"Seems that he's decided to get serious about you."

Christina frowned and stroked the cat. "What do you mean, serious?"

"He asked my permission to ask you to marry him."

Christina's frown turned to a look of distaste. Mrs. Peterson said, "I know you've had your doubts, but it's serious now. He's coming calling tomorrow. Are you interested in him?"

"He's doing well in his business, and I suppose I should be flattered that he asked me to marry him, but I don't want to be married yet. I'm too young. Besides, I find it hard when I'm with him to think of anything to say. He's always polite but all he can talk about is business. If I mention a book I'm reading, he doesn't answer. When I talk about America and how Trina is doing, he changes the subject." Christina shook her head. "Sometimes it's like I dropped a rock into a bottomless well, a long wait and no answering plunk."

Mrs. Peterson understood. Her Carl hadn't been much of a talker. "You know how Norwegian men are; they want to show a woman they love her, not talk about it. It's just their way."

"I know many men have a hard time talking to women, but Hans goes too far. All he talks about is making money. There's no doubt he's going to be rich someday. He always knows where to buy cheap and where to sell dear, but sometimes he takes advantage of people. I don't like that."

"Then you should think twice about marrying him," Mrs. Peterson said setting her coffee mug down with a decisive thump. The cat looked up from where she was sleeping on Christina's lap and stared at her.

"Oh, Mrs. Peterson, there's so much to think about. Pastor Erickson said that if I find a good man here in Norway, it's my duty to marry him and raise good Norwegian children. Like everybody else he knows Hans is interested in me. For over two years now everybody but Hans has known he's going to ask me to marry him. He looks at me like Bossy used to. I don't know what to do." Christina put her hands over her face, unable to sort out her feelings. I wish I had a mother to help with all this she thought.

"Wait, wait a while longer; the answer will come to you." Mrs. Peterson said gently.

Christina put her hands down and absentmindedly stroked the cat. "I'm not pretty, Mrs. Peterson. I can't afford to wait. Hans may be my only chance to ever get married. I don't want to be an old maid, and if I marry Hans I could have a good wooden house like Linda lives in."

"You're only eighteen, child. Besides, it isn't only pretty women who get married. Sometimes it doesn't seem like it, but there are men who know beauty is only skin deep. Those are the best ones."

On Sunday, Hans Stammerud again walked up the path to Mrs. Peterson's cottage. His hair was slicked back, and he was still wearing the better of his two dark gray suits. That morning he had carefully washed and shaved. Shaving for the second time in two days with his straight razor had left his face looking pink and chapped with several bloody nicks on his chin.

Christina and Hans decided to walk along the cove. For a long time they concentrated on picking their way among the rocks and neither spoke. Hans cleared his throat at several points as if he were about to speak but remained silent. Finally he said, "The weather is good for this time of the year."

Pausing as though she were giving the subject deep thought, Christina replied, "Yes, it's very nice. This warm weather is unusual for this time of the year."

Now that he had now gotten the required small talk out of the way, Hans quickly said, "I have some soft goods coming in that I can make a good profit on. In a year or two I'll be able to build a big house like some of the ones in Vardo. Would you share it with me?" He stopped and placed a hand on her arm.

She jumped at his touch. "Are you asking me to marry you then?" she asked staring at the ground, suddenly too shy.

Hans blushed, looked out to sea, then without looking at her said, "It could be a good deal for both of us. Would you think about it?"

"Yes, Hans, it's very good of you to offer. I'll think about it." The two completed their walk in silence, and Christina returned to Mrs. Peterson's cottage more confused than ever.

The proposal from Hans Stammerud added to the pressure she felt from the pastor not to go to America. At least Hans wasn't a fisherman so she wouldn't have to worry about losing him to the sea. His business was doing well, and he would be able to provide a comfortable living. In a few years she could have the kind of house Linda Golseth had. The idea of rugs on the walls and a brightly painted ceiling was tempting. She asked herself, "Why can't I be content with that? Why can't I decide?"

There was no sense asking Hilma who clearly wanted Christina to stay. Christina absentmindedly hung her hat on the peg and went to find Mrs. Peterson. The older woman was at the kitchen table knitting a sweater. The cat was batting lazily at the yarn as it unwound from the skein. Christina marveled that Mrs. Peterson could still knit despite how gnarled and twisted her fingers were from the arthritis.

"What should I do?" Christina sighed, dropping into a chair across from the old lady. "All the good reasons are for staying here. I don't have any good reasons to leave."

Mrs. Peterson set her knitting down. "What are your poor reasons for wanting to leave Norway and go to America?"

Christina thought for a minute and spoke slowly, "Well, to start with I don't like it here very much. All the places I read about in the books look like nicer places to live."

"Why?"

"It would be warmer, food would be easier to get and... " her voice trailed off. "Oh, I don't know. It just would be better."

Mrs. Peterson was silent. When she finally spoke her tone was reflective. "If Karl and I had left Norway, our lives would have been better and Karl would still be alive. This place is my home, but a man and a woman can make a home wherever they are. But child, I can't tell you what to do. You have to find your own answer."

Wayne P. Anderson

The Dream

Finally a dream helped Christina make the decision. On a Sunday morning toward the end of winter she was drifting in the half awake half asleep stage. Then she felt herself wafted into the air through the roof of the cottage and high into the sky. She was looking down at a richly dressed woman walking with two teenage children. The woman entered a house much like Linda Golseth's where a man waited for her. Both the man and the woman had sour expressions on their faces. She couldn't hear what they were saying, but she knew it was about money. The clothes and the furniture indicated they had enough money, but it was not making them happy.

Then she was wafted to a place she didn't recognize. Again she saw a women walking with several children on a farm with many animals. In the door of a two-story wooden house a man appeared and the couple talked. Again she couldn't hear anything, but she knew it was something about the weather. There was some kind of danger, but the woman smiled and reached out to touch the man.

Her spirit self moved back into the room, and Christina found herself lying in bed staring at the ceiling. As she got up she knew she was going to America no matter what the cost. Something was waiting for her that she wasn't going to find in Norway.

Her sister's letter promised that Dakota would be different. That was appealing because Christina couldn't walk around the island, see fish drying, or a boat leaving the cove without painful memories of her father and Olaf. It hurt too much to stay on the island.

Her elation at having made the decision was immediately dampened by the problems she must solve before she could leave. There was no one who wanted to buy the cottage. The money from the sale of the boat had helped for a short time but had dwindled away to almost nothing. Her father's years of hard work had not resulted in much of an inheritance.

Christina thought about the thirty U.S. dollars she had carefully hidden in a sock in her hope chest. That would have to be enough. Being poor wasn't going to stop her.

Word got back to Pastor Erickson that his sermon had not changed Christina's decision to go to America. A message was sent to come to the church office to discuss her plans. Christina dressed in her Sunday dress, and Hilma helped her dress her hair in a style that made her look five years older. When she was shown into his study, he was sitting at his desk with his back to the window, the light surrounding him like a halo. She squinted into the brightness, but it prevented her from seeing his face clearly.

"Sit down, Christina," he said gesturing to a chair next to the desk. "Christina, as you know I am very interested in your welfare and the state of your soul. I have heard that you intend to do a very dangerous thing, move to America. It is my wish that you stay here in Norway."

The light surrounding him and his deep sonorous voice made Christina feel that she was talking directly to God. Then she remembered his sermon at the memorial for her father, and he shrank back to a normal-sized human being.

"I understand, Pastor Erickson, but," she began.

He interrupted, "Christina, do you understand me. I don't want you to do something rash. Leaving will be a dangerous thing for both your body and more importantly your soul."

"This has not been an easy decision. I have prayed and thought about it, Pastor Erickson, and it's what I need to do. I have no family here, no chance to make a decent living. Petrina is my only family and I want to be near her."

Having defied the pastor she sat silent, afraid that God

might strike her. Pastor Erickson waited as though he were considering her argument. Finally, he said, "If you must go, Christina, then I will give you my blessing, but I don't want you to fall into sin. In America there are many churches which are not the true church. Before you go I want you to sign a vow that you will remain true to the Lutheran Church that follows the Norwegian doctrines."

He reached across the desk and handed her a square of paper which read:

Will you, Christina Gunnerson, promise that in the future you will not accept or recognize anyone as your pastor and spiritual guide but a person who can prove and clearly show that he has been rightly called and properly ordained by the Norwegian Lutheran Church ritual and will you promise to obey the clergyman, whom you as a part of the congregation choose for your pastor, as your spiritual authority in what he demands of you in accordance with your native country's (Norway's) church ritual?

Christina signed the paper, rose and left the study.

CHAPTER TEN

TRONDHEIM

Preparing for the Voyage

Mrs. Peterson rocked slowly in her chair trying to ease the pain of her arthritis with the gentle back and forth movements. Christina was working at the loom making a tablecloth for her hope chest. At nineteen she had matured into a large boned, physically strong young woman with an unlimited capacity for hard work.

Mrs. Peterson broke the silence. "I fear you're going to have a terrible time on this voyage. Things will get much worse for you before they get better. My Karl said it's a long dangerous trip just to get to the Lofoten Islands; then you have to sail south another five hundred miles before you get to Trondheim. You'll be worn out before you even start that dreadful voyage across the North Atlantic."

"But, Mrs. Peterson, the Vikings did it in their small open boats. I'll be on a big ship." Christina enjoyed the rhythm of the shuttle as she passed it back and forth on the loom. The cloth she was weaving was a simple one suitable for daily use.

"Our men were different then. Besides, you forget, many of them died on those voyages. Big ship or not it's a rough ocean to cross. You're a brave girl, but you're also an innocent babe who doesn't know all the pain that can come from doing risky things."

Christina paused in her weaving and looked fondly at the old woman. "I don't feel brave, Mrs. Peterson, but what more pain can I have than what happens here. Things can't be any worse in America and they might even be better."

Mrs. Peterson stood up slowly, walked to the stove to pour herself some coffee and hobbled back to the rocker. "I know you must go to America and do whatever you must do. It's still a big step for such a young girl to set off alone for a foreign country."

"Alone when I go, yes. But Trina and the Nilsens will be waiting for me." Christina felt she could not tell Mrs. Peterson the fear inside her was an iceberg chilling her soul. It would make it too easy to stay if she put the fear into words. She loved the old woman and was sad knowing she would never see her again when she left the island. She did feel young and powerless, but the need to escape was stronger than her fear.

Later that day Christina sat on the floor in front of her heavy wooden trunk. Arne Vollen, the boat builder, had carefully made the chest by hand for her mother. The pieces were fitted tightly together like the seams of the sailing ships so that it would last a lifetime. It was a large trunk about thirty-eight inches long and twenty inches high with a heavy iron key for the lock. The year, 1851, was painted in large numbers on the front, and the sides were brightly painted in a design similar to the rosemaling that Christina had admired on Linda's ceiling and walls. Mrs. Peterson had a similar trunk made a hundred years earlier that had belonged to her grandmother.

There were too many things that had belonged to the family to take all of them with her and difficult choices had to be made. As Christina sorted out the items, she placed them into two piles: those that would go with her to America and those to be left. She sternly reminded herself to take only what she needed, not the things that she loved because they were reminders of her family.

She finally decided to take one memory piece from each person in her family. From her mother the trunk itself. Her father's fishing knife went into the trunk, the last thing he had touched. She held up the necklace of wolves' teeth Olaf had been given by Wolfman on their trip to Russia. Tears came to her eyes. They had been so happy that time. She carefully tucked the necklace in the trunk. Next she neatly folded her good Norwegian clothes and laid them in the trunk.

She, like most Norse, was disdainful of machine made clothes. The letters from America emphasized how soon store bought clothes wore out, and she was determined to be prepared. She packed some heavy woolen knit sweaters with a design that other Norwegians would recognize as from Finnmark, the family tablecloths and a few usable utensils. Wrapping them carefully she put in some dried cod and a few sausages to eat on the long sea voyage.

Her packing finished, Christina stood up and looked at the trunk. It seemed so small to be holding everything she needed to begin her new life. Sighing deeply, she closed the lid and turned the lock.

The First Leg of the Journey

Ivar and his group of fishermen were going to the Lofoten Islands for the spring run of cod. From there she could catch a boat to Trondheim and find a ship that would take her to New York.

It was still mostly dark all day when they left Vardo. Coming from Vardo, Ivar's group would be coming from the farthest distance of any fisherman for their winter fishing. Daylight lasted only two hours this time of year, so they counted on the northern lights to show the way. The aurora borealis fanned out across the sky almost every night. Sometimes it was only faint feathers of lights, but some nights full curtains of light would drape across the sky. When this happened, they could see almost as well as if the sky were lit by a bright moon.

On one such night they sailed past the North Cape, and in the greenish light Christina could see the tall cliff of blackish granite towering over the shoreline. Her chest filled with pleasure. It felt good to be alive. "Ivar," she said, "it's so beautiful at sea, it's hard to imagine that it can turn so dangerous."

"It's a tricky master, this old sea. It's not to be trusted, but on a night like this we can forgive some of its fickleness."

It was the middle of February when they finally arrived in Svolvaer in the Lofoten Islands. In the twilight the shadows of hundreds of boats drifted around them like the ghosts of lost Vikings. Christina was wide-eyed at the sheer number of boats she could see in the dim light. "Ivar, all the fishing boats in Norway must be here."

"You bet. There're thousands of them of all kinds and sizes. If there's some strange way of getting fish out of the water, someone will be using it on one of these boats. They come from all over to fish this coast. Svolvaer is sure the fishing capital of Norway, maybe even the fishing capital of world."

"But, Ivar, surely there aren't that many fish."

"I used to think that when I was a boy. I'll never forget the first time my father brought me here. I asked him the same question. There's plenty of fish for everyone. No matter what a man uses to catch fish here, he'll return loaded to the gunwales."

They came into the docks before light. As she jumped onto the landing and looked around, Christina was surprised to find that people were already hard at work. There was movement all around her. Part of the embankment was swarming with women working on yesterday's catch. There were tons of cod being cleaned and processed; split cod were being hung up to dry into torr'fisk. After the long voyage all the activity around her was very exciting. She moved her head quickly from side to side trying to take it all in. So many things attracted her attention as she began moving quickly in and out of the crowds of workers.

As a hand grabbed her shoulder, she turned to find Ivar right behind her. "Whoa, young lady, I'm not as young as I used to be. Slow down, we have plenty of time to see everything."

She stopped; her legs were with excitement making it hard to stand still, "Oh, Ivar, it's all such a wonder. It's beyond anything I've read in my books." She continued to bounce up and down trying to see everything. "Oh, look. There are so many cod they just spread them out on the bare rocks along the shore." Ivar and Christina had to pick their way carefully among the fish. "Look, Ivar, so many they have to dry them as cliff fish."

Ivar stopped to talk with several of the old salts, establishing that a good place for Christina to stay was with Mrs. Gullickson, one of the many widows in the village. Another widow, Christina thought. Their cemetery must look like the one on the island, all women and children, no men.

They had worked their way past the fish to one of the narrow streets. Christina was still looking, too excited to say much. Ivar went on talking, "Yes, we'll all live well this year." They turned into a narrow street. "We'll have to find you a place to stay until we find a boat to take you to Trondheim." Ivar stopped to ask directions and they walked in silence for a while.

Ivar continued, "You'll find Trondheim a very old town. Did you know it was the Viking's first capital? That's where they used to sail out from on raids that carried them all over the world." As Christina looked up at the sky, the old buildings on the narrow street leaned in over her head. Ivar noted her looking up. "They lean in so they can pull loads up for storage without hitting the sides of the building." Christina let out a small yelp as a large rat ran across the lane in front her. Ivar laughed. "It's a big one. It will take a tough Tom to kill that one."

They turned down another street as Ivar cautioned, "It may take me some time before I can find someone going as far as Trondheim. It's almost four hundred miles and there's always danger of bad weather. I don't want you to go until I can find someone that I can trust to get you there."

Once established in a small room at Mrs. Gullickson's, it was no problem for Christina to find a job preparing fish for drying, so she was soon back at her old job of cutting off heads and gutting fish. She was comfortable with the people she met; they were so like the people she knew back on the island. Mrs. Gullickson reminded her of Mrs. Peterson and soon adopted Christina as one of her own.

It was the middle of March before Ivar made the contact he had been looking for. One day Christina looked up from gutting fish and saw him strolling down the dock. With him was an old man with a deeply wrinkled face and a short white beard. Staying a short distance back to keep from getting blood splattered on their clothes, Ivar introduced the newcomer.

"Christina, this is my old friend, Bryngel Estensen. Everybody calls him Bry. He's been sailing anything that will float over these waters for sixty years. He's proof that it's possible for a sailor to live to a ripe old age."

Out of the sea of wrinkles shone a pair of bright blue eyes with a sparkle of mischief in them. "So, you're the young lady that wants to go to America. Why are so many good Norwegians going to that land of wild Indians and flat prairies? Too bad we can't flatten Norway out; it would be as big as America and you could all stay here." He laughed exposing a deeply stained irregular row of brown teeth.

"You don't like America?" Christina asked.

"America? America is all right. I just don't like all our good young people leaving, that's all. I know there is nothing for them here, but I can't wish us into being a rich country. No, you must go, but our wealth goes with you."

Christina was puzzled. What in the world was Bry talking about? She couldn't smell any alcohol on his breath, but he talked like men in the village did when their tongues had been loosened by alcohol. She thought, "Maybe it's what happens to men when they get older; they say more of what is on their minds."

Bry saw the blank look on her face. "Never mind, young lady, we'll get you safely to Trondheim, and I'll make sure that you get on a boat to America with a good captain so you can walk on the streets of gold and live like a queen."

"Well," thought Christina, "this is certainly confusing. I don't think I understand what he's telling me at all."

CHAPTER ELEVEN

THE SHIP

"This is the one'll take you to America," Bry said. Christina and Captain Bry Estensen stood on the wharf looking up at the ship. "It's one of the new ones with an engine to push you along when there's no wind." He took a weathered pipe out of his shirt pocket and tamped tobacco down firmly in its bowl. It took several matches to get it going to his satisfaction.

Christina stared at the ship in open mouthed wonder. "I've never seen any building that stretched so far into the sky. It goes on forever; it must be the biggest ship in the world."

"Outa the way, lady," the gruff voice of a dock worker shouted. Christina jumped and hastily stepped forward to the edge of the wharf to let by the crate of live chickens he was pushing.

"Bry, this ship is made of iron. What makes it float?" Christina asked, her eyes sweeping the boat from bow to stern.

"Ya, sure, it's pretty big. It goes over two hundred feet long, but when you go to Bergen or New York you'll see even bigger ones. Soon no one will remember when there were real seamen who sailed wooden ships." His voice was sad as he continued. "By the time you get married and got babies we'll have ships maybe twice as big as this one and sails will be a thing of the past."

Christina was so engrossed in the size of the ship that his words passed by her unheard. "It's got such little sails for such a big ship. What's that big chimney in the middle for?" she asked, pointing to the sooty black pipe with smoke coming out of it. Again she didn't wait for an answer to her question before she fired another one. "Is this really the boat that will take me to America?"

"This is really the one." He nodded and puffed on his pipe. He smiled at her disbelief, enjoying the opportunity to show off his knowledge to what to an old sailor was an attractive young woman. "On this trip you'll see some of Norway's upper class. This ship has cabins for one hundred quality people who can afford the best. Too bad those of you without money will have to travel in steerage. They'll shove five hundred of you in below decks. It ain't much for comfort but you sure can't beat the price."

He knocked the ashes out of his pipe and after carefully stepping on the ashes that fell on the dock stowed it in his shirt pocket. He started toward the ship's gangplank. "Come along," he said over his shoulder. "I know the captain. He'll let us go aboard and look around."

A ship's officer who was supervising loading looked over at Bry and Christina. At first he seemed confused at seeing them, but this was followed by a broad smile. "I'll be damned. If it ain't Captain Bry Estensen himself and with a lady young enough to be his granddaughter. You old sea dog, I heard you were food for the mackerel some years back."

Bry pumped the man's hand. "The sea spit me back up again. I did lose some good sailors when that one went down. This young lady, Christina Gunnerson, will be one of your passengers. I'd like permission to show her the ship."

The officer waved them up the gangplank. "Permission granted."

As she stepped onto the main deck, Christina's eyes widened at the swarm of activity, men putting boxes and bales into a cargo hold, others repainting bulkheads. Still others were just moving with no obvious purpose, adding to the general confusion. She had to step carefully to avoid tripping over equipment or getting in anyone's way. "It's so big, it would hold everybody in the village and everybody in Vardo all at one time."

Bry nodded, "Almost, Christina, almost. It's a good ship and you'll appreciate its size a lot more when you start to roll on the high seas. The small ships toss passengers about a lot more. Most of the real sailing ships are gone. Now we got these monsters that don't know if they'll steam or sail. But this kind of ship is sure faster and safer. I remember, how in the old ships the waves would wash over the deck so bad the passengers had to stay below with all the hatches closed for a week at a time. Air used to get so foul that everybody would get sick."

Bry paused and scratched his beard. "I can't remember making a trip to America when someone didn't die. A captain always had to keep his Bible handy to do the burial service." He stared off over the harbor. "Ya, I've seen many a poor soul, sewn up in sailcloth, rocks at his feet, dropped into the sea."

"Oh, how awful." A look of distress crossing her face, Christina wondered if someone would die on this trip.

"More awful for the poor souls I was sewing up I would say." Bry was silent for a while, remembering the nameless people with great expectations for a new life in America who never made it across the Atlantic.

He turned back to Christina and pointed to an open space on the foredeck. "If you're going to be aboard for three weeks, you'll need some space for exercise and fresh air," he said. "The captain will have you up on deck every day if he can. It looks big now but this'll seem awfully crowded before you get to New York."

Christina watched as a slender young man walked up behind Bry. He cleared his throat and Bry turned around. The young man saluted, "Seaman Ole Swenson reporting for duty, sir. The captain sent me up to find you and show you around the ship. It's been awhile since I last saw you, Captain Estensen. How have things been up in the Lofoten Islands?"

Bry smiled broadly showing his yellow stained teeth. "Even darker and drearier than down here." He turned to Christina. "This is my friend Ole. He started out a few years ago sailing with me from Tromso to Trondheim. We tried to make a real sailor out of him, but he could never remember the names of the sails, so he had to take up arranging the supplies for these big ships. I think he's really a landlubber at heart."

The young man grinned at the teasing and bowed in front of Christina. She blushed as he ceremoniously took her hand and said, "Welcome aboard. Don't take this old salt too seriously. He's just jealous because he never moved beyond sails. He's too old to learn to be a modern sailor where we use our brains instead of muscles."

Christina glanced at Bry and saw him hiding a smile behind his gnarled hand. "It's all right, Christina," he chuckled. "Some little fish never learn to respect their elders. We just have to overlook their jabbering." Christina sensed the good feeling between the men but was puzzled by their banter. Ivar and her father never talked like this.

The younger sailor was eager to show off his knowledge to Christina. His eyes wandered slowly from her bonnet to her shoes, and he smiled into her eyes pleased with what he saw. She blushed and stared down at her feet suddenly unable to think of anything to say. Christina, for the first time in her life, wondered if she might be attractive. As Ole chatted about the ship, Christina had trouble following some of what he said. His pronunciation and use of words were different than what she was used to in Vardo. Also, Ole was far less taciturn then the young men from the island.

Ole first led them up the ladder to the superstructure on the main deck. "The people with money and position who act like they know it all will stay here. You won't be allowed on this deck after we sail. These people only want their own kind around and a few servants to carry out their orders, so they won't get their hands dirty."

Christina frowned at the bitterness in his voice. She was unsure of how to react to this kind of openness from a stranger. Ole moved on and opened the door to one of the staterooms. Stepping aside to let them go in, he said, "See, they have everything they need right here."

The room was small and crowded. A double bed filled most of the space. There was a sink with a blue and white pitcher. Sunlight streamed in the small round window over the bed. "When you're with them, you have to remember to say, yes sir, no sir, by your leave, ma'am. But sometimes they give us money, so we do what they ask with a smile."

Christina hadn't met many people with money, but she knew they were somehow different. She could remember her father telling her, "We're just as good as they are, and maybe just a little bit better cause we do honest work, so don't you hang your head around them."

Her father's advice fell on barren ground. Christina still felt uncomfortable around well dressed, well spoken people and tended to keep her eyes down and her mouth shut. They always knew what to say and do. In this strange new world in which she now found herself she was never quite sure what to do, and she didn't want to offend anyone.

Ole's voice pulled her back from her thoughts. "Come on, let's get to the heart of this lady." He led them down narrow passageways, down ladders, deep into the central part of the ship where he announced, "This is what drives it. This is the engine room." It was filled with more walkways, pipes, dials and wheels.

Christina looked around and tried to ask intelligent questions, but much of what she was seeing was not registering.

There were too many new sights that she had no background to understand. Ole pointed out parts of the ship and gave them names that vanished from her mind almost before they were out of his mouth. What she did remember was the noise and heat and the sense that she would suffocate if she had to work this far below the surface. She looked at Ole with admiration for all the things he knew and wished she could be as comfortable as he was with everything.

She noticed that Ole was concerned for her safety, taking her arm whenever there was a difficult passageway or ladder. She glanced at Bry who winked at her. When Ole placed a hand on her arm or shoulder, it sent a charge of excitement through her. How could the touch of a simple sailor do this to her and not the touch of Hans Stammerud? She glanced up at Ole through her eyelashes and flushed when his amused blue eyes met hers. This was awful. She was acting just like that lovesick Petrina when she was around Lars. She kept her eyes on her feet as they climbed down ladders, up ladders, through passageways and around corners. Christina had no idea where she was in the ship.

Ole paused and said, "We're now in midship." Christina didn't know what that meant but couldn't force herself to ask.

Ole went on, "We're going into the ship's barn where the stock is kept. Most of what we keep here are cattle and chickens so that the passengers can have fresh meat. We'll also take on some horses which will be used in a state called Iowa for breeding stock."

Christina stared at the crates of chickens and the cows placidly chewing hay. One of the cows that returned her stare looked just like Bossy. Christina felt tears prick her eyes as a wave of homesickness flowed over her. Grateful that neither of the men had noticed, she turned to follow Ole out of the barn.

Finally they reached a large room packed with beds. "Here's your new home," he said, "You'll be living here in the women's quarters for the next three to four weeks. We're in the aft of the ship. Married couples and families are in the middle of the ship one deck up. The single men will be living in the forward part of the deck we're on now."

Christina looked around the room. The cots were so tightly packed together there was little room for walking. Personal items would have to go under the beds. There were no portholes to let light into the room, and it was dimly lit making it mostly shadow and dark. It gave her the same closed in feeling she had had in the engine room.

As they looked the sleeping area over, Ole said, "Captain Winjum is a good man. He cares for the comfort of even his steerage passengers. Not like some of the captains I've heard about who treat cattle better than they do people. You're lucky you're on a good Norwegian ship with Captain Winjum.

"The captain wants you to be comfortable. Look how he's laid out the space for the beds. There's so much space here between decks that I barely have to stoop down. See there are only three bunks in a row and never more than two high."

"It looks crowded to me," Christina said. "Aren't people going to be awfully close?"

"You should see what it's like on other ships. Some lines crowd in bunks three and four high with hardly any space between them. This ship carries three quarts of water a day for each passenger, and you won't even have to carry much of your own food on board with you."

Christina had never worried about whether they would have enough food or water. I wonder what else I've taken for granted she thought. Ole went on, "For the sick we keep vinegar, wine and sugar. There's no doctor for this trip, but we got a sick bay with instructions in case anybody gets sick."

The sun was setting as they came back on deck, leaving orange and red clouds feathering out from the horizon. They stood for a while leaning on the railing looking at the lights in the harbor and in the windows of Trondheim.

Bry said to Ole, "Christina was placed in my care by a friend of mine. Her father was Anders Gunnerson, a good sailor and fine man. The captain knows she's aboard, but can't give her any special attention. I would appreciate it if you'd watch out for her during the voyage."

With no hesitation Ole answered, "It would be a pleasure to help her." He took her hand and bowed to her.

Christina felt her cheeks flame red. The pounding of her heart echoed in her ears, and her chest tightened against her lungs shutting her breath off. A feeling of dizziness momentarily swept over her, and she reached out her free hand to get support and grabbed Bry's arm. She stifled the urge to giggle. What was the presence of this man doing to her?

The way these men talked and acted when they were sober was the way her father could act and talk when he was drinking. Were most men like her father or were they like Ole and Bry? She saw she had a lot to learn about men and ships. Right now learning about men seemed more important.

CHAPTER TWELVE

THE ATLANTIC CROSSING

Knowing her way there, Christina arrived in the women's quarters minutes before the rush. In the dim light she tried to decide which would be the best place to make the journey. Ole had told her the captain placed families with the smallest children midship where the dipping and rising of the ship was not as extreme. Seasickness would be less severe.

She looked at the bunk closest to the bulkhead toward the center and hesitated. Top bunk or bottom bunk? Bry had said, "Take a top bunk. When you hit rough water everyone becomes seasick. Some will be so sick they won't make it to the slop pail. You don't want to be down below when that happens."

Christina threw her traveling bag on the top bunk. When Ole brought it down, her trunk could go under the lower bunk. Women were now coming into the section and claiming other bunks. Christina crawled onto the top bunk to see how difficult it would be getting in and out of it. The mattress was very thin. Her bones were going to ache a bit before she got used to it.

She sat on her knees watching the other women come in. Her attention was drawn to an attractive, small dark woman, who looked to be about Christina's age of nineteen, standing in the entrance looking carefully at the women already there. Her eyes lit on Christina. The woman smiled and nodded at her and then started working her way through the increasing disorder toward Christina's bunk.

The woman didn't look much like the Norwegians that Christina knew, and she was still debating what to say when the woman placed her bags on the lower bunk, looked up at her and said, "I hope you don't get seasick. I hear it can get messy on the lower bunk."

The abruptness of the opening startled Christina. She jerked back slightly and raised her hand to her face, the introduction she had started to compose in her mind gone. Seeing Christina's reaction the woman added, "Oh, I'm Maria Amundson. We might as well get acquainted. It's going to be a long trip."

Up close Christina could see the woman was no longer in her teens. She might be as much as eight years older than Christina. "Wouldn't you be better off in a top bunk?" Christina asked, "There are others still not taken."

"Don't be concerned about me: I want the lower bunk anyway. I don't like heights, and I do want a bunk mate who looks like she's got some life in her."

Remembering her manners, Christina said, "My name is Christina Gunnerson, from Vardo."

Maria looked up from checking her mattress. "Doesn't feel very comfortable. You look awfully young to be traveling alone. Where are your parents?"

Christina slid off the top bunk and lit heavily on the deck. "I need practice getting up and down. Both of my folks are dead. I'm going to Dakota Territory to join my sister and her husband."

"Too bad. About your parents I mean. I'm going to a place in America called Wisconsin to be married to a Norwegian bachelor who already has a house and animals on his farm."

"Were you promised before he left Norway?"

"No, I was just a little girl when he left. He remembered me from when I was a child and wrote my parents about marrying me. I didn't like the job I had in Trondheim, and there were no young men interested in me." Maria laughed, dimples forming on both sides of her generous mouth giving her a mischievous appearance. "My mother says they are all afraid of my tongue. I think their mothers never taught them to have a sense of humor."

All this personal information from a stranger made Christina nervous. Would she now be expected to tell Maria everything about herself? Christina decided it would be better to be embarrassed by asking questions rather than by answering them. "Do you remember much about the man you're going to marry?"

Maria shook her head. "Only that he's a big man, never talked much when I was around. He seemed nice enough." She paused and stared into space. "I think it will be a good match."

By the time they had been at sea two days, Christina knew that this trip across the Atlantic was going to be a difficult one. So many people. She was used to being alone; now there were people everywhere, all the time. As she had suspected, what Ole said were generous quarters, quickly became cramped and uncomfortable.

She didn't like being surrounded by strangers. Here were hundreds of people who didn't know anything about her and she nothing about them. Most of them were not friendly like

Maria or Ole. They were typical reserved Norwegians, and it was obvious to her that there was not going to be enough time to get to know many of them. Most of her fellow passengers went around acting like they didn't have a care in the world. If they wept with sadness at leaving their homes and friends, they were doing it at night into their pillows.

The human noises bothered her: farts, snoring, laughter, arguments. These were private sounds that she didn't want to hear. Sometimes what she heard would just make her back stiffen, but other times her face reddened in acute embarrassment.

Christina did enjoy talking to Maria. Maria accepted as natural the sounds people made and couldn't understand why Christina would be embarrassed. "Gosh," Maria teased, "that's the closest thing we have to entertainment on this boat. You can be such a stick."

Maria knew about things that were seldom talked about like sex and was learning even more in some of her trips to other parts of the ship. In spite of her twenty-six years Maria by braiding her hair and putting on a short dress of a child looked like she was in her early teens. Being small, she could blend into the dark corners to do her listening.

Christina thought that what Maria was doing was very sinful, but she couldn't help but be entertained by her reports of what she had seen. Some of the things she reported seemed better than the made up stories Christina liked to read.

"Don't look now, but you know Nina, the tall women that has the bunk against that wall?" Maria whispered. In spite of the warning Christina glanced over at Nina. Maria went on, "You know how she's so high and mighty, she doesn't like to speak to us? Well, last night she snuck out, acting real mysterious like. I followed her and saw her meet a sailor who works on the horse deck. Then I saw them go into a horse stall together."

"They didn't! Then what happened?" Christina's eyes were wide with curiosity.

"I couldn't get close enough to see, but the thumping noises I heard weren't coming from any horses' hooves."

"Oh, Maria, you're so naughty."

The trade-off in the relationship was that Christina knew about ships and what to expect at sea. She told Maria, "Bry said that just a few years ago we would've been making this trip on a sailing ship that wasn't driven by steam. That would have taken us a much longer time and a lot more people would have died from disease on the trip. One trip he was on Bry said forty-nine people died from cholera. Someone was bound to die on every trip. He says even these steam ships won't be around long."

"But this is modern." Maria protested. "What could be better?"

"Well, he said it would be only a few years more before all of the passenger ships would be driven by steam alone, and they won't need those poor excuses for sails we've got topside."

Seasickness

The gentle rocking of the ship for the first two days had been misleading. On the third day out everything changed. The gentle movement became a series of sudden dips and sharp rises as the ship began plowing through the rough water of the North Atlantic.

By the time the rough waters hit, the passengers housed in the cramped quarters had already begun to smell of sweat and unwashed clothes. The younger people showed the symptoms of seasickness first. Shortly after the up and down movement started, a few of the younger women complained of being nauseous. They became pale and restless and soon were throwing up their most recent meal.

At first they had the energy and the will to make it to strategically placed buckets. By the time they were throwing up the third or fourth time they no longer cared if they made it to the buckets. Within an hour the quarters reeked of vomit. Some of the older women who hadn't felt seasick at first were pushed over the edge by the vile odor. It was then that Christina appreciated the wisdom of being in an upper bunk.

At first Christina felt superior and thought that because of her previous experience aboard boats, she wasn't going to get seasick. Then her stomach began to roll and a wave of nausea swept over her. The urge to throw up was so strong and so sudden that she barely made it to one of the buckets. The relief was instant but short-lived; within minutes the irresistible urge to throw up grabbed her stomach. This time she slowly worked her way back to her bed with the boat swaying and rocking. At the end of the second hour she was confined to her bunk praying for relief. Her experience in smaller boats had not prepared Christina for the extent of her own and others' seasickness when it hit. Few people escaped from seasickness, not even the sailors, although most of them had only a brief bout with it. The seasick crew couldn't keep the area clean and soon the floor was slippery with vomit. Within days the young and very old came down with various ailments brought aboard by the other passengers. There was much coughing and moaning. Christina tried to help with the ill and found some so uncomfortable that they asked to be left alone to die in peace.

The foul weather lifted briefly on the fifth day which allowed Christina and a small group of hardy souls to struggle up on deck for a breath of fresh air. The cold air, the smell of the sea, the sight of the horizon restored her strength. Reluctantly she descended to her quarters where the heavy odor of unwashed bodies engulfed her. In the dim light she felt her way toward her bunk, grabbing the metal bed frames to keep from falling in the slop.

She crawled into her bunk and sat staring off into the

dimly lit surroundings. As her eyes adjusted, Christina found they were fixed on the woman one bunk over from her. The woman was lying very quietly, in the same position she had been in when Christina and the others had left over an hour ago. Christina and the woman hadn't spoken to each other, but Christina knew from Maria that the woman was a widow, Ellen Stormo, who was going to Wisconsin to join her son's family.

Christina got down from her bunk and made her way over to the woman. The woman seemed to be asleep with her eyes wide open. She had missed breakfast and it was nearing supper. Christina leaned over and asked gently, "Mrs. Stormo, can I bring you anything, maybe some soup?" Mrs. Stormo continued to stare at the deck above.

Tentatively Christina reached over and touched Mrs. Stormo's arm. It was cold. Christina grabbed the arm and began shaking it. "Mrs. Stormo, wake up, wake up. It's time for supper." There was no response. A cold chill ran down Christina's back. She turned to several of other women who were sitting on their bunks. "Would you help me? Mrs. Stormo is not waking up."

Two of them came over, went through the touching and shaking process. One turned to Christina and said, "I think she's dead. We had better find one of the ship's crew."

Within minutes one of them had found a steward. He came to the door, studied the situation carefully, then placed a handkerchief over his nose and came over to where Christina was standing by the body. He placed two fingers on Mrs. Stormo's throat and felt for a pulse. He shook his head and lit a match and held it in front of her eyes. The pupils didn't change size; the woman didn't blink. He turned to the anxious group which clustered around the bed. "This woman is dead. Everyone stay back. We'll get her out of here before whatever she had spreads to anyone else." Within minutes all signs of Mrs. Stormo were gone.

The following morning the captain conducted services on the foredeck. Mrs. Stormo's body had been sewn into a canvas sack with rocks at the feet. Beside Mrs. Stormo was the body of a baby who had died on the deck above theirs. Because the parents of the baby were present, the crew had taken special pains. They had put the body in a small wooden coffin weighted with sand.

The baby's family stood by the coffin as the captain read the service. The mother had a dazed look and showed no sign of emotion. The father held another child in his arms and another by the hand. He was staring at something unseen a thousand yards away. A girl of about ten stood to one side sobbing intensely. The captain finished reading, and the small coffin with its tiny passenger and Mrs. Stormo in her canvas sack were assigned to the sea.

As the assembled group broke up, Christina heard the mother say to the father, "It's your fault. You're the one who had to go to America and drag us along. Now look what your wanderlust has done." The father continued to stare into the distance.

The next day was spent cleaning out the quarters. The decks were washed down with seawater and then scrubbed with vinegar water as a disinfectant. Maria and Christina, along with the rest of the steerage passengers, brought their bedding up on deck for airing where they stayed while their quarters were allowed to dry out. Later when they went back below, the smell of seasickness lingered unhidden by the vinegar.

On the seventh day another storm hit the ship. Rain and sleet came pouring down the ropes and through the hatches. Waves broke furiously over the deck. All passengers were sent below and the hatches were battened down. In spite of the smells the passengers felt safe and snug below decks.

Christina was bored. Lighting was too dim to read by.

Christina poked her head over the edge of her bunk, "Maria, talk to me. Tell me something, anything to keep me from going mad."

"Well, let me see. What if we were going over on a boat with an English crew and all the other passengers were Russian. Wouldn't that be terrible?"

"I like the crew. They're friendly."

Maria laughed, "If I were a young sailor, I'd be friendly to a nineteen-year-old Norwegian girl, too. Didn't your mother ever tell you what men are interested in?" she teased, her dimples carving her cheeks.

"Maria, you don't mean it?" Christina was shocked.

"Christina, you are so innocent. Don't they know anything up north? Haven't you ever seen how male dogs pay attention to a female? Men are just like that."

Christina's cheeks flamed. "These are good Norwegian bachelors, not some kind of foreigners who do awful things to women. Now stop talking like that."

Later Christina was standing at the rail deep in thought; her eyes fixed on the waves, when she was startled by the arm of someone brushing against her. A deep voice that demanded attention asked, "Going to America to make your fortune?" She turned to face a man whose thin blond hair was just at her eye level. The man was standing much too close. She could feel his sausage laden breath on her cheek. As she stepped back, she thought, "He's too short. More Maria's size."

The man didn't seem put off by her retreat or her silence. In a voice that insisted on a response he went on. "I'm glad the seasickness is over. It was bad in the men's quarters. I've been noticing you and wanting to say hello. Are you promised in America?"

"No, I'm going to live with my sister and her husband in Dakota Territory," she said cautiously. The talk with Maria about men's intentions had put her on guard.

"I'm going to take up land in Minnesota. You know how to care for animals, keep a garden?"

This is getting awfully personal she thought, but he seemed nice enough, and she didn't want to be rude. "I kept a cow at home and I had a small garden. Mostly it grew potatoes."

"You know how to keep a house then?" he asked.

"Yes." He asks too many questions she thought. I've had enough of them. The man moved closer again, his unpleasant breath again confronting her. Annoyed she turned her back and moved away. "I've been on deck too long, I'm chilled. I'm going below now. Goodbye." She left him standing alone with his mouth still full of his insistent questions. Guilt at her rudeness descended on her.

The men's questions became a subject of conversation below in the women's quarters. Feeling guilty at her rudeness to the man on deck, Christina mentioned him to the woman in the bunk next to her. "Oh, old barnyard breath," she said. "So he's checking you out now. I don't think I would like living with a man whose every statement sounds like an order. By now he's looked all of us over. With us all avoiding him, I wonder who he's going to breathe on for the rest of the trip?"

The short man with the big voice and bad breath didn't approach Christina again, but he must have spread the word to others that she was free to marry and knew how to do farm work because now when she came on deck one or another of the Norwegian bachelors would find occasion to come over to her and start up a conversation.

When Christina commented on this to a group of the women, Maria said, "When men find out I'm promised they quit talking to me. I noticed they don't talk much with women who don't know anything about farming either. You have to ask yourself do they want a wife or a hired hand."

One of the other women laughed. "I think they want both. They're very practical—they just know that a good pioneer woman should be both."

"I still think they're more interested in something else," Maria interjected." I wouldn't go into a darkened part of the ship with them alone."

"Maria, you're awful," Christina said. "These men have good Lutheran upbringing; they've no intention of 'foolin' around. Courting is a serious business, and when a decent young man pays attention to you; you should expect he's got marriage on his mind."

Maria looked at the other women and winked.

The ship provided food but it was inadequate. Most of the passengers in steerage knew they needed to bring extra food to supplement what the ship supplied. Maria found Christina digging in her trunk. "Lose something?" she asked.

Christina straightened, her hands on her hips, "I can't find a sausage I know I had in here yesterday. I don't know where it could be."

"Other people are complaining about missing food. When we're out, someone is getting into our things."

Christina was confused. "You mean we have to lock up our stuff if we want to keep it. We never had to do that at home. That's not right."

Maria shrugged, "You have to live with people the way they are. When they're hungry, they'll do things they wouldn't do if they had lots of food."

"But wouldn't they feel guilty or fear God'll punish them."

"Maybe later. But don't count on it to save what food you got left. Use that big iron key to lock that trunk."

Sad Thoughts

Christina was ready for the trip to be over. The crowded quarters, the lack of privacy, the constant questions from men about could she milk a cow, grow a garden, all combined to make her pull into herself and avoid talking to the other passengers. She lost interest in the men who had been chatting with her and now felt no guilt when she excused herself from a conversation and walked away before the man was done questioning her.

Despite Christina's avoidance of others Maria continued to be a close confidant. As the two women stood on the upper deck watching the endless sea go by, Christina's air of competence was washed away by waves of homesickness. "Maria, I'll never see my home again. I've jumped from the frying pan into the fire. I can't go back and even if I did there's nothing there for me."

"That's true, but the reasons you left haven't changed. You're right. Things won't be any better even if you could go back. You'll just have to keep moving on."

"I wake up from dreaming of my old cottage, my father, Olaf, their boat, my friends, and I can't stop crying." Tears welled in Christina's eyes and Maria put her arms around her. For a few minutes the two women clung to each other in their shared misery.

The depression was made worse by a minor incident that left Christina feeling all was hopeless. It happened when she was standing on deck breathing deeply of the fresh salt air. The ship was lurching in high seas and to keep from falling on deck she hung to the railing. Only two other passengers were on the deck, hunching their shoulders against the brisk wind.

Shielding her eyes from the glare and salt spray, Christina saw a bird struggling to get to the boat. What was a bird doing this far from land? Perhaps the storm had blown it out to sea. The bird was faltering in its struggle to reach the boat and was dipping closer and closer to the water as it fought the wind.

Christina stared at the bird, trying to will it the strength to make the final few yards. She could feel her energy reach out and touch the bird, who with a surge of power, made it the final distance. It dropped to the deck, safe at last. As it lay on the deck exhausted, Christina moved toward it to pick it up and keep it safe.

Just as she was about to touch the tiny creature, the captain's dog leaped on it crushing it in his teeth. She stared unbelieving at the feathers whirling across the deck.

Was this an omen? A voice in her head said, "It's all for nothing, Christina. You can struggle all you wish, but before you reach your goal, you'll be crushed. You can fight a while longer, but in America you're going to be destroyed."

Christina stumbled back to her bunk, curled up in a ball and pulled the covers over her head. All the next day she was silent and nonresponsive. All offers Maria made to bring her food were ignored. On the morning of the second day Maria brought her some bread and cheese and pulled the covers off her. "Christina, you're being a baby. You've got to take care of yourself." Christina moaned, and turned her head away.

Maria shook her gently. "You've got to eat at least a little bit." Christina pulled the covers up again. Maria dug in Christina's bag and found her Bible. "Let's read something that might help you." She paged to the book of Job and read it to her. Still no response.

Maria began to recite the 23rd Psalm. Near the end Christina was mumbling along with her. That gave Maria the opportunity to ask Christina to pray with her. Together they prayed for strength to get through the black times. The familiar ritual and sense of God's presence restored her.

Shortly there was a shout from outside in the passageway. "Man coming into the women's quarters." A moment later Ole, was standing by her bunk. "Maria says you're not doing so well."

She buried her face in the mattress, embarrassed to be seen by a man when she looked such a mess and felt so low.

Ole went on as if she were paying attention. "It's not good to stay down here in the dark too much; you might find yourself with too many black thoughts. Let Maria help you get fixed up and come up on the deck. There are things I want to show you." He turned and worked his way past the beds.

Sighing deeply, Christina swung her legs over the side of the bed and chewed for awhile on the bread and cheese Maria had brought her. Finally she smiled weakly and began brushing her hair.

Maria brought Christina a basin of water to wash up in. Then she dug in Christina's trunk and found a nearly clean dress and helped her into it. Christina numbly followed Maria up on deck where Ole waited for them. At first she heard nothing that was said to her. Ole led her to the rail and kept talking. Gradually his voice began to form sentences in her mind. The blue sky, the bright sun and cool breeze revived her spirits.

"See that big hunk of ice out there?" he said, pointing to a glistening white iceberg. "Well, most of it's below the water. We hit that and we join the mackerel."

Christina shuddered at the idea of the mackerel. "I didn't come this far to be food for the mackerel," she muttered, her voice cracking.

Maria and Ole both jumped at her voice. Except for the prayer with Maria neither of them had heard her speak since she had seen the bird killed. When she didn't say anything more, Ole went on, "We'll see a lot of these now, but we keep a careful watch. Unlikely any ship would be so poorly captained that's they'd hit one." He went on talking about the sea and the men who sailed on it.

The next morning Christina woke, her spirits revived. The dark mood had gone with the ice floes. From now on, she told herself she must spend as much time out of this gloomy steerage as possible. If she stayed down here with the gloom and smells, the stupor might come back again.

She was eager to get up and out of the quarters. Her plans were to be on the deck when it was possible; but when bad weather came, she would go to the ship's barn and help with the animals. The decision to be more active kept her spirits revived, and again she began to enjoy meeting people especially the young men who worked in the barn. They respected her sway over animals. An hour or two in the barn and she would leave smelling of cattle or horses but feeling attractive.

An Invitation and Warning

Ole came to the entry of the women's section and stood a moment while his eyes adjusted to the dimness. He stopped at the bunks of several of other young women before he reached Christina. "I'm glad I found you." He said. "The captain sent you an invitation." He handed her a card carefully written in script that said, "Captain Lamberg requests the pleasure of your company for coffee in his cabin at the change of watch tomorrow morning." Ole stood waiting for an answer.

"Of course I'll come. I wouldn't miss it," Christina said.

She was excited. Getting to have coffee with the Captain, even for those in private quarters was considered a special event. Some of the other women who hadn't been invited mumbled their discontent just loud enough for the Christina to hear.

"The captain has an eye for the young ones. Probably up to no good."

"Well, that certainly is going to make some people feel pretty high and mighty."

"Doesn't that old dog know his attention is wasted on children?

Most of the women pretended that it was unimportant. Christina guessed that each of those invited probably had a friend like Bry who knew the Captain and had asked him to keep an eye on their young lady. Whatever the reason for the invitation, it was obvious that the Captain was taking a personal interest in each of the six.

The next morning Christina pulled her trunk out from under the bed, unlocked it, took out her best dress, shook out what wrinkles she could and got ready. Maria fixed her hair in fresh braids, pulling the hair on the front of her forehead tight as she worked the braids into a bun at the back.

The six women who had been invited were nervous and self conscious as they entered the Captain's cabin. They were aware that everyone on board treated the captain with special respect. Even the rich people in the private cabins deferred to him. They knew that any man who got that reaction from others must be very powerful and wise.

The cabin was finished in attractive woods, oiled and highly polished, which Christina didn't recognize. After having been packed so closely together in steerage, Christina was delighted to be in a compartment with only six other people.

Captain Lamberg smiled but seemed oddly ill at ease with the young ladies. The muscle under his right eye twitched, and he rarely looked directly at them. His voice reminded Christina of her father's, deep and resonant, and made her feel warm and protected. She thought, "How can he give orders that are obeyed so quickly? He talks more like I wish Pastor Erickson did."

The women did not chat with each other as they sipped their coffee. Awed by their surroundings they were content to let the captain do most of the talking. He began by commenting on the weather and asked if they had all been able to watch the icebergs move by. The twitch under his eye became more frequent, and he flushed slightly as he said, "None of you have your parents here to give advice. I want you to think of me as sitting in for your father in what I am about to say." The women leaned forward curious about what he might reveal.

"New York City is a very dangerous place. There are many men who prey on newcomers. They count on your innocence of America and your trusting natures to take advantage of you. I must insist, that for your own welfare, you don't talk with anyone when you leave the Castle Garden entry point. You should be particularly suspicious of men who come up to you and want to take you to dinner. They want to recruit women to their houses."

Captain Lamberg coughed and his face reddened as he said this. He paused to regain his composure. Christina didn't know what he was talking about but was too shy to ask him to give more of an explanation.

She could see that the captain's discomfort was stopping the others from asking him questions. She found herself wishing Maria was with them to help get the Captain to clarify what he meant. There was an embarrassed pause in which they all stared down at their coffee cups and concentrated on finding something in the depths of the coffee's blackness.

The captain cleared his throat and continued. "My men will see that your luggage is moved to the train station." Having given his lesson on how to survive in the New World, the Captain stood up, excused himself and went out on deck.

Back in steerage Christina immediately looked for Maria. "Maria, the Captain told us men would come up and offer to take us to dinner, but we weren't to talk with them because they were trying to find women for their houses." She paused to catch her breath. "He didn't tell us what he meant and got all red when he was telling us about them. I don't understand."

Maria started to laugh and said, "Christina, you are such a baby. Didn't they tell you anything in Vardo?"

"Maria, tell me."

"You know what the bull did to your cow when you wanted her to have a calf? Well, there are men who pay money to do the same thing to a woman. If you go with those men, they'll kidnap you and put you in a house where men come and pay to have sex. They won't ever let you go out, and they'll make you do it all night long."

Christina shook her head in disbelief. "Maria, you tell such stories. That doesn't even make any sense."

"That's why the Captain was embarrassed. He knows that some women have become slaves to these men. Even if you escape from one of those houses, no God fearing man will ever want to marry you."

That night Christina awoke sweating from a dream in which she was running down a narrow street with a giant bull chasing her as well dressed men grabbed and pulled at her trying to get her into their houses.

CHAPTER THIRTEEN

THE ARRIVAL IN NEW YORK

One morning Ole came into the women's quarters to announce, "After breakfast the Captain wants all women on forward deck. He has some important things to say to you before we arrive in New York."

As they gathered on the deck, there was much primping of hair and smoothing of dresses. One woman was cleaning a smudge from another woman's face with spit on a handkerchief.

Appearing as if from nowhere, the captain was in front of them. He cleared his throat, which brought them to complete silence. Christina could feel the tension of the women as they moved forward to hear him above the wind.

"We'll be arriving tomorrow at Castle Island which is at the south end of Manhattan Island in New York City. The American immigration officials will meet you there to check your papers. They will examine you to make sure you are healthy. If they find you have a serious illness, you will not be allowed ashore. Let us pray that you are all healthy. The official will also ask you questions about yourself and what you intend to do. Do not tell them if you already have work; instead tell them that you will be looking for work."

The personal concern shown by the captain in their reaching their destination safely increased the intensity with which the women listened to what he had to say. The Captain paused. He seemed hesitant to continue as if he didn't quite know how to make them believe what he had to say. There was shuffling of feet as the listeners picked up his tension.

Finally he took a deep breath and began speaking more rapidly than usual. "Once you are through immigration and into the city of New York, some people, even women, will come up to you speaking good Norwegian and claiming they want to be your friend. I don't like to say this about a fellow Norwegian, but most of these people are criminals. They're called runners and will try to get you to stay in overpriced hotels or eat in bad restaurants. If you don't watch them closely, they will steal your baggage or anything else they can get their hands on. They may try to sell you something. Don't buy it. Our experience is that it will be junk. Some of the men will promise to get transportation for you to where you're going at much better rates than I or my agent has gotten for you.

"It's true these men will get you fares on trains or boats at half a dollar below those designated by the Established Emigrant Transportation Company, and even so they pocket half a dollar per passenger. But the truth of the matter is that the transportation they'll get for you is not safe and might take eight to fourteen days longer than what we've arranged. They've been known to load so many passengers into their boats that many have gotten sick and some have died. We've had reports of emigrants being put ashore only halfway to their destination."

Christina saw several women take each other's hand for support as the captain was giving his warning. He paused to give his words time to sink in. When he started to talk again, the group leaned forward as one.

"You've already heard stories of the pickpockets in New York. The stories are no exaggeration; the city is overflowing with them. My advice is get out of New York as soon as you can; it's not a fit city for decent young Scandinavian women."

Without waiting to answer any questions, he turned and disappeared down a hatchway.

After he left the women stood silent, as if overwhelmed with dealing with the hazards of New York. A pinch-faced woman said, "Forewarned is forearmed. Let's get on with it." The tension broke and women gathered in groups of three and four. There was the buzz of voices as they discussed the implications of what the Captain had just said. Maria and Christina agreed with the pinch-faced woman, who had joined them, that they would take no chances on anything other than the arrangements that the captain had made.

Two mornings after the Captain's talk the girls awoke to great excitement in the quarters. Women were quickly pulling on clothes to go on deck. Word had quickly spread that the skyline of New York was growing out of the darkness. The morning weather was fair, and the passengers from steerage crowded the deck to get the best view of their new country. Maria took Christina's hand and pushing and shoving they worked their way close enough to the rail to watch the skyline.

Christina looked around at the people; some were laughing, some had tears running down their cheeks and several were both laughing and crying. She turned back to the skyline and felt a cold hand of fear run down her back. Maria felt her fear and squeezed her hand. "There's so much to do, so much to remember," Christina said. "I can't believe I'll ever get to Petrina's; it seems further now than when I started."

"Everything will be all right." Maria reassurance fell on deaf ears. Christina's heart was beating so hard that it blocked out the sounds around her.

Late in the afternoon they were allowed to disembark at Castle Garden, the American immigration station. Maria and Christina came down the gangplank together. Once on the wharf the solid ground kept coming and jarring their legs. "Maria, I can't get my feet to hit the ground right."

"I'm having the same problem." They went inside the building where they would be processed. "It feels like the building is moving."

"I know," Christina replied. "When I had been on the boat from Vardo, it was days before I got over the feeling that I was still moving over the water."

They entered a large circular auditorium and became one with a mob of immigrants from other ships. Christina looked at the high ceiling and distant walls. "This one room could hold passengers from many ships," Christina said.

"Maybe seven or eight thousand people." Even Maria was impressed with the room's size. The area was full of immigrants from other countries already waiting to be processed by the American officers. One of the officers saw they were confused and came over. He pointed to a group in the middle of the auditorium, "You Norwegians who just arrived, you stand over there in that line."

The interpreter who processed them showed them where there was hot water in the washrooms and food at low prices. They were allowed to sleep on the floor overnight.

The next morning as Christina left Castle Garden, she saw crowds of people gathered to watch her and the other disembarking immigrants. Some of them were obviously

124

relatives or friends of passengers, but others seemed to have different reasons for being there. A line of carriages with handsome matched teams of horses were lined up along one side of the street. Women in expensive clothes sat in the coaches staring at the passengers as they disembarked. One lady in a black satin dress conspicuously covered her nose and mouth with a lace handkerchief as the new arrivals came out into the street.

When Christina reached the street, she went over to a sailor who was helping the passengers get their baggage aboard a van on its way to the train station. "Who are the grand ladies sitting in the coaches?" she asked.

The sailor gave them a quick glance and said in a low voice, "They're the cream of the city. Very rich. Watching you immigrants come ashore is like entertainment for some of the wealthy."

Christina walked closer to the spectators and returned their stares. She was enthralled both by the fine silks and satins the ladies were wearing and the beauty of the matched teams of horses. She couldn't remember ever seeing their like in Norway. The lady she was staring at withdrew into the carriage and spoke to her groom who shouted at Christina. The sweeping gesture of his arm coupled with his scowl indicated she should move on.

She turned and walked back to stand by her luggage and just listened to the sounds around her. She recognized some of the languages being spoken because they had a Scandinavian sound to them. She had been told that other immigrants would be arriving on ships from Finland, Germany and Sweden. She recognized Swedish when she heard it because it sounded much like Norwegian. She knew that with a little care she would be able to talk to Swedes, but the thought bothered her.

Her father had once said to her, "Swedes are an irritable lot, people who have inflated ideas of their own worth. They're the kind, who once they get in control, will hold you down. We would be better off if we could get free of the Swedes."

She was a little surprised that the captain hadn't warned them against talking to the Swedes. Another time Christina had asked Anders, "Papa, the Swedish king tells us what to do and sends his people here to enforce his rules. What are the Swedes like when they're in Sweden?"

Anders took the question very seriously. "The Swedes? The Swedes are great brooders. They are very formal, not at all a friendly people. Even when a Swede becomes rich, he stays miserable. The only good Swede is a drunken Swede; then he sings and will talk to a Norwegian."

The thoughts of her father's advice were interrupted by a well-dressed man speaking English who came over to her. He was wearing a fancy black suit with a high collared white shirt and a red tie. Only in Trondheim had she seen men so well dressed. There was a feminine air about the man as if he were as soft as a woman. The man came and stood very close to her causing her to step back a step. When he saw she didn't understand English, he switched to halting Swedish.

"I have job for attractive young lady. You can earn good money and buy nice house in few years. Come with me and I will buy good meal for you in best New York restaurant."

Christina turned away. She knew intuitively that she didn't want anything to do with this man in spite of his nice manners. White slavery in a house of prostitution had never been talked about at home, but the Captain's lecture and the chat with Maria had convinced her that the man was dangerous. The man seemed unabashed by her turning away from him. He made a comment that with her looks she should be flattered to get an offer. Sighting another young woman standing alone he moved off down the line.

In a few minutes another man approached her. In good Norwegian he said, "I have a good place for you to stay here in

New York." He reached for her bag, pulled it from her hands and moved off down the street calling back over his shoulder, "Hurry up, you need to come early if you're going to get a room."

Taken by surprise, she stood gaping after him for a moment. Then seeing her bag disappearing, she sprung forward, and in a few long strides had the man by the tail of his coat. "Stop, I don't need a room. Give me my bag." The man kept moving.

Ole, noticing the commotion, came running up and placed himself in front of the man ready to hit him with a pry bar he had in his hand. The man set her bag down. "Here, here," he said, "no need to get so upset. I was only trying to help the lady. I'm just a good Norwegian trying to be kind to a fellow immigrant."

With Ole's help Christina's baggage was finally put aboard a wagon with that of some of the other passengers. The four horses pulling the load were old and undernourished. This work was probably the end of the road for horses which once pulled the fine ladies' carriages Christina thought. She was helped up onto the baggage by the driver. She, Maria and five other women began their trip to the train station. None of them planned to stay over in New York.

Christina felt defenseless and vulnerable; the captain's talk, the approach of the well dressed man and the runner, the sheer confusion of the streets of New York made her feel that danger was everywhere. Once they were in the streets working their way toward the train station, she kept her eyes on her brightly painted trunk. In the last hour she had learned that anyone might attempt to run off with her few treasures.

Christina was finding New York overwhelming, and her mind was working double quick to keep up with what she was seeing. She knew if she stopped to relax and take a breath she would miss something important. There were thousands of people moving in all four directions. Unlike a Norwegian city few of them had blond hair and pink skin. Dark hair and light brown skin seemed to be normal here. As a group the men seemed quite short; many of them were not tall enough to look directly in her eyes. And the fast way they moved surprised her.

Everybody was in such a hurry to get somewhere. She saw a man dressed like someone who had just gotten off the boat stop to look up at one of the buildings. First someone bumped him on the right side, and as he turned two men pulling a wagon shoved him. Losing his balance the man sat down hard on the ground and the mob swept around him. No one stopped to help him, and he was still struggling to get up as the wagon moved them around a corner.

She returned to watching the scene unfolding around her. There were hundreds of other horse drawn carts and buggies. It was amazing to her how the driver could move about in this confusion. She looked up to examine the buildings and saw people leaning out of open windows shouting to people below. As they went through an intersection and she got a chance to see the tops of the buildings, she saw smoke pouring out of chimneys giving the air its gritty, unpleasant quality.

Maria was taking the same train as far as Chicago. Christina could feel a surge of energy much like that she felt during the time of the midnight sun. She knew that it would be days before she would be able to sleep regular hours again because she was so churned up inside by all she was experiencing.

"Maria, the people are dressed so strangely and they look so different from the people at home. Look at all those men with black beards and funny hats."

As usual Maria was amused at what she saw as Christina's innocence. It made her feel worldly wise to be able to explain things to her. "The men with the funny hats are Jews. They are fleeing to America not only because of hunger, but because in some countries people are killing them because of their religion."

"Look, those men are all covered with something black."

"Those are Africans. They were once slaves in America. There are lots of them here."

Christina's head was in a spin. So much was happening so quickly that there was no time to worry about what was to come or to be sad about leaving Norway and her friends there. Even the loss of Anders and Olaf was pushed into the back of her mind.

As soon as arrangements were made to get a train ticket, she would be on her way to the end of the railroad line in Brookings, a town in Dakota Territory. Soon she would finally be back in the arms of a family that she could call her own.

CHRISTINA's SAGA:
BOOK TWO
DAKOTA TERRITORY

NORTH DAKOTA

DAKOTA TERRITORY

Watertown •
Hayti •
Lake Poinsett • Estelline
• Brookings

SOUTH DAKOTA

CHAPTER FOURTEEN

THE ARRIVAL IN DAKOTA TERRITORY
1880

$\mathcal{M}$aria left the train shortly after they got into Illinois. During their last conversation Maria joked about the fun she would have teaching her new husband about sex without him knowing he was being taught. As was now usual for her, Christina was both shocked and amused by Maria's comments. She didn't break down and cry until hours later. She was watching the passing countryside and began to remember Maria's warmth and humor. She thought, "I only just meet people and they're gone from me forever." Suddenly the tears welled up and spilled over.

It was late in the day when the train arrived in Brookings, the first station in Dakota Territory. As she stepped down off the train, the fine dust made her sneeze and then sneeze again. Everything around her on the station platform was in disorder, and she was engulfed in noise, moving bodies, dust and the stench that heat draws out of animals and people. Her senses were overwhelmed.

People were moving around like two schools of fish swimming through each other. Baggage was being loaded and unloaded, carts being pushed to and fro on the platform. Standing with her baggage amid all the confusion, Christina felt dizzy and bewildered. She bowed her head and put her hands over her eyes to allow herself time to regain her presence of mind.

As she took her hands away from her face, some stray hair fell over her face blocking her view of the chaotic scene. She poked at the unruly strands; her inner thoughts fluttering from one dead end to the other in the maze of her mind. "Oh, my back aches so. My legs are stiff. My hair is dirty: it's out of control. I'm sure I look even worse than usual." Out loud to no one in particular she asked, "What on earth do I do next?" The question was lost. Her voice was only a whisper in the wind of sound that surrounded her.

She took a deep breath and allowed the activity to swirl around her without trying to make sense of it. The paths of a few well dressed men in suits and ties interlaced with those of men in rough working clothes.

She scanned the moving mass and found a stationary figure to focus on. He was dressed in a leather shirt and canvas pants. He had a face that reminded her of what one of the Devil's helpers had looked like in an illustrated Bible she had seen as a child. A hat pulled down to his pointed ears cast a shadow over deep-set eyes and a prominent nose. Evil leaped out from his face pushing warmth away. He saw her recoil, moved his jaws firmly up and down and spit a stream of brown juice in her direction. It lit some distance away but fell among previous spews. She saw that if she didn't lift her skirt when walking she would soon have a wet, brown hem.

On both sides of the station, wagons and carts pulled by horses and oxen waited for loading. A little girl with two small boys chasing her ran by. Christina stepped back to avoid them when a heavy blow hit her from behind. Her weeks at sea had tuned her sense of balance, which kept her from falling. When she had steadied herself, she turned to see a young man. He had been walking backward pulling a cart loaded with boxes labeled Dr. Roback's stomach BITTERS. He blushed and said something to her in English. The two boys she had avoided stopped to watch but scurried off when the young man yelled something at them. He then bowed in her direction, leaned into the weight of the wagon and this time faced forward as he pulled his load into an area marked "Baggage."

Christina knew that Brookings was temporarily the end point of the railroad, and as such, the jumping off point for homesteaders who were just now taking up claims in Dakota Territory. Much of what she knew had been translated for her by Maria. Christina admired the ease with which Maria could get men to talk to her. Her look of wonderment at their knowledge led them to tell her what she wanted to know. Even on subjects she knew about she would listen intently, her head cocked in admiration.

A ticket agent Maria had questioned at their final change of trains had told Maria that business was booming for the railroads. He had said, "The railroad owners can hardly help but make a fortune. Capitalism is booming and making new millionaires every week. You've come to the right country to get rich."

Maria had asked, her voice full of respect, "How are they getting so rich, when we come over with so little money?"

He had spit tobacco juice at a brass spittoon sitting on the platform, missed, but didn't seem to notice or care. "Well, young lady, a lot of people with a little money adds up to a lot of money. We now got two passenger trains a day into Brookings. Each train has from seven to nine coaches. Within a year the Chicago and Northwestern Railroad is goin' to finish a branch line from Brookings to Watertown, and then with all you Norskys and Germans coming in you bet they're goin' to begin building beyond Watertown. All you newcomers are hard workin' people; you'll make good farmers. Yup, some people goin' to make big money in this country." The man had run out of breath, and chewing hard on his wad of tobacco had made out their tickets.

Maria had then gone into the waiting room to stay with Christina until her train left. A man in an ill-fitting wool suit, who had a prominent red nose with the veins showing, had approached the two girls. "Buy you ladies a cup of coffee to pass the time away? My name's Bay, Josh Bay. I'm a drummer, sell plows."

In spite of his red nose he acted like he was a real lady's man, and Maria had put on her best seductive smile and tilted her head in an admiring angle.

His chest swelled and he smiled as if he were a fellow conspirator in some secret plot. He paid no more attention to Christina but focused all of his charm on Maria who used this as an opportunity to get more information about Dakota Territory for Christina.

When they had settled down at a table over coffee, Maria had asked, "Plows? You sell plows for the farmers?"

"Yup, young lady, and to carry all the plows I sell, they needs lots of trains. Well, there are also some stoves, furniture, baggage and other implements for the new landowners and between us they got to run nine or ten freight trains a day going through to Brookings. Why they got small settlements springing up on the prairie almost like magic. We got Europe moving over here to the great prairie. Way things is goin' soon won't be nobody left where you came from."

Then Josh added, "Even running that many trains we're behind in getting goods in. We just can't keep up with demand. This is a great time to be a salesman. We're all goin' to get rich. You ladies want you a good man, who's got money, you marry a drummer, not some farmer."

That business was as good as he had said it was, had been evident to Christina on the train trip across Illinois. At almost every station after Chicago she saw goods piled haphazardly in every direction on the platform and sidings waiting to be moved out to the homes of their owners.

Wayne P. Anderson

Transportation into the Wilderness

Standing on the platform at the Brooking Station amid the confusion, Christina asked, of no one in particular, "What will be left of Europe if so many people are coming to America?" She shook her head and refocused on the matter at hand. Where did help lie in all this muddle?

By continuing to watch carefully Christina saw there was a pattern in this commotion. Much of the activity centered around the barn-like area the cart with the BITTERS had gone into. Boxes and crates were piled in a more orderly fashion; and after watching the people moving in and out for a while, she saw the action centered around a tall, thin man in a worn gray uniform. He had on a hat that looked to Christina like it was official.

He had a long mustache pointed at the ends. She had not seen one quite like it before and was entranced by the way it moved when he talked. The eyes above the mustache met hers. He smiled. Having been caught staring made her squirm with embarrassment. She chided herself, "Christina, you're too bold."

His friendliness to those people coming up to him helped her gain the courage to approach. She told herself, "You been standing around long enough. It's time you started making arrangements to get to the lake."

Once the decision was made she lifted her skirt above the platform with its still damp tobacco juice and took quick strides over to the baggage master and asked him in Norwegian if he could help her find some way to get to Lake Poinsett. His smile turned to confusion as if trying to figure out what language she was talking. Christina was frustrated. How can there be so many people and so few who know how to speak Norwegian? They stood looking at each other, neither quite sure about what to do next.

The baggage master's face relaxed. He gave her a fatherly pat on the shoulder and motioned her to wait. He disappeared into one of the side rooms reappearing a few minutes later leading a thin, blond boy of about her age who was carrying a broom. His face was covered with so many red and yellow pimples that it was painful for her to look directly at him. He became instantly better looking when he began to speak in Swedish. "I'm Tod. Mr. Jamison said you speak some kind of Scandinavian."

Her eyes teared up with relief hearing him speak. Now she could get something done. She nodded yes to his question and said, "I understand Swedish."

Seeing the tears in her eyes, he blushed and dropped the broom. He stooped to pick it up and backed into Mr. Jamison, which caused him to redden even more. Finally with the broom under control his own control returned, and Tod pulled his shoulders back, cleared his throat in order to produce his best adult voice, and said, "He keeps me around to talk to immigrants from Scandinavia when I'm not loading the train or sweeping out the dirt that keeps blowing in. What do you want?"

It had been hours since she talked with anyone who understood her. Her first impulse was to tell him everything that had happened to her since Maria left. Instead she told herself to keep it simple. "I need to get to Lake Poinsett. I'd like help finding someone with a wagon going that way who can take me and my trunk. I'm going to live with my sister and her husband on their homestead."

The boy translated for Mr. Jamison. Jamison looked directly at her and spoke for a while in English. She stared at him intently, fascinated by the variations of black in the shine on his handlebar mustache. What kind of oil or wax must he use to give it such a fine shape?

When he had finished Tod said to her in Swedish, "Mr. Jamison says that many farmers are here to haul their equipment and baggage. Some of them will be going close to the lake. He will ask around to find someone to haul you and your baggage. He says for you to wait outside on the platform for a while. When he finds someone, we'll come and get you."

Within the hour Mr. Jamison and Tod came out with an older heavyset man with well-muscled arms who was introduced to her as Mr. John Fennern. He was wearing a heavy homespun shirt buttoned at the wrists, well patched pants and a tattered straw hat which had not kept his face from getting reddish brown from the sun. His color contrasted with the white skin of Mr. Jamison who seemed to spend most of his time inside the baggage building.

Tod told her, "Mr. Fennern, he's a German homesteader in town to pick up a stove, a new plow, several hundred pounds of flour and things like salt and sugar. He says his wagon's pretty full but he can get your stuff on the load."

One of the wagons she had looked at earlier turned out to be Mr. Fennern's. Two oxen the same dull beige as the dust on the platform stood flicking their tails against the flies. Her baggage would just fit in the small space left in the wagon. Tod continued to translate. "It's about forty miles to where you want to go. He said with the heavy load it will take almost three days."

Christina nervously ran her hands over her unruly hair, tucking in stray strands, hoping to look more mature than she felt. She was getting ready to do business. Money was concerned so her shyness had to be placed on the back of the cupboard and her resolve brought to the front. With Tod as intermediary they made their offers. Tod said, "Mr. Fennern will carry it for $1.50."

Christina countered, "I think it's only worth a dollar." She didn't really know if it was a good offer but her father told her people usually asked too much.

Tod talked with Mr. Fennern a while. Mr. Fennern glanced

at her, drew his furry caterpillar eyebrows into a line across his forehead and made a short statement to Tod, who turned back to Christina, "He said since you're a young girl he's already made his best offer. If he knew you were a haggler, he would have set the price higher. For the money he will take you right by your sister's homestead." Tod added, "I think he's making you a good price; you'd be wise to take it."

She reexamined Mr. Fennern who continued to stand with his thumbs in his belt, elbows set wide and looking down at her from his full height. Christina caught a twinkle in his eyes. He seemed amused that she wanted to dicker. The eyes made Christina feel safe with him. She said to Tod, "Tell him I'll pay what he asks."

Having made the deal the mantel of shyness slipped over her again, and she averted her eyes from Mr. Fennern. The travels of the past year would not have been possible if she had not learned to rely on the kindness of strangers. Experience told her that for some reason older men were willing to help and protect young girls. After all, where would she be without Ivar, the two Norwegian captains, Mr. Jamison and now Mr. Fennern?

Tod translated Mr. Fennern's last statement, "I'll be ready to go at daybreak tomorrow. You be sure and be ready." She watched as Mr. Fennern moved a sack of flour and wedged her trunk into a spot behind the driver's seat.

To save her scant reserves of cash Christina slept sitting up in the waiting room of the railway station. At first she fidgeted in the hardwood seats. Her muscles ached and she could find no way to sit to make herself comfortable. Finally using her carpetbag as a pillow she found a spot where her body hurt less and being on the edge of exhaustion fell into a sound sleep. The light of the dawn woke her, and she came out to see Mr. Fennern feeding the oxen. He stopped to help her load her baggage into the wagon.

Just as Mr. Fennern was laying out the harness to yoke up the oxen, Mr. Jamison came out to talk with him. Again she found her attention fixated on Mr. Jamison's mustache, and as his mouth moved she saw light glisten off the ends from the new wax he had used to shape it this morning. Christina's attention was drawn away from Mr. Jamison's upper lip adornment by a movement off to her side where she noticed a short dark man not much older than her was also watching the conversation.

At first Mr. Fennern shook his head, and said, "Nein." Mr. Jamison continued to talk motioning toward the dark man. Finally Mr. Fennern turned, looked at the wagon load and then at the two duffel bags standing by the young man and said, "Ya."

The young man was motioned forward, and after a bit of moving and shoving, his bags were placed on the wagon between the plow and the stove. Without being asked, the young man immediately began to help Fennern yoke the oxen. When they were ready to move, he crawled up on the wagon and sat on a sack of flour behind Mr. Fennern. Christina was already sitting on the other side of the wagon seat. In clear Danish that was easily understood by Christina he said, "My name's Paul Christinson."

Her heart jumped at the sound of Danish. She was delighted to have someone who would understand her on the trip. She turned to face him, "I'm Christina Gunnerson."

Silence. Her eyes met his briefly which gave him encouragement to go on. "I've been a sailor on a Norwegian ship. I jumped ship in Baltimore to come here and join my older brother Arron, who came over here three years ago. His homestead is close to Mr. Fennern's."

Christina leaned closer to him. She felt drawn to Paul, whom she immediately saw as kinfolk. She was so lonesome for the sound of good home talk that she had even responded to Tod, a Swede, as if meeting him were almost as good as meeting someone from Norway. She told Paul, "I'm going to live with my sister and her husband who have a claim near a Lake Poinsett."

She hitched herself over on the seat to get still closer to Paul. When she did his large ears, which stood out from his head, reddened slightly. She saw that his skin was weathered, a sign that he had probably worked top deck on the ship.

Mr. Fennern got into his seat, shouted a command and cracked his bullwhip on the oxen's rumps. The oxen strained to get the wagon moving. With a creaking of wheels the wagon inched forward. Christina could see that the oxen were in for a hard four days. Wind, she thought, wasn't so sure as oxen but was faster.

Two miles out of Brookings the wagon began crossing grassland with only a suggestion of a trail. Before them stretched vast empty space; there were no trees, no fences and for mile after mile few buildings. The land was so featureless that Christina expected Mr. Fennern to take navigation instruments out to chart his course. When they did see a rare building, it was often a twelve by twelve foot claim shack in pinewood or a sod shanty. Only once did they pass a building that looked like a real home.

She had been so used to leaning her eyes on the walls of the fjords that flatness with its lack of trees and buildings was disturbing to her. Unlike the sea she just had crossed, this one was untroubled. A few birds wheeled in the sky above. There was no place to hide and the sheer immensity of this New World frightened her. All she saw mile after mile was waves of knee high grass ruffled by a steady breeze that any sea captain would have been overjoyed to have in his sails.

After the first flurry of conversation Christina and Paul pulled back into mutual shyness. They had been so eager to talk that their Scandinavian reserve had dissolved too quickly, and they now needed time to themselves to rebuild an appropriate social barrier.

Christina watched the sky. It was very clear, no clouds and blue beyond anything she had seen before. The sun beat down on the slow moving wagon. As the day heated up Christina's throat dried out, her lips cracked and she became preoccupied with water. She didn't want to be a bother to Mr. Fennern but there was no sign of a water keg. Finally she turned to Paul, "I need a drink; I'm dying of thirst."

"I'll ask Mr. Fennern to find a waterhole. I need a drink too."

Paul tapped Fennern on the shoulder and with hand signals and the word "wasser" got him to understand. Fennern grunted and pointed up ahead, indicating that soon they would find water. Another half mile and they saw cattails ahead indicating a slough. The young couple jumped off the wagon and rushed ahead. They reached the waterhole only to find it covered with a green scum with bugs skating over it. Christina felt a flash of anger. Her face reddened. "Is Mr. Fennern playing a joke on us? We can't drink this water."

Paul agreed, "Looks like a swamp."

A half-hour passed before Mr. Fennern and the wagon arrived. The oxen were his first concern and he unhooked them and led them down to the water. They stuck their noses deep into the water and began to suck it up. When they raised their noses to take a breath, green slime hung down like gangrened snot. Mr. Fennern came over to where Christina and Paul stood with a tin cup in his hand which he used to clear some of green away, dipped water up and drank with apparent relish.

Paul pointed to the green scum and bugs and made motions as if throwing up. "I want him to know that this water might make us sick."

Fennern shook his head, "Nein." Then he pointed to his eyes and closed them. Paul said to Christina, "I think he means if you close your eyes, you won't find it so bad."

"Paul, I can't drink it and I need water."

"I think we can do something. Have you got some kind of cloth? We'll strain the bugs out." When Christina had found a cloth, he placed it over the tin cup and showed her how to strain water into her mouth. For the first time on the trip they saw Fennern smile. Christina then took the cloth and squeezed water into the cup for Paul. When she did, Mr. Fennern burst out in a loud laugh as if he found the daintiness of the newcomers comic. The laugh embarrassed Christina, and she had a picture of Mr. Fennern telling his wife and friends about the crazy Scandinavians who were afraid of a few bugs and a little green slime.

Later when she told Petrina about it, Trina said, "The same thing happened to me, but I didn't know about straining out the bugs so I passed up the first waterhole. By the time we reached the next hole, I did just what Fennern told you to do; I shut my eyes and drank."

After the adventure of the waterhole Christina and Paul felt closer together and found things to talk about. Tired of riding they got off to walk. The oxen moved so slowly that they could take side trips to explore the land and still catch up with the wagon. Christina was excited to be back on the ground after the weeks she had spent on ships and the days on the train. Now she was in control of where she went.

"Paul, the ground feels different when you walk on it."

He walked in silence for a while before he said, "It's soft, and you can almost feel yourself bounce when you walk on it. I'll bet it's the dead grass built up over the years." He jumped up and lit hard. Christina could see the tremor of the impact for several feet around.

With enthusiasm she said, "Paul, look how black the dirt is where the farmer has broken the sod. It's so different from the rocky soil we had on the island."

"My brother says he can grow most any crop here. He says if it grows grass that thick it will grow oats, corn, wheat, potatoes, anything you can think of to plant. With dirt like this to work we will all become rich beyond anything we had in Europe. We won't need to be servants to anybody anymore."

The sun was on the horizon directly in their eyes before Fennern stopped to make camp for the night. They ate hard bread and cheese with mold on it and a fatty sausage that Fennern smacked his lips over. When it came time to lay out the blankets, Mr. Fennern pointed firmly to the places where each of them was to bed down for the night. He then very pointedly placed his bedroll halfway between theirs.

Paul commented to Christina on this, "He's a Low German, probably over from Russia. They think young people can't be trusted."

"Trusted with what?"

Paul looked at her as if trying to find a polite answer she would understand. His look of discomfort brought back a memory of Maria's statement on the sea voyage over, that she was awfully naive about sexual matters. That made Paul's meaning clear to her. She blushed and said, "Oh."

The look of enlightenment that accompanied the "Oh" took Paul off the hook, and they made their arrangements for bedding down. It was an hour before Christina could fall asleep. The stimulation of talking with Paul, the noises of the night and anticipation of seeing Petrina again made her mind race in circles pushing sleep away.

The next day and the next night were like the first: flat grasslands and occasional sod shanties. She felt they were passing a giant picture painted on a roller that was being run past them over and over. Nothing changed; it had all been fixed for eternity.

It was late afternoon when they reached the northwest shore of Lake Poinsett. In the greetings with her sister and Lars she hardly had time to say goodbye to Paul. Mr. Fennern was in a hurry to move on. He had another day on the road before he would reach his farm. He dropped her trunk and bags on the ground, declined Petrina's invitation to stay for coffee, watered the oxen and slowly moved off into the distance. An hour later they had just disappeared below the horizon.

CHAPTER FIFTEEN

DISCONTENTMENT

𝕴n her dream the ship had hit choppy seas and Christina was holding on to keep from being thrown into the cold water. Instead she woke to Petrina shaking her shoulder. "Christina, you're oversleeping again."

Petrina's tone was getting more unfriendly by the day. "Oh, Trina, I need more sleep. I can't get up; I'm too tired." Christina pulled herself into a ball and stuck her head under the pillow.

Petrina slapped her on her bottom and shouted at her, "Lying in bed all day is for rich people. We're trying to make a farm out of this desert. You got water to carry for the corn and chickens and a cow to feed. Now, no more nonsense, get up."

Christina clenched her fists under the covers and attempted to keep the resentment she had of Petrina's lordly commands off her face. I am not a slavey, she thought. I think they asked me to come over here so they could have themselves a free field hand. She crawled out from under the blanket and pulled on her old brown dress.

Lars was already off somewhere, doing heaven knows what. What she did know was that she and Petrina seemed to be doing most of the work around the homestead. Now, with Petrina five months pregnant and an one-year-old to attend to, Christina felt the homestead was a monster eating up her energy. Without her daily sweat to feed it; it would starve and return to prairie again.

"Trina, there's too much work." She lifted her callused hands to show her sister.

Petrina didn't even glance at them. "You complain too much. Remember we didn't leave you to go hungry in Norway. We feed you good and give you a decent roof over your head, and all you can do is be ungrateful." She looked as if she were about to cry at Christina's ingratitude.

Christina had to allow Petrina her point. They fed her, but they made sure they got it back in water carried and rows of corn hoed. She resented that Lars made comments about her eating. At dinner last night he had said, "I swear, Christina, I think you'll eat anything that wouldn't eat you first."

Although Christina ate ravenously in the two months she had been with Trina and Lars, she was still hungry most of the time. As she sat on the edge of the bed pulling her shoes on, she studied her arms. Freckled from the sun, they had become even leaner and more wiry than they had been when she arrived. Her menstrual periods had stopped, and she wanted to sleep many more hours than Petrina would allow. Fatigue had become a constant companion.

She wanted to scream, "You're using me all up; there's nothing left of me," but she kept her mouth shut. Christina stuck some pins in her hair to hold it out of her face, went out to the privy, and still sleepy eyed came back inside and sat down at the table. A steaming bowl of yellow corn meal and a hunk of dark bread had been set out for her. Christina began to eat.

As she began to mix bread dough in a large bowl, Petrina continued, "We need to work hard now. We're not like the grasshopper who expects the industrious ant to take care of him. You'll have plenty of time to rest when winter comes and we get snowed in. You'll be impatient to get back in the fields when spring gets here." As if in offer of reconciliation for her sharp tone, Petrina stopped mixing and poured a cup of coffee from the pot on the stove and placed it in front of Christina.

A whimper came from the other room. Mennie had wakened and was ready to start her day. Christina looked up as Petrina went to get the child. Her sister was hard on her, but then she did have others to worry about. Christina's feeling that she was a welcome guest in Petrina's home had lasted a month before they had begun to quarrel. Maybe it was impossible for two grown women to live comfortably under the same roof.

The space they shared was only a simple two-room frame house, but it was Petrina's house. There was no way to avoid feeling like a visitor. She was welcome, but she was expected to work. It was apparent that Lars and Petrina felt she was indebted to them for more than just the money they had loaned her to come to America.

At first Petrina began harping on little things. If Christina was not busy, she pointed out things that needed doing. More and more Christina found that she could only enjoy herself when her sister was not around. Despite how tired she was, Christina took long walks, carrying a gunnysack, collecting buffalo chips for fuel. It was comforting to be alone; it reminded her of the walks along the water picking up seaweed for Bossy.

Christina's main job for the day was carrying water for the family garden. They were growing peas, carrots, potatoes, beans and cabbage. Except for the peas, most of it would keep well over the winter in the root cellar under the house. Her muscles no longer hurt; now it was just the fatigue and the boredom.

She looked forward to tomorrow. One thing she could say for Lars and Petrina was that they respected the Sabbath. Sundays, Christina could sleep as late as she wanted. Then Lars would hold a little church service for them, reading from the Bible and leading them in hymns. They knew it was important to keep contact with God even if no minister was available to hold church services.

Jacob

Christina had met Lars' younger brother Jacob while she was still a small girl, but she remembered little about him. Now twenty-seven, he was considered by his neighbors to be one of the leading citizens of the area. He had already been elected one of the county commissioners. Whatever Jacob set his mind to do, he did well. When neighbors needed help he was there, not only to lend a hand, but to share ideas about how to build a better addition on a barn or show them an easier way to break a horse to harness. He and his wife, Lilly, lived two miles south of Lars' place, also on the shore of the lake.

That Sunday after services Christina strode the two miles to Jacob and Lilly's home. She stayed as close as she could to the lakeshore to enjoy the sight of the water, so like the sea at home.

The birds also attracted her attention, birds like they had never had in Norway. She stopped to watch the gentle stirring of the water as the wind passed over it. A shadow moving across the water broke her concentration and she looked up to see a large bird flying erratically. It was a hawk who was avoiding something. As it came nearer she saw the hawk was trying to get away from a much smaller bird that kept flying at its head. "How strange. Why is the big bird so helpless? I must remember to ask Jacob."

The roof of Jacob and Lilly's house could be seen from a mile away. The house had become a regular part of Christina's dreams. Now when she dreamt of how she wanted to live in the future with her husband and children, it was in a house like this one.

The house stood tall and unprotected from the elements. It was the largest hulk on the prairie, not designed to be a part of it but defiant in its resistance to wind and hail. There were three rooms downstairs and two bedrooms above. A cook shed had been attached to the side of the house so that cooking could be done in the summer without turning the rest of the house into an oven.

Lilly saw Christina walking along the lake and hastened out to meet her. Lilly had on a rust colored linen dress with a lace collar, elaborate embroidery down the front and a bustle down the back with a small bow on it. Goodness, thought Christina, that's her best go-to-meeting clothes. Maybe I've come at the wrong time. They must be expecting company.

"Christina, I've so glad you could come over. How are Petrina, Lars and Mennie?"

"We're all working hard to make the farm go. Mennie is well but cries a lot." Christina couldn't stop staring at the beautiful dress.

Lilly smiled and said, "Oh, my dress. I like to remind myself of how it was before we became homesteaders. It would be so easy to let go. Wearing my good clothes makes me feel that I'm still a lady under the dirt and sweat."

There was warmth to Lilly that drew people to her. While a bit jealous of her ease with people, especially men, Christina was also pleased to have a chance to be with her. "Let's go down to the boat dock; Jacob's going fishing." Lilly headed down the hill toward the lake. "He's real proud of how good the boat he made turned out. Get more settlers in the area and we might even make some extra money selling them boats."

The boat was not very large. It had no sails and was rowed by two oars. Two could sit comfortably, but three would have been hazardous. "Oh, Lilly, do you think he'll let me ride in it?"

Lilly laughed. "Jacob let you go out in it? That man wouldn't accept no for an answer. He loves to show off his handiwork."

When they reached the small dock, Jacob gave Christina a hug. She blushed. She knew it was rare for a Norwegian man, even a relative to touch a woman, much less give her a hug. But then Jacob was different, more outgoing and spontaneous. While his warmth embarrassed her, she looked forward to being with him.

If he hadn't been married to Lilly, he was just the kind of man she would have wanted as a father for her children.

Last Wednesday when they had been washing out clothes together, Christina had made the mistake of saying to Petrina, "I'd like to find a husband as nice as Jacob."

She was surprised to see that this angered Petrina, who snapped, "What's the matter? Isn't a man like Lars good enough for you?" Trina had stopped scrubbing and had gone into the other room to pout.

Jacob now pointed to his boat. "Would you like to take a ride in my masterwork?" He beamed like a little boy showing off his favorite toy.

Christina looked at Lilly for permission. Lilly nodded. "Go ahead, I've had all the rides I want in that washtub. I prefer something bigger."

Christina climbed aboard the small craft and Jacob pushed it into the water. She said, "The boat is so much smaller than anything we had in Norway. Is it safe to go way out in it?"

"This isn't the Norwegian Sea, Christina; we'll be safe." Jacob rowed with long powerful strokes. Several hundred yards out into the lake he stopped to rest. "The lake has a lot of fish in it, and I can't reach them with shore fishing except in the spring. The boat will help me bring in a good catch. Fish have kept us from going hungry many a time. They've been our salvation since we got here. I don't know what those immigrants coming later who can't get a claim on the lake are going to do until their first crops come in."

The surface of the water was polished steel, marbled by the reflection of the sky and clouds. Its beauty was enhanced by the dancing gold flecks from the sun straight overhead. Jacob took out a cigar box from under his seat and untangled two fishing lines. He set the floats on them, baited the hooks with a bit of colored rag, checked the sinkers and dropped them over the side.

"We've over an area where the water is cooler underneath. In this weather the big ones go down to the coolness. We'll catch us a couple for supper."

"What do you do when the lake freezes up in the winter?" She asked leaning forward to watch the floaters bob on the surface of the water.

"No problem. They're even easier to catch. We cut a hole in the ice and drop a line with a bit of fat bacon on it. The fish are so hungry they bite at anything."

Jacob was the most talkative man she had met since Bry had helped her get to Trondheim. So not to scare the fish he was talking very quietly. "We ate so many fish in '77 we thought we might develop scales. I'm sure that fins had started coming out of my back."

"Why so many fish?"

Jacob shook his head. "I've never seen anything like it. That was the year of the grasshoppers. They came out of the west like one of the plagues that God sent on the Egyptians. They filled the sky with black clouds. There wasn't a blade of grass left when they got done with us. The birds were the only ones who profited. We thought we would lose everything, but we had the fish. It's what saved us."

The gentle rocking, floating sensation of the boat and Jacob's quiet voice was making Christina drowsy. It was an effort to keep her eyes open. Her mind drifted to the small bird chasing the hawk. "I saw a small bird attacking a hawk. The hawk seemed to be afraid of it. Do you know what was happening?"

"Oh, that, the Americans call that a King Bird. It doesn't seem to be afraid of anything that comes into its nesting range. I once climbed a tree with one in it and thought it was going to peck my eyes out. It was scolding me the whole time like a bad tempered fishwife."

Christina saw the float dip under. "Look, I think something's taking your bait."

Again it went under and stayed. Jacob reached out and began to draw the line in. A brief struggle and a bullhead landed on the bottom of the boat. Christina gasped.

Jacob gave a laugh. "Ugly looking thing, isn't it? But quite tasty."

"Pa never taught me to fish. Olaf was going to be the fisherman in our family. I want to learn. Will you teach me how?"

"You come around on Sundays. I'll show you how to do it. If you're living on the lake and know how to fish, you'll never starve." He paused, cautious, as if not sure how she would react to his next question. "How is it living with Petrina and Lars?"

"Hard. She rides me all of the time." Feeling a bit guilty, she added, "Being a mother in a two-room house, even if it is wood, isn't easy. Having a baby does make us awfully crowded; and when the new one comes, I don't know what I'll do."

"Your sister is a fusser all right. I figured you'd have some problems. Why don't you get your own homestead? They've got some good ones unclaimed over on the east side of the lake. You came to America at the right time. You wait very long, someone else'll grab it up."

"I'm not old enough."

"You will be by next spring. Go over and look the land over. You can fish to get by. Lars and me can help you build a shanty. All us kids and ma took homesteads when we got here, and it's worked out just fine. Fellow by the name of Bjorklund got a claim there. Nice enough family considering they're Swedes. He was a shoemaker in Sweden. He ain't much of a farmer; even his wife would agree on that. Anyway, he don't know fishing either, but I bet he'll be a good neighbor. Why don't you go over and meet him one of these Sundays when you're free?"

Christina looked puzzled. "I need to think about it."

"Don't think too long. With the extension of the railroad to Watertown north of here we can expect a new flood of immigrants. The Germans and Scandinavians come into New York, buy tickets to the end of the line and make their claims. I figure it won't be long before all the good claims will be gone."

Christina stayed to eat the fish they caught and some boiled potatoes for supper. It was late when she got back to Petrina's, and she had to walk part of the way by starlight. When she came in, Lars looked up from the book he was reading by the light of the hearth fire and said, "You're late. We were worried, thought maybe the wolves had got you."

156

She smiled at his teasing. "They're not hungry enough to eat me this time of the year. Besides I got no fat meat on me. I wouldn't make a good meal."

Petrina gave her a sharp look as if to say, "Don't get sassy with my husband, young lady. It's not your place."

Christina went to sleep happy, dreams about learning to fish from Jacob swimming through her mind.

A Swedish Family

Taking Jacob's suggestion she started out early from Lars and Trina's on the next Sunday morning without waiting for the Bible reading and hymn singing. Lars grumbled at her about not being careful enough about her soul. As she walked she conducted her own service with a prayer and a hymn. Two hours later she had crossed the top of the lake and started to move south.

Homesteading a piece of land on this side of the lake appealed to her. Far enough from Lars and Trina that they wouldn't interfere in her life. Close enough that she could visit them or Jacob and Lilly when she wanted to. There was brush to use for fire, water was readily available from the lake and with the fishing skills she was going to learn from Jacob, food when she needed it. A number of the quarter sections along the lake had already been taken. Lars suggestion that the Bjorklunds would be a good family to know had stimulated her interest in meeting them.

Christina paused on the edge of a wash and looked across the gully. It startled her to see a man skinning a coyote. His head was down, and he was intent on pulling the skin away from the body with his bloody hands. The blood shocked her and her first impulse was to flee. As she turned to go a limb cracked under foot and the man raised his head. His face was covered with a black beard. He hollered, "Hello," across to her in Swedish. "Come on over. Meet your neighbor."

Too polite to refuse but tense from the unexpected encounter with this fierce looking stranger, she was not careful crossing the wash. She stepped on some loose gravel, which sent her sprawling on her back. She stopped sliding only when she crashed into a dead bush at the bottom of the gully. For a moment she was confused and frightened. Closing her eyes she took a deep breath and checked her body mentally for any place that might be hurt. All the parts were still there and functioning.

She opened her eyes, looked up and saw a black beard leaning over her with a concerned look on the owner's face, not what she expected from a Swede. His deeply tanned skin was almost olive, and under his straw hat his hair was as black as his beard. There was a spot of white below his lower lip, which at first glance she thought was food left over from his breakfast. Looking closer she saw that the hairs were white. His left eyelid drooped giving him a sinister look. She shivered as if a cold breeze had hit her.

"Hello, young lady. That was quite a performance. You didn't have to do it on my account."

His statement took her by surprise. His next words made it clear he was teasing. "Are you all right? That was some fall."

His voice didn't fit the face; it was light and pleasant.

She relaxed and noticed that the air had not turned cold. She rearranged her dress and sat up. "I'm all right. Just clumsy."

He continued to stare at her, as if he wasn't sure if she really was undamaged. To reassure him she went on, "I'm Christina Gunnerson from across the lake. I live with Lars and Petrina Nilsen."

The man looked away as if slightly embarrassed by being alone with a young woman. Christina thought, "He's shy, just like some Norwegian men."

The man looked back at her, swallowed and said, "I'm Peter Bjorklund. My wife Carrie and I got a homestead over toward the south. I'm just finishing up here. Caught this varmint in one of my traps by accident. Would rather have gotten something to eat instead. Was hopin' to get me a big jack. The kids like rabbit meat."

Bjorklund rubbed his bloody palm on his jeans and offered her a hand to help her up. Her first impulse was to reject it, but he seemed to expect her to take it. When she was on her feet standing next to him, she found they were the same height. Her hand felt sticky, but she didn't dare rub it on her dress for fear of leaving stains on it she couldn't wash out.

Bjorklund took his knife, spit on it and wiped it on his pants. The red colored spit blended in with various stains that he had put on his overalls earlier. He stuck the short skinning knife into his belt, shook out the coyote hide, then rolled it up and stuck it in a sack. "Hides not much good for anything but killing 'em keeps 'em from eating my rabbits. 'Course this year there's plenty of rabbits for all of us."

Another pause. She could feel his unspoken question. "What's a young women doing out alone on the prairie?"

"I'm out looking the land over. My sister's brother-in-law, Jacob Nilsen, says there's good land on this side of the lake that hasn't been claimed yet."

"Yup, a quarter section just south of mine, more below that." Again the long pause. Having given all the important information about themselves, neither could think of anything else to talk about. There was a tension as if each were reaching for something appropriate to say but not finding it.

Finally Bjorklund said, "You're a far piece from home. Why don't you come back to the soddy with me and meet the missus and my mischief makers. Wife would enjoy a chance to chew the fat with you. Might even find we got something to eat. I'm hungrier than a weasel in a hen house."

The offer to share food was not unusual even when there wasn't much in the larder. Accepting an offer was taking a chance on not getting much, but refusing the invitation would be bad manners. Besides, she knew that if Mrs. Bjorklund were like most prairie women, she would welcome a chance to chat.

Bjorklund picked up a dilapidated gun that was standing against a tree. He saw her staring at it. "Ya, it's a bit old and beaten up, but it keeps us fed. This is a cap and ball gun. It can hit anything you want if it's not more'n fifty feet away. Don't cost me much to shoot because I can put gravel down the barrel if I ain't got no lead shot." He laughed showing even white teeth. "If'n we got prairie chicken for dinner, you could be picking rocks out of your teeth.

"I'm lucky to have the missus I have. Mrs. Bjorklund is from a family with money. Why she married me I sure don't know. What with the hard times in Sweden, I knew I'd never make us a good living. She deserves more so we came here. It's not what either of us expected."

Christina encouraged him to go on, saying, "I expected hard work here but more food than we had in Norway."

"The missus and me heard stories told of how there had been a plague that had killed most everyone in the Midwest and that farms complete with buildings were just there for the taking. When we found that we had to build our own house and that all there was to build it with was sod, why Carrie just sat down and cried. If I hadn't known so much about trapping and had this old gun here, we would have starved to death."

Like so many others that Christina had met since she had left Norway, once the initial tension was broken Mr. Bjorklund was eager to have someone new to talk to. She knew from listening to her Pa and his friends that most men said very little about personal matters unless they were drinking. She'd also heard wives complaining that their husbands didn't tell them anything.

Christina was young, attentive but not beautiful enough to threaten either the husband or the wife, so they felt free to talk to her. She had learned from talking with Maria and other attractive women that men were more cautious about saying much about themselves to women who were attractive. With beautiful women men seemed to only say things about themselves which put them in a good light.

They were plowing through the tall grass now, Bjorklund leading the way, the path closing up as quickly as his body moved through it. "You said you have young ones?" Christina asked.

"We got three. Boy nine, girl seven and another boy five. Carrie says we can't have no more until we get more space to live in. The soddy's a bit crowded."

They broke out of the grass to a clearing where the wheat was cut and put up into shocks. Carrie Bjorklund came out to meet them wiping flour off her hands on her apron. "I'm mighty pleased to see another woman," she said smiling warmly. "It's been a time since I've had a real grown-up to talk to. My soddy's a mess what with the kids and the dirt and all, but come in and sit a spell. We've got the coffee pot on."

Christina studied the soddy. Mr. Bjorklund seemed proud of it. "Built it myself with the help of a neighbor. Didn't have the money to haul in lumber from Brookings, so we figured why not use what God gave us; so we used the sod."

Lars and Jacob had both explained to her how lucky they were to have wood houses. She could see that the Bjorklunds had dug a hole in the ground, saving the sod that they had cut into blocks. The blocks were then stacked on top of each other to make the walls.

"You two women folk go on in. I'm gonna stretch this coyote skin."

Christina followed Mrs. Bjorklund into the soddy that was indeed a bit crowded. It would have been uncomfortable for a couple, much less for a family of five. When she stepped inside it was dark; but when her eyes adjusted to the light coming through the single window, she could see that boards had been laid across the walls, then covered with straw and more sod laid down over the straw to make a roof.

Mrs. Bjorklund watched as Christina's eyes moved around the room. In an apologetic voice she said, "This isn't what we expected when we came here. I'm hoping we can have a real house before long. This is warm enough; but when we get a big rain, the floor turns to mud, and we have to cut more sod to put the roof back on."

Mrs. Bjorklund was flushed with excitement over having a real guest. "Pull up a stool and sit. The oldest boy there lying on the bed is Earl. I'm afraid Earl does look like death warmed over. He's been suffering from the trots for some weeks and has no energy."

The other two children were poking at each other with boards that looked like the one Peter was using for stretching the coyote skin. The girl poked hers at the boy's face. He didn't pull back quickly enough and got a sharp whack on the nose. He immediately set up a wail. The girl gave a frightened look at her mother.

Carrie Bjorklund didn't look at him but raised her voice to say, "For pity sake, Moses, stop making all that noise."

As Mrs. Bjorklund turned to get cups, Christina saw that there were only three intact coffee cups left. She suspected that the rest probably died at the marauding hands of the children. Mrs. Bjorklund filled two of these remaining tokens of a better life with coffee. She handed Christina the cup that still had a handle on it.

"Coffee might not taste like what you're used to. We've been using some burnt flour to stretch it. I have something here that will help it." From a private hoard Carrie brought out one of her treasures, a box of lump sugar that she handed to Christina. Christina took one and placed it in her coffee.

Carrie went on talking. "I've been hungry to sit and talk a spell with another woman."

Christina nodded as Carrie said, "It's been a hard three years, but I think we're going to make something out of this piece of prairie even if the Mister's not much of a farmer. Sometimes I think he's kind of like a blister; he don't show up until the work is done. Still our crop was good this year. We got taters, beans and some wheat to take to market."

There was no anger in her statement about her husband not liking work. Christina wondered if any man really liked the hard life of farming. Carrie went on, eager to share her thoughts with her new audience. "He likes trapping and he's really good at it, knows a lot about animals and their habits. This winter we'll likely get a load of furs that we can sell for staples. Maybe get ahead a little. We figure in a year or two we'll be able to start building a house out of wood."

The sun was in mid sky when Mrs. Bjorklund fed the three children their noon meal and then reset the small table for the three adults. Dinner was a chowder made with prairie chicken, potatoes and corn. As Bjorklund had predicted, Christina found gravel shot in pieces of her chicken.

They talked about prairie life, and the subject of animals came up. All of them allowed as how they listened to the coyotes singing to each other in the night.

This set Mr. Bjorklund off telling them of his experiences with coyotes. "I respect the coyote. Smartest animal on the prairie. The other day I watched two of them catch a big jack. Now you know a rabbit can outrun a coyote if he'd go in a straight line. But a rabbit circles, always comes back to his home territory. So what these two coyotes do is, one chases him until they get back to the starting place, then the other takes him for a while. Pretty soon the rabbit's getting pretty tired and movin' slow. Then the coyote runs up to him and knocks him in the air with his nose and catches him in his mouth. A circus juggler couldn't have done it better. Damnest thing you ever did see."

"What do you know about wolves?" Christina asked.

"Well, I ain't killed none yet. But there's money to be made from the bounties. They're hard on cattle and sheep, and if you got a good rifle or know poisons they're not too hard to kill."

"Are they dangerous?

"Mostly not. Hear tell they eat an occasional Indian in the winter when they got nothing better to eat. But I suspect they got to be pretty hungry before they'd do that."

"Would a woman living alone be safe?"

"Like I say, they prefer other kinds of meat. I just wouldn't want to be caught by one in the dead of winter when other food's hard to find."

It was late afternoon when Christina said her goodbyes and headed back for the Nilsen farm more than ever convinced that come spring she would find some way to take a homestead on this side of the lake.

CHAPTER SIXTEEN

ICE FISHING

With the harvest in and winter approaching there was, as Petrina had predicted, less work. They still had to get up early to attend to chores and make preparation for cold weather, but the backbreaking work of harvest was done. Christina continued to eat two portions of everything put on the table and began to put on weight. Her periods started again, and as the days grew shorter and colder the return to her natural weight helped her stay warm.

As Petrina grew heavier with her second child, she became even touchier and more difficult to be around. Not only did she complain more, but Christina noticed that she wouldn't leave Lars alone with her for more than a few minutes. With the crowded conditions in the shanty and Christina's newfound energy, it became more difficult for Christina to put up with Petrina's constant irritation. She felt that if she were to keep from blowing up and murdering her sister, she needed to find a place of her own. But there was winter and the birth of a new baby to get through first. She had to pray regularly for God's help in controlling her anger.

With less work around the homestead Christina could now visit Jacob two days a week. Often they went fishing, but sometimes they just kept each other company. One afternoon Jacob broke the silence with, "I been thinking, if you're going to be having your own place, you'll need to know something about tools." They were sitting on the front stoop drinking the bitter yellow tea that Lilly made from local plants. She said it was good for nervousness. Christina didn't like the taste much, but it was better than plain hot water.

Neither woman responded to Jacob's statement. He went on anyway. "I been thinking that you're going to need a small boat for fishing when you move, so why don't we catch two fish on one hook and make you a boat so I can teach you how to use a drill and a hammer."

Lilly looked over at him. "That's man work, Jacob."

"Well," he said, "if she don't learn some man's work, she won't be much good by herself on a claim, now will she?"

Jacob had built a lean-to on his barn especially for his carpentry work. There, one morning a week, he put Christina to work learning the basics of woodworking.

At first the proper use of the plane perplexed her, but soon her arms got the rhythm of it, and long spirals of wood curled smoothly off the planks she was working on. "I was right, Christina," Jacob said. "You got a good feel for wood and tools. We're gonna make us a fine craft."

"You're such a good teacher; I'd have to be a real dummy not to learn the way you show how. Why don't more women learn how to do this?"

"No need for most of them. Mostly we keep the work divided. But if you're going to live alone, you got no choice. There's men out there don't know near what you already know. You'll do fine."

In early October she and Jacob were in the boat. The water was choppy and a stiff breeze kept trying to push them toward the shore. Jacob was explaining again about fall fishing. "These cold nights have cooled the lake down. It's pretty much the same temperature all the way down. It'll stay that way until the ice forms later this month. The fish will be close to the surface now. You might even be able to see them and toss your hook right at them."

She asked, "Will it be the same in the spring?"

"Almost. I'll show you some new tricks then. But it's pretty much the same." He handed her the fishing line so she could set the depth. "How are things with Petrina? We seldom see her now that she's so far along."

Christina didn't answer at once. She didn't want to say too much about her plans. She concentrated on the line, adjusted it and dropped it over the side. Finally she said, "She's touchier than ever. I need to move out. I been looking." She stopped in mid-sentence to attend to a fish. It was buffalo fish, lazy and easy to land. "Will these be good to eat in the spring or tasteless like they were this summer?"

"Most suckers are not good eating in the summer. They'll be all right in the spring, and it's easy to catch them. Put a worm on your hook and fish near the surface, you'll almost always get one." He spent a few minutes resetting his own lines then asked, "You say you been looking?"

"I been over to the other side of the lake a couple of times. Like I told you I've met the Bjorklunds, the Swedes on the north side. They've built a pretty good sod shanty, but it's small for five. I keep wondering how they keep from knocking everything apart."

"Lots of practice, I guess. Add a room and they'll feel like they're in a palace."

"Mr. Bjorklund doesn't like the farming much. He lets the older boy do a lot of the work."

"Well, like I said before, he's not much of a farmer."

"Even his wife agrees with that. Anyway, right south of his place is an unclaimed quarter section. I haven't told Petrina yet, but come spring I'm moving out. She's so touchy now that if I told her she might send me out into a snow bank."

"She's a little tough on you, Christina, but she wouldn't do that. Besides if she did you could always come and spend the rest of the winter with us."

"That's a comfort to know, but I'm going to keep my mouth shut about my plans to leave. Petrina can blow up about it when it happens."

"What about her babies?"

"Lars will have to do more. If I stay through spring planting, I'm there for the next year, and I want to get started on my own place." She paused. "Don't you think I should move? You're the one who suggested it first."

"I know. I was just thinking two babies will be a chore for her, and Lars is not one to help. He may be my older brother, but he's not going to do anything that's women's work."

The next Saturday Christina made a trip into town to the general store. She checked the availability of tools and seed and their prices. The following week Petrina got sick and took to her bed. Christina took over the cooking and the care of Mennie so she couldn't get down to Jacob's farm.

The next Friday the temperature dropped sharply, and the wind started to blow with gusts filled with a light sharp snow that cut into the skin and worked its way through cracks. For three days everyone who could, stayed inside. Then Jacob and Lilly made a visit to see Lars and Petrina, so it was a month before Christina could get another lesson in fishing.

When Christina finally was able to set out for Jacob's, there was light grainy snow on the ground and the lake was covered with ice. The air was crisp but with her large mittens, heavy men's boots with extra socks and double sweaters under her winter coat she was comfortably warm. Jacob had insisted that she pay special attention to warmth for today's lesson since they might be standing out in the open unprotected by a windbreak for some time.

After a hot cup of coffee with Lilly they walked out on the ice carrying their gear and a hatchet. As they walked he said, "The top water is too cold for most fish. Deep down it's doesn't have enough food so we have to find the spot with the best combination of temperature and food. I figure on this lake it's where water meets the land about thirty feet down." He stopped thought a moment, moved just a few feet further out. "This is about it, Christina. You chop a hole. It should be only about half a foot wide."

The chips of ice flew as she attacked the spot. Four inches of ice later she broke through to the water. Jacob took out a hard boiled egg, took off his gloves and began to peel it. He popped the egg in his mouth and began to chew. Christina gave him a questioning look. "Oh, the egg? No, it's not my lunch. I need the shell." He broke up the shell in his fingers and dropped it over the open fishing hole. "The glitter of the egg shell attracts the fish. In a minute or so if we've hit the right spot, we'll have some company. If not, we'll try another hole closer in, and you get to eat the egg."

They broke out their line, set it for thirty feet, put fried bacon rind on the hook and dropped it into the hole. Jacob continued the lesson. "Pull your line slowly up and down to attract the fish's attention." Within minutes her line was hit and within the hour they had taken enough fish for both families. "Petrina will be happy to get more fresh fish," Jacob said. "She must appreciate your fishing."

"She admits it helps pay for part of my keep. It reminds her of home. I think she gets homesick for Pa and Olaf. Sometimes she talks to me about them as if they were still alive back on the island. It just doesn't seem real to her that they're dead."

Jacob looked serious. "And even here in America, Christina, death visits when you least expect it."

Neither of them realized that his words were a prophecy.

Deep Winter

More snow fell and the temperature stayed below freezing. Blizzards came and rearranged the fields of snow into giant drifts that buried houses and barns. The snow was so deep and the landmarks so few that without knowledge of where the farmhouses were and a good sense of direction a visitor would have been lost in the white desolation. Lars and Petrina made arrangements for Mrs. Bjorklund, who had experience as a midwife, to come and stay before Petrina was expected to go into labor.

Their well-laid plans were upset when a blizzard arrived before Mrs. Bjorklund. As the blizzard began its rampage, Petrina's water broke. Outside the small house the air sucked up snow that quickly became a weapon in the fierce breath of the wind. It cut into the skin and drove the ten below zero temperature through the warmest clothes. As the fury of the storm rose, Petrina moaned, clutched her middle and doubled over. Labor had started.

At Petrina's moan Lars paled. His hand shook splashing coffee from his cup onto the floor. "I can't go out in this for Mrs. Bjorklund; even Lilly is too far away. What's going to happen to Trina?"

Christina looked at his white face and thought, for people who go off to pillage and plunder, men certainly get upset about things. Faced with home problems men are sure helpless. A baby chick two hours out of its shell can do a better job of taking care of itself than a full-grown man.

Once over coffee when Jacob was out fishing alone, Lilly had told her that even he couldn't stand to be around when a woman was in labor. She laughed and said, "They probably feel guilty that their lust is causing us so much pain."

After censoring her thoughts, what Christina finally said to

Lars was, "Petrina and I will handle it. You just keep Mennie out of the way."

Petrina gave another low moan. Christina shivered. The goose bumps on her arms could have been a nervous reaction to the moan, but more likely it was from the cold wind fighting its way into the room. Frost was forming on the walls and when she stood close to the wall she could feel the heat draining out that side of her body. Lars had laid in a good supply of buffalo chips and wood from the lake bushes, but it was going to be burning up fast.

Christina went over in her head everything she had seen when helping with the birth of animals and everything she had heard from other women about childbirth. With the process straight in her mind she settled down to wait.

Petrina raised her head from the pillow and arched her body in response to the contraction that had seized her. Her body had been working and straining for four hours. Both women knew that a second birth could go from a few hours to a whole day. This baby was acting like he was in no hurry to come out into the cold.

"Does it hurt much?" Christina asked.

Petrina grimaced, took a deep breath and laid back on the pillow. "Not so much yet. It will get much worse before the baby comes."

Christina took her hand and held it. Petrina's lordly attitude was gone. Now it was just her frightened sister in need of support and care. In the next room Mennie was crying because she couldn't be with Mommy. Petrina said, "Let her come in and see that I'm all right. It'll be fifteen minutes before another cramp."

Two hours later the contractions were closer together. In spite of the cold from the walls, Petrina was sweating. "I'm tired. I need a rest. I want it to be all over."

The next contraction came; she gasped, her muscles tightening. A minute later she said, "It's close, they're getting worse."

"I'll tell Lars to make sure there's water to clean you up and to wash the baby in."

When she returned Petrina had a worried look on her face. "Something is wrong, Christina. I should have had another cramp and it hasn't come. I feel like everything's stopped."

"Are you sure?"

"The baby's stopped moving. Christina, is the baby dead? Am I going to be all right?"

The chill that passed over Christina did not come from the cold in the room. She had no idea of what might be wrong. All they could do given their resources was to wait. She began to talk to Petrina of old times. "Remember how I never wanted to take my cod liver oil? I was just doing that to make you angry."

Petrina smiled at the memory. "I know. You were really a rotten little kid. I learned a lot about being a mother trying to make you behave."

They talked on, Christina trying to keep Petrina distracted. When the scream broke from Petrina's lips, they were both surprised. "That was a hard one. Something is happening again."

The contractions now came close together. Within forty minutes the head of the baby appeared. Christina took hold of the baby and pulled gently twisting to help the shoulders come out. The baby slipped easily out into her hands.

Christina shouted, "Lars, come in with the water. Your boy is here." Lars brought the water and cotton rags. Christina held the baby upside down and slapped its bottom to clear its throat and nose. The boy let out a squall protesting his entry into such a cold world. Christina tied a string around the umbilical close to his body and another closer to the mother and cut it with the scissors. She then washed the white covering off the baby. Finally she placed the baby on Petrina's breast where it immediately began searching for a nipple.

Christina chuckled at the sight and Petrina gave her a weak smile in return. "We've just got the afterbirth to worry about now," Christina said. "It should come out soon." They didn't have to wait long, and Christina caught it in a scrap of cloth from a worn old petticoat. Despite the anxiety they had had when the baby seemed to have decided not to come and the icy conditions of the room, Petrina's delivery had been a relatively easy one.

The addition of the baby to the already crowded house brought Christina to the limit of her patience. With the baby's crying it was worse than steerage. The noise, the lack of privacy, Petrina's nagging, combined to shrink the house around her to where she could barely take a deep breath. She was trapped. There had to be some way out of this.

CHAPTER SEVENTEEN

DEATH

$\mathcal{T}$he new baby was named Anton. He was small at birth, overactive and irritable. To add to this he suffered from colic, and Petrina spent many of her waking hours holding and rocking him. His crying made it difficult on many nights for anyone in the shanty to get much sleep. While feeling sorry for her sister, the confinement in the two rooms with the constant demands of the children caused Christina to feel like a dinghy in a storm in constant danger of being dashed under the waves. She could hardly wait to leave Lars and Petrina and stake out her own claim. She knew it would be hard to get a proper building and twenty acres broken to the plow, but solving those problems would be easier than staying on here.

Winter was breaking up. There had been several thaws and no new snow. Christina had to get away and decided to visit the Bjorklunds. She set off on the four-mile trip to their homestead on the old pair of skis she had gotten from Lilly. The surface of the snow was hard and she was able to move swiftly.

In little more than an hour she came upon the sod shanty. At first she had trouble seeing it because no smoke was coming from the tin chimney to guide her. As she came up to the snow covered soddy, there was only the sound of her skis gliding across the frozen surface. She shouted, "Anybody home?" No answer. From the ice in the foot tracks around the house she estimated that it had been at least a week since anyone had been here.

Did the Bjorklund's have any other place to go? She didn't think so. Yet it was obvious they hadn't been at home for some time. Where could they be? She heard the devil speak in her ear. "If they've left the county, their claim will be free for you to take over. Think how nice that would be. It's already got an acceptable soddy on it, and they've broken the twenty acres."

Christina shook off the corrupt thought and walked around the soddy and peeked in the window. In the gray of the room she saw a pile of something on the bed. It could be someone lying on the bed sleeping. She rapped. No answer. She pushed at the door. It resisted, then she saw it was nailed shut.

Several miles north of here was the homestead of the Efraimsons, a family of Finnish immigrants. She had met them and knew that they spoke some Swedish. Perhaps they would know what had happened to the Bjorklunds. She turned north.

The exercise of cross-country skiing brought her spirits alive. It was exhilarating to feel her body working smoothly again. Getting away from the confinement of the house, she was like a hawk freed from a cage. She soared. In the distance smoke was coming from the stovepipe in the roof of the Efraimsons' sod house. Good, she thought, even if they don't know about the Bjorklunds, maybe they'll have coffee on the stove.

The Efraimsons' sod shanty was large by local standards, but Christina felt it was still too small for the family that lived in it. How could seven people live in a space no more than sixteen by twenty feet? As she got closer, she could see they had added a wooden lean-to on one side.

Although there was only the one family living in the sod shanty now, when they first arrived there had been three families plus their cow and an ox. Christina had been told that during their first winter they had all lived in the one room dugout. She was not sure where they bedded down for the night. She tried imagining three families and a cow and an ox in the one room. She got a picture of them all lying on the floor; and when one turned over, all the others changed position. "How cozy," she thought. "Wall to wall bodies."

A hundred yards away from the sod shanty she hollered, "Hello, the house!" Mr. Efraimson appeared at the door and waved. As she came up to the house, he asked in Swedish, "You're the Nilsen girl?"

"That's my sister. I'm Christina Gunnerson. Have you seen the Bjorklunds?"

"Mrs. Bjorklund is inside. She not much for company right now. Her man is dead."

"Dead?" was all Christina could say. She paled and reached out a hand to steady herself. She had liked the black bearded man with the sinister eye.

Mr. Efraimson stood outside with her. "I think you should know what happened before you see her." He said in a low voice. "Ya. He was out trapping and crossed a creek and broke through some rotten ice. He come home half froze but didn't last the night.

"Mrs. Bjorklund is taking it real hard. After it happened, she just sat with the body and stared at him. When the children couldn't get her attention, the oldest boy came to get me. We found her mumbling something about he had no right to do this to her. That she hadn't come all the way to America for him to die on her.

"She's been talking out of her head ever since, and this ain't one of her best days. When the weather gets better, we'll take her and the children to Brookings. If she doesn't get better, they'll probably put the three children up for adoption. The two older ones are almost of an age where they can work for their own keep."

"Was that his body at the shanty?"

"Ya. The ground's too hard to bury him. Come into the house. It's crowded but you can warm up and have a cup of coffee."

As soon as Christina got inside, Mrs. Efraimson said to Mrs. Bjorklund, "Well, this is a surprise. Christina Gunnerson has come to see you." Carrie Bjorklund paid no attention, her eyes remaining unfocused.

During the time Christina was in the soddy Carrie would occasionally start talking, but it was to the dead Peter Bjorklund. "My mother said I shouldn't marry you. She said someone of my station would be better for me. I was too crazy about you to know what was good for me. Why did we come to this land where God doesn't exist?" Her voice sank to a mumble.

The Efraimsons and the Bjorklund children continued their activities as if Mrs. Bjorklund weren't there. After coffee with some bread and butter to give her energy for the trip back, Christina put on her skis and headed back to the Nilsens.

Her return trip was seen though a mist of tears which kept freezing on her cheeks.

The Ice Storm

The ice on the lake began to break up early that spring. The water was still almost at freezing, but it would now remain open for fishing from the boat. Eager to get some early fishing done, Jacob sent a message to Christina via Lars to come down and go out with him. Anton was sick again, and Petrina needed her to stay to help with Mennie.

Early on the Saturday afternoon Jacob had expected Christina to go fishing with him, without warning, a sleet storm hit the area. Christina, who had been chopping brush down at the lake, felt the sharp wind driven ice beating on her back. When she turned to face the storm, it felt like the razor-edged blast was stripping the skin from her face. Covering her face as best she could with her arms, she ran for the house and got to the door at the same time as Lars.

Christina stood at the window watching. She could see the water on the lake form claws, which reached up from the lake to seize anything floating on it to pull it into its maw. An image of Jacob's little boat flipping in the air jumped in and out of her mind. She shivered and tried to shake the picture away. Petrina, carrying a whimpering Anton, came up behind her and stood watching with her. She turned to Petrina and said. "I hope Jacob has gotten back from fishing. In that little boat I don't think he's safe."

Preoccupied with Anton, Petrina hardly heard her sister's concern. "Jacob is one of the smartest fishermen around. He'll be all right. Go pick up Mennie; she needs some attention."

Next morning before first light there was a pounding on the door, and they opened it to see a wild looking, frenzied Lilly. She sobbed out, "Jacob is dead."

Christina felt her mind go numb; she was sure she couldn't be hearing right. Why was Lilly saying something that couldn't be true?" Petrina turned white. Lars stiffened. "What happened, Lilly?"

It was difficult for Lilly to answer because of the sobs that were choking her words off. "I told him not to go out; the weather was going bad. He wouldn't listen. Hans Bergson came by and he wanted to be the first to go out for the open water fishing. Jacob was always so crazy about fishing. He felt he had to go. Then that horrible ice storm came. I waited and waited. He didn't come home and he didn't come home. I knew something terrible must have happened."

Her voice broke and her body was racked with sobs. Christina put her arms around her. It was some minutes before she blew her nose, wiped her eyes and found her voice to go on. "After the storm I went looking for him. I found him; his poor body was all caked in ice. He was frozen to death and still lying on that awful boat."

Lars left Lilly with the sisters and went out to where she said she had left the body. It was hours later before he came back with the rest of the story. "I found the boat with Jacob on it. The boat must have tipped over and he managed to swim back and crawl on top of it. The wind must've pushed it into shore. There's no sign of the other man. We just got to expect he's dead too."

The weather stayed cold the next day and the next. On the third day Jacob was buried in a grave on his land. His brothers Lars and Bernt had fought with the frozen ground and won a shallow grave from it. Christina had watched in silence as they broke into the hard ground.

On a break Bernt came to stand by her and in an emotion filled voice said, "I was only six when Dad drowned while fishing. Ma brought us to America so we wouldn't suffer the same death. It's almost as if God decided that Jacob was going to die a Norwegian fisherman's death no matter where he went. Perhaps we can't escape our lot."

On the day of the burial the family and friends stood shivering and muffled to the eyes around the grave. Christina looked at the mound of earth beside the grave and said to Petrina, "It seems like such a small piece of earth to hold a man who was so big."

Petrina misunderstood. "He wasn't that big a man; he'll fit the grave just fine."

Christina tried again. "I meant, he would have been one of the most important men in the territory. We don't have many around here could match him for leadership."

Petrina's voice choked on her answer and she only nodded in assent.

The Homestead 1882

Christina had talked with Bjorklund and Jacob about the homestead laws. She knew the homestead rules said that the homesteader must be age twenty-one or head of a family and a U.S. citizen, or have declared intention to become a citizen before filing. She would be allowed to claim 160 acres for her home, but she had to live there for five years and make improvements. This included building a livable house, cultivating twenty acres for crops and showing other evidence of residence such as a well and fences. She would have to live in residence seven months each year with no absence of over six months.

Three weeks after Jacob's death Christina returned from one of her wanderings. Petrina was washing clothes at the washtub. Mennie played near by and Anton lay in a box on the stoop. "Where have you been off to now? You've been gone all day. With Jacob gone we thought we might see more of you. Don't you see that Lars needed you to carry water for the animals?"

"I walked around the north end of the lake and crossed the dry bed of the old lake. On the east side of the lake there's land which hasn't been claimed yet. I'm going to stake out my own homestead."

"You're talking crazy. You're too young. Besides a woman can't run a farm by herself. You'll never be able to do what you need to do to prove up the land. You can't build a house; you can't break twenty acres of ground; you don't know anything about putting in a crop. You'll starve to death."

"I'm healthy and I'm strong. I'm not going to stay here and work as a maid. I've talked with the Efraimsons; they'll help me make a sod shanty."

Petrina became quiet. The realization that Christina might really leave was a new idea. She had assumed that she had no place to go. Her thoughts burst out in words. "But we like having you here. I know I've been hard on you, but it's only been for your own good. You must understand that. I feel responsible for you. Lars and I both want you to stay. The children love you and will miss you if you leave us."

The arguments washed over Christina. Was she mistaken? Was something wrong with her that she saw only the bad side of living here? She thought of the long hours in the field, Lars' teasing, the crying babies. The thoughts strengthened her resolve to move.

Softly Christina said, "I need to be out on my own. If I leave now and get my own place, we can still be friends. If I stay here, I'm afraid we'll end up hating each other. You've got to see that we can't live under the same roof."

Petrina shook her head. Her face went white, and she clenched her hands as if to strike out. "Christina, you are a strong willed, ungrateful, wicked child. You can go, but if it doesn't work out don't come crying back to us begging for a place to stay."

The gossip spread quickly through the township that Christina was going to leave the Nilsens and start her own homestead. A week later Lilly came over. She had aged years since Jacob's death. Her face was lined, her movements slowed and her hair was limp and specked with gray. Tears would gather at the corners of her eyes and spill over even when she was discussing business affairs. Despite this she was already carrying on the work at the farm, keeping business affairs in hand and planning not only how to keep it going but how to add more land to her holdings.

She asked Christina to go for a walk. Christina noticed that Lilly avoided the lake and walked west away from it. When they were some distance from the house, Lilly finally said, "Christina, Jacob often said how much you needed to be on your own. That it wasn't good for you to stay as a servant in your sister's house. I've got good news for you. The Efraimsons sent word that Mrs. Bjorklund is better. She's found a place in Brookings and doesn't want to return to the farm. She'll sell you a quit claim for $75."

Christina's stomach responded first. It cramped. She thought, poor Mr. Bjorklund. It's not right he died and I should get my wish. Then a lightness came into her breast and a feeling of freedom. "I want the claim, but I don't have $75."

"I've thought of that. The Nilsen family will get the money together for you somehow, and you can pay us back later."

The offer was a Godsend. So much would be taken care of with the purchase of a quit claim.

Within the month she had moved into her new home. As Jacob had told her, taking land on the lake was a good choice. She not only had easy access to water but a source of food. This side of the lake was as rich in fish as the other, and because of the lessons from Jacob she now knew how to catch them.

The Bjorklunds had left a patch of rhubarb and horseradish. There was cultivated ground near the soddy they had used for a large family garden. Christina's first job was to put in a garden with beans, carrots, cabbage and peas. Then, in the small field over toward the lake, where the Bjorklunds had grown wheat, she used a stick to punch holes in the ground and planted potatoes and corn. Wheat and oats would have to wait until she could find someone to plow the twenty acres.

CHAPTER EIGHTEEN

LIVING IN THE SOD SHANTY

$\mathfrak{T}$he mouse scurried across the dirt floor and dove for the hole just as Christina brought the broom down. Dust flew. She carefully raised the broom, but there was no mashed or disabled mouse under it. Christina muttered to herself, "Uff dah. Another one missed. They're too fast for me. I've got to get me a mouser." Living alone she had gotten into the habit of talking out loud to herself.

She looked around the room. They had gotten in her breadbox, a precious book had been chewed on, they had nibbled on her flour bin, and one morning she found mouse droppings on the table. "These mice are going to ruin everything. Now who do I know who would have an extra cat?"

A picture of the Efraimson homestead flashed into her mind. She could see chickens, their cow, a large black dog and cats. They had a yard full of cats. "Ya, the Finns have cats. I think it's time I give them a visit."

Since this was to be a formal visit, she took off her apron and dug her favorite sweater out of the chest. Next she spent half an hour unpinning, smoothing and repining her hair, then covered her head with her straw hat to keep her skin from getting burned.

Having done what she could with her limited resources to make herself acceptable, she set off in a northerly direction for the Finn's claim. With her ground-covering stride the two miles would take her just over half an hour.

Marching across the windblown prairie, she knew she could be seen from the Efraimson farm while she was still some distance away. Christina saw no signs of life around the yard and was wondering if she had made the trip in vain when she heard someone yelling in Finnish. She caught her name in the din, but the rest of the sentence was just noise.

Not too far ahead she saw the oldest Efraimson boy pop out of the grass. This was followed by the barking of their large black dog, who saw his main job being to serve as welcoming committee. He accepted the family's assignment as their coyote chaser, but his real talent was in greeting strangers.

With the dog's announcement of her arrival the other members of the family began appearing, out of the grass, out of the barn, and out of the house. The other four children appeared eager to see the Norwegian lady with the braided hair.

As she approached the soddy she could hear Mrs. Efraimson's voice raised in anger. Mr. Efraimson was making pacifying sounds, which Christina imagined to be, "Yes, dear, of course, dear, whatever you say dear." Emma Efraimson definitely seemed to be in command of her family. When the Efraimsons talked with each other in Finnish it sounded like gibberish to Christina, but she could tell if it were angry gibberish or friendly gibberish. On the other hand German sounded like a real language to her, but the tone often seemed angry. The older Finns' command of Swedish allowed them to carry on conversations with her about basic matters like crops, buildings and food.

Finished with their discussion, the elder Efraimsons came out of the shanty. They saw that she was dressed for a formal visit so they shook hands with her and asked her, "How goes it down your way?"

"I'm feeling fair to middlin'."

The children gathered around them, their eyes glued on the adults. They could understand almost nothing of what the grown-ups were saying, but the appearance of Christina had broken the monotony, and they were fascinated by her strange way of talking. A visitor, even a young girl visitor, was a major source of entertainment.

After the obligatory comments about the weather and their chances for a good crop this year, Christina got to the point of her visit. "Mrs. Efraimson, I need a cat. The mice are a real bother. If I don't do something soon, they will chew up everything I got. Have you got one you can give me?"

Emma Efraimson looked over at their small wooden barn. After spending the winter with a cow and oxen inside the soddy, the Efraimsons decided that separate housing for their animals was of primary importance. Emma nodded at the spot where six cats lay sunning themselves. Christina followed her gaze.

Emma said, "Cats we got in plenty." She pointed to one that sat some distance from the rest. "Take the big yellow one with the bent tail. It don't get along good with the others. You keep it hungry, it will make you a good mouser."

Scandinavian rules of hospitality could now be followed and Emma said, "Come into the house; let's get out of the sun." The eyes of the children followed them. Once the adults were inside the soddy, little faces appeared at the windows and one on each side of the door. There was some giggling, and one of the boys had a laugh that was like the cackling of a chicken. The sound made Christina smile, and she placed her hand in front of her mouth. The idea of others seeing her large front teeth still bothered her.

While talking Emma Efraimson was setting out cups for coffee. "What you doing about getting you a real window 'stead of that oilcloth you using now?"

When Christina had taken over the soddy, the window that had been in it last winter was missing. She figured some family passing through had added it to their wagonload of supplies. For the time being an oilcloth stood between her and the weather.

"Window? You know I don't have money for a window."

"Well, when the homestead man comes around to check if you done the right things to prove up the land, he's goin' to want to see a window. I think we found one you can get a part of. Over north there's a family got one they rent out when the government man comes by. They get word where he's going to be, and then they pass the window around so you got it when he comes by your place."

Christina shook her head. "No, I think I can find some way to get one of my own. I want a good one that will keep the wind and snow out when the winter comes. I want as much light as I can get. The federal inspector won't be around for a while. I got time."

The one-room sod shanty they were sitting in was little more than a large, damp, dark hole. As she sat looking around the room Christina was becoming obsessed with trying to figure out the mystery of how they had ever gotten three families, a cow and oxen in here. Did some of them sleep sitting up? Maybe after the children went to sleep, they stacked them in a pile or perhaps stood them in the corners. She was dying to know how they had done it, but was too polite to ask.

As far as it was from a real wooden house, Mrs. Efraimson was still proud of her dugout. She began talking about the advantages. "The nice thick walls make this a good home. We're nice and cool in the summer and cozy and warm in the winter."

Christina almost blurted out, "I think if you were warm it was all those bodies you shoved in here. I bet that's what gave you good heat on those cold winter nights." She bit her tongue and kept her mouth shut.

Mrs. Efraimson sipped her coffee and went on bragging about her sod shanty. "Look how sturdy it is. We're not likely to be blown down by a high wind."

Christina continued the dialogue in her own mind. "Yes, and with all this dirt for walls and floor we got creepy-crawlies, mice, and bedbugs. We might not be blowed away by the wind, but we might get carried away by all the critters living with us."

What she said out loud was, "V. G. has made hers nicer by whitewashing the walls, and she's going to get her man to put real wood shingles on the roof."

The idea pleased Emma. "Oh, won't that be nice."

Christina went on. "Well, some day we'll all be able to build real wood houses like Meyer Pearson built last year."

Emma's voice took on an irritated tone. "Well he must of brought a bundle of money with him to be able to bring that lumber all the way from Canby, Minnesota. If they got that kind of money, what are they doing homesteading? Besides I don't much like the way Olga Pearson lords it over everyone because she has a frame house. It's not Christian to be so high and mighty."

Christina hadn't noticed that mousy Olga Pearson lorded it over anyone, not even her children. While she kept her mouth shut about it around Emma, Christina could hardly wait until she had money so she could smash down her soddy and build a real wooden house. The spot where the soddy stood would make a good flower garden.

Coffee finished Christina went outside and gathered up the yellow cat with the bent tail and headed back to her claim. The children and the dog followed for several hundred yards until they were distracted by a large jackrabbit. The dog gave a yelp, the oldest boy a whoop and they took off after the fast moving rabbit.

The cat took to Christina immediately and made itself comfortable in her arms. "Cat, you just got yourself a job. No more lying in the sun; now you're going to earn your keep by stopping those plundering mice from spoiling everything." The cat began to purr.

CHAPTER NINETEEN

NEIGHBORS

Christina bent to enter the sod house through the low door. She blinked, temporarily blinded by the dazzling after images of the sun dancing in front of her in the semidarkness. The dirt walls absorbed much of the light that managed to slip in the door and the one small window.

Christina sat down slowly on the lone stool and wiped the beads of sweat from her face. She sat slumped forward, her head cradled in her palms. She watched droplets of sweat form tiny wet spots on the packed dirt floor. Tears of weariness prickled behind her eyes.

Her twenty-one-year-old eyes adjusted quickly to the murky light of the room. Was that Cat? The animal was so still that at first Christina almost couldn't see her. Cat was sitting alert, poised for action with her left front foot outstretched. "What are you doing, Cat?" Christina asked the feline.

Cat responded to Christina's Norwegian with a Finnish "Meow." As Christina watched, she saw that the cat's foot was holding something. She squinted, leaned forward and made out the shape of a mouse. Cat was holding the mouse by its tail, intently watching its futile attempts to escape. Cat turned to Christina and meowed in a tone that said "Watch this."

She lifted her paw and freed the mouse; but before it could disappear under the wood box, the velvety gold paw streaked out and batted it back.

With Christina as her audience Cat began to perform using the mouse as a prop. Each time, she held the mouse by the tail watching it struggle frantically to pull away, then lifted her paw, letting it run a short distance before reaching out to bat it back. Cat repeated this move four times as if experimenting with how far she could let the mouse run and still catch it.

Before Christina could become bored with the display of skill, Cat rolled the mouse into a ball of fur that she batted back and forth between her paws. The speed with which the cat moved pleased Christina. She felt no sympathy for the mouse. "Good Cat, you'll get rid of those messy old mice." The sound of Christina's voice distracted Cat who missed the mouse. It quickly dove into a crack in the sod wall and disappeared.

Having Cat around had made a difference in Christina's life. Besides being a good mouser, she was also a good listener. When Christina talked, Cat looked at her, cocked her head and stared without blinking. It helped ease the loneliness.

Christina's thoughts moved to her need for company. There weren't many people around yet, and those few were some distance off. Although they had arrived in Dakota Territory only four years ago, Petrina and Lars had arrived early enough to get one of the best claims in the area. Lars' mother, brothers and sister who had arrived four years earlier had come to a land virtually empty of people. Even now, eight years later when Christina filed her claim, there were still only 700 settlers in the entire county.

Christina remembered her conversation with the land agent who told her, "Well now, young lady, you're lucky to be getting in early on the land rush. With the railroad coming into Watertown we're going to have Scandinavians and Germans grabbing up all the claims that's available. Why, in ten years we'll have four maybe five thousand people living right here in this county."

"Well," she said to Cat, "all those people, that's the future. I'd like some neighbors right now. You're not much for answering back." She smiled, "And I'd guess that you and I couldn't start much of a Lutheran Church." In her prayers at night Christina prayed that God would send some God fearing Norwegians to live close to her.

One morning when Christina came out of the soddy and looked to the south, she saw a strange object sitting on the horizon. She couldn't make out what it was, but from its size it was sure to mean that there were people with it. Her heart jumped. Cat had followed her outside and Christina turned to her. "Cat, I think maybe people are moving in south of us. I think I'll go see."

She went to the piece of mirror she kept on the outside wall above her wash basin and pail of water. She scowled at her reflection. Her hair was flying about her face in wispy strands, and she had smudges of soot from the stove on her face. As she began to clean up, she said to the image in the mirror, "You've been away from people too much; you look like a homeless waif. You've got to take better care of yourself."

Pulling on a light shawl she moved off with her broad stride across the grasslands. Meadowlarks called to each other, bees searched industriously for nectar and field mice scurried into the tall grass as she passed.

As she approached the mysterious dark shape, she saw it was an unhitched wagon. When she got up to it, blankets were lined up under it with four small still bodies wrapped in them. No sign of adults. She shaded her eyes with her hand and turned toward the lake. There was a team of oxen up to their knees in the lake with their noses deep in the sparkling water. A man and a woman stepped out of the brush and started toward the wagon. Seeing her they froze and waited silently.

The couple stood alert, their eyes darting first at her and then at the wagon. They were poised to move quickly away. Christina could see that her unexpected appearance here in the middle of nowhere made them nervous.

The man and woman were about the same height, both just slightly taller than Christina's five foot seven inches. The man wore a beaten felt hat, overalls from which all color had been washed out and a tattered jacket from what was once a fancy wool suit. He wore a thick brown mustache over his well-formed lips. A line of tobacco juice marked the right corner of his mouth.

The woman had on a bright green dress, which was a contrast to the usual grays and browns worn by pioneer women. Her face had the relaxed look of someone who smiled often. She was heavier than the man and, Christina guessed, probably stronger.

Hoping her Norwegian could be understood, Christina said, "Hello, my name's Christina Gunnerson. I live on the claim just over north of here."

The man stared at her as if she had just stepped out of the spirit world. His wife spoke first. "Close your mouth, Andrew. It's just a young lady, not a naked savage." She turned to Christina. "I'm Lizzie Bakke; the man here with the open mouth is my husband, Andrew." Christina was delighted that Lizzie had answered her in good Norwegian.

Lizzie Bakke stared over Christina's shoulder as if trying to see where Christina had come from.

Christina answered the unasked question. "Oh, you can't see my place from here because it's a soddy and blends in with the ground. You got to be real close before you know anyone lives there."

Lizzie Bakke asked, "You live with your folks?"

"No, my folks are dead. It's my homestead. I live there by myself."

Wayne P. Anderson

"Your folks, they weren't killed by Indians, I hope. Andrew, he don't much like Indians."

Christina could see that the Bakkes were still unsure how dangerous this country might be. They weren't the first couple she had met who were concerned about Indians. While Christina had yet to see a wild Indian, she knew that the Custer battle had been only five or six years ago. "No, there aren't any Indians I know of around here. Both my Ma and Pa died in Norway. I'm on my own here."

"You look too young to be living by yourself. How can you be safe in this wild land without someone to take care of you?" Christina's mouth was full of words, but she didn't get a chance to use them before Lizzie went on. "Well, we came from Norway, too. We been livin' up at Albert Lee, Minnesota. But Andrew has convinced himself that we can do better here in Dakota Territory."

Andrew still hadn't said a word but had been nodding his head along with what Lizzie was saying. Now he walked to the wagon box, threw back a tarp disclosing a disorganized pile of equipment and household goods. He began moving it around with no apparent goal. Finally after he handled some of the pieces several times, he pulled out a shovel. He still didn't say anything to acknowledge Christina's presence, but he glanced at her from time to time to be sure she was following his actions. His slow movements suggested some kind of ceremony.

Lizzie went to the four blanket robes and shook each of them in turn. The four boys who emerged were yawning, stretching and rubbing the sleep out of their eyes. They had slept in their shirts and pants. When they saw a stranger, they each tried to smooth their white hair with their hands; then in unison they yawned. Lizzie lined them up in order of their height opposite Christina, then came back and stood beside her.

Andrew Bakke stepped between the boys and the woman, put the spade in the ground, checked Lizzie and Christina to make sure they were paying attention, then bowed in the direction of the boys and said, "This land is going to be my homestead, and I claim it for myself and for my heirs forevermore. It is my wish that the Bakkes will always abide here."

Christina looked at Lizzie Bakke who was smiling with pride and treating her husband's strange behavior as if it were the most normal thing in the world. The ceremony over, one of the boys pushed the smaller one to the ground and took off running. The other three gave a wild whoop and took off in pursuit.

Lizzie turned back to Christina. "We traveled to Dakota in this covered wagon pulled by that yoke of oxen. I walked all the way and still kept the family supplied with bread, baked in the oven of our big cook stove. Now why don't you just pull up a plot of ground to sit on, and I'll brew some coffee and we'll have some of that bread for breakfast."

As they started to eat, the boys were introduced to Christina as Elmer, Carl, Albert and John. Lizzie pointed at Elmer, the oldest boy. "Elmer, he likes to make things. Put some tools in his hands and give him a piece of wood, and he'll make most anything. We get around to building us a house, we already got us a good hired hand."

Elmer blushed with pride. This gave Christina an idea. "I'm pretty good at catching fish. I have my own boat. Would Elmer be willing to help me build a chicken coop if I catch you some fish?"

Lizzie looked at Elmer who nodded eagerly. "Looks like the boy would be pleased to get a chance to do some real work with tools," Lizzie said.

"Couple miles off to the east I know where there's an old deserted claim shack that's not completely picked over," Christina said. "I'll bet we can find enough boards to make me a coop for the broody hen my sister is going to give me."

Before she left, Christina had made arrangements with

Andrew Bakke to use his oxen to plow the twenty acres of land that Bjorklund had broken. In return she was to supply them with fish for the summer, introduce them to their neighbors and help carry the sod for their sod shanty.

Cat

Christina was learning about farming the hard way. Her hands were callused and her muscles even stronger than they had been. Once again she was lean and wiry. Getting the homestead had been a lucky break. The Bjorklunds' tragedy was her good fortune and enabled her to avoid some of the problems Petrina had forecast.

There were numerous wild animals around the homestead, most of which presented no danger: coyotes, skunks, jackrabbits, gophers and prairie chickens. The rabbits and the prairie chickens were a source of food. A big rabbit could serve a couple of people for several meals. Christina and Cat could eat off one for days.

The first few times Trina had served rabbit, Christina refused to eat it. It looked too much like a skinned cat to her. When she finally did eat it, it was because she had been working hard and was extremely hungry. Trina had covered it with flour and lard gravy that make it look more like chicken. Since then she had learned to like it.

Prairie wolves also roamed the grasslands and although she was afraid of them, Mr. Bjorklund had explained to her that it was only rarely they ever killed a human. In spite of this, the night sounds of coyotes and wolves howling at the moon sent shivers down her spine, and she pulled the blankets closer around her.

The chicken coop gave her growing brood of chickens protection from most marauding animals: foxes, skunks and coyotes. Once she closed the door of the coop at night, none of these animals could get at them, so it was a surprise when she opened the coop one morning and found one of her chickens had been killed. There was a bite mark at the base of the skull, and the blood of the half grown chicken had been lapped up.

Christina looked over at Cat. "Cat, I think we got us a big rat of some kind. I think maybe you should sleep with the chickens tonight."

Toward morning when the first fingers of light were crawling above the horizon, Christina was jerked awake by a scream that sounded like a child in pain. Still confused by sleep, she rushed outside to be met by sounds of spitting, hissing and shrieking coming from the coop. She ran for the coop and saw a small dark animal slip out of a hole in the side and head for the lake.

Inside blood was splattered on the walls and there was a vile smell that made her gag. Cat lay on her side trying to get to her feet. One ear was almost tore loose, there was a gash on her face and blood was seeping from wounds on her body. She scooped Cat into her arms and began running the quarter mile to the Bakke place still dressed in her nightclothes. She began hollering for Mrs. Bakke when she was still several hundred yards out.

Both Lizzie and Andrew were coming out the door when she arrived at their soddy. "Christina, what's the matter?" Lizzie asked.

"It's Cat. She's all cut up. Some animal got into the coop and was killing chickens. Cat's bleeding something fierce."

Lizzie took Cat from Christina and examined her. "I think we can fix her up. I'll need to do some sewing on her where the skin's been cut too deep. Should be able to save her, but you'll need to feed her lots of liver to get her blood back."

Andrew Bakke carefully examined the cat and then delivered his opinion. "Weasel. Ounce for ounce meanest fighter there is. Sure did tear Cat up some."

With needle and thread from her sewing basket Lizzie put

Cat back together again. To keep her still they had to wrap her in a towel and both Andrew and Christina held her. Ever after when Mrs. Bakke came to visit, Cat would leave the soddy and go hide.

Later Christina brought some bullheads over to the Bakkes. She was still paying off Andrew for plowing her twenty acres of land. She cleaned them for Lizzie out back of the Bakke's new sod shanty.

Watching how quickly Christina cut off the heads and gutted the fish, Lizzie said, "You do that good as a man. You gutted a lot of fish?"

"I learned the hard way. I've cut a lot of fish in Norway."

"Do you ever feel you would like a man to share the work with you?"

"That would be nice, but I can do whatever a man does."

"Well, you won't start babies without one. Do you want to live on the homestead alone forever?"

Christina sighed and set the knife down. Her eyes were troubled as she said, "I don't like living alone. But I can't live with Petrina and Lars. I'm not pretty, and I don't know any good Norwegian men. I don't know when I might get married." She shrugged. "I may just be an old maid." She glanced away from Lizzie and saw the Bakke's cats lined up in a row, their ears perked, their eyes watching her hands cut up the fish. Christina threw the fish heads to the cats who pounced on them.

When the din of the cats had died down, Lizzie continued. "Maybe we can find a good man for you. There are some unmarried and widowed men living around here. I hear that over northwest of here near Hayti, there's a new settler, Daniel Sour. He was a carriage and wagon maker, but when his wife died two years ago, he gave up his shop and came to Dakota to claim land."

"I been thinking too, Lizzie. I'm looking but I don't talk about it. I know about Mr. Sour. But he's German and doesn't speak much English and no Norwegian. Besides he has three grown sons, one almost my age. I heard at the store last week that Sarah J. Sundy's been giving him the eye. I don't think I got much chance even if I wanted it."

Talking about marriage was making Christina nervous. She couldn't look directly at Lizzie for fear she would blush. In spite of her embarrassment she went on. "I had a chance to get married in Norway. Some days I think I made a mistake not marrying him. I'd be living in a nice wood house and have pictures on the walls and no calluses on my hands."

"Don't give up. You're strong and do your share of the work, not like some of those lazy ones who count on their good looks to get them by. You can get a good man from around here." Lizzie paused, thought a moment, then went on, "Well, some I know maybe ain't so good."

They worked in silence for a while. Christina thought the subject had been dropped when Lizzie said, "Maybe you should go work in Watertown or someplace. Lots of men there so you'd have a choice."

Christina remembered her dream before she left Norway that she would find a man in America. No one resembling him had entered her life, but she trusted the dream and felt that she would find him. She took the fish livers she had carefully set aside and took them home as a treat for Cat.

It became a good summer for new neighbors. Two miles to the north the Danes, Bertel and Elsa Andersen, and their three children moved in. They build a dugout for the family and a separate one for livestock on the north side of a hill located near the Dry Lake shore. Elsa was quick to let everyone know that Bertel had served in the Danish Army and been awarded a medal of recognition and a Veteran's Honorary Donation of one hundred crowns that he received annually.

Another Norwegian family, the Bergersons, moved in to the south of Bakkes. John Bergerson not only claimed a quarter section under the land act, but under the Timber Culture Act got an additional 160 acres of land for planting ten acres of trees on it.

The neighbors she had prayed for were arriving at last. Cat's wounds were healing nicely. The weasel hadn't come back. Her chickens were growing. The crops were coming up. Life was good.

CHAPTER TWENTY

INDIANS

When she walked across the prairie near the farm, Christina would occasionally see deer who would bound out of sight when she came near them. At night she could hear the howling of wolves. Several times when she standing at the window looking out in the late evening, she had watched two of them cross the field south of the chicken coop.

One evening after seeing them, her thoughts went to Wolfman and her trip across Norway to Russia. She wondered if he had finally missed as a wolf leapt at him, been crippled and left to die alone in a tent, then to freeze and be buried when the clan returned in the summer. She turned her head away from the path the wolves had taken to keep from thinking about it.

In late September Mennie knocked a lamp over, and Lars and Petrina's house caught fire. The dry wood lit like kindling, and they saved only themselves and the clothes they were wearing. The family had to stand and watch their precious mementos of Norway go up in smoke. Lars, Petrina and the two children moved in with Lilly.

They decided to rebuild at once a house bigger, stronger and warmer than the old one. Christina came over to take care of the children while Lars' brothers and sister's husband all helped put up their new home. By the first of November two rooms were finished enough for them to move in. Two more rooms were framed in, and they planned on finishing them as soon as the spring thaw allowed them to bring in more lumber from the new railhead at Watertown.

Caring for the children stirred Christina's need to have her own. After she had been with them for a week, it was painful to leave them and return to her soddy. Anton and Mennie also made it obvious that they loved having Christina as their nanny, a fact that made Petrina jealous. "You get to play with them and give them permission to do whatever they want. I'm the mother and I'm responsible to make them behave themselves."

Again she began to worry about finding the man in her dream. It seemed he would never come here, and she didn't know how to go somewhere else to look for him.

Petrina went back to being bossy and picky, and by the middle of November the two sisters had had enough of each other. Despite her love of the children Christina went back to spending most of her time at her own soddy and visiting with the neighbors in her area.

Christina's neighbors a mile and half due east were Meyer and Olga Pearson and their two daughters. It was Olga Pearson's wooden house that Emma Efraimson felt indicated too much wealth for them to be homesteaders. The Pearsons had come to Dakota Territory in 1879 and built one of the first wooden houses in that part of the county.

In the spring of 1883 just after planting time, Meyer Pearson got an offer of a job in Michigan to earn money so they could keep the homestead going. Olga stayed behind with the two little girls to work the farm.

Christina was feeding the chickens when Olga and her two daughters came hurrying across the prairie. She had a girl's hand in each of hers and was practically dragging them along. They stopped, out of breath in front of Christina. The dust on Olga's cheeks had pathways that were still damp from tears.

The five-year-old's head was lightly covered with wispy white hair. Ella's large soulful blue eyes made even the most reserved want to pick her up and take care of her. Her need to elicit protection was in part related to her seven-year-old sister Anna's ability to cause accidents to happen. The older girl with her freckles and reddish cast to her blond hair had a look of potential mischief about her.

Under calm conditions Olga was high strung. When things went less than well, she reacted with panic. The girls seldom saw strangers and had picked up some of their mother's tendency to overreact. Now they stayed silently behind their mother, the littler one hanging on to her skirt and peeking out from behind her mother at Christina.

Olga caught her breath and gasped, "Christina, are the Bakke's home?"

"No, they and the boys have gone off to Brookings. They won't be back for two or three days." Christina waited for Olga to explain the emergency. She knew Olga had trouble in knowing what was a real crisis. There were times she had been very fearful one day, and on the next couldn't have told you what she was so worried about.

Still out of breath from the exertion, Olga said, "We're all alone out here then?"

"I guess. Why?"

"A man rode by our farm this morning. He said we should all pack up and go into town. Some of the Indians left the reservation and have gone on the warpath again. He said they're likely to come here killing and burning."

"I never heard of Indians around here giving us any trouble," Christina cautioned.

"Christina, it's only a few years ago that they rose up in Minnesota and killed all those poor settlers. Those awful savages are born to raise hell and kill. They don't want us around these parts. This was their hunting grounds. They're still mad at us for coming and using it like God intended, to grow food and raise God fearing folks like my girls here." The thought gave her strength; she squared her shoulders and a look of pride appeared on her face.

"You think we should go to town then?" Christina asked as she scattered the last grains of corn to the chickens.

"No, I don't want to leave my new home. Meyer and I worked too hard to build it for some beasts to burn it down and steal everything. I don't know what to do, but I'm not leaving!"

Christina thought a moment. "I think we should go to town. If they burn the house, you can always make another one."

"If we try to walk to town, they could catch us in the open, and we'd be worse off," Olga protested. "I won't go. If I can't find nobody to help me, I'll just stay at the house with the girls."

Christina looked at her soddy. "Well, if the Indians want my sod shanty, they can have it. If it was a nice house built of wood, maybe I wouldn't leave either."

The four took off across the wind swept grass for the Pearson farm. The light breeze carried vestiges of the land it passed over, a light smell of skunk, dry grasses, newly turned sod. If they had stopped and let the odors envelop them, they would have found traces of the smoke of a far off grass fire.

Christina turned and saw the Pearsons falling behind. Olga's face was flushed with the exertion of trying to match Christina's pace. Christina had to slow down her long stride so that the Pearson girls could keep up. The little girl's eyes were still wide with fright. Silently they trotted in their bare feet attempting to stay close to their mother.

It only took thirty minutes to get to the Pearson house. Fifty yards from the house Olga stopped and examined the buildings and the yard for anything that was out of the ordinary. From that distance all appeared normal. The women still approached the house cautiously. When they were in the yard, Olga jerked her head toward the house. "Might be Indians in there."

Christina walked up to around the house and cupped her hands against the glass. "It's all quiet in there. There's no sign of any movement."

Olga pulled the children closer to her side and picked up Ella. "Christina, you go in first."

Pushing the door open with her foot, Christina stepped in. All was quiet in the room. Her eyes checked every corner. Against the wall next to the hearth was a long, heavy looking rifle. She went to the door, "Olga, do you have bullets for Meyer's gun?"

"I don't know. He hides them somewhere so the girls can't find them." She cautiously entered the room. "Let me think. Maybe he's got them in his box he calls his useful this and thats." She went into a bedroom, pulled a large box out from under the bed and began to search in it. "I don't know how he ever finds anything in this box. Look at this mess, nails, hammers, pinchers, steel spikes, tongs and all kinds of junk jumbled together."

She took pieces out until she found a box containing the large bullets labeled "Springfield rifle." She handed the box to Christina who tore it open and put a handful of the large cartridges into her apron pocket and picked up the rifle and stepped outside.

Olga followed her and in a voice filled with awe asked, "Can you really shoot that?"

"I seen Bjorklund do it. I can figure it." She set the gun against the wall and straightened her dress. The respite allowed her to become aware that her hair had come loose and was getting in her eyes. First she took a deep breath to collect her thoughts, and she took a moment to readjust her hair. Finally she said, "We're not going to see any Indians, but I got to know how to use the gun anyway."

She pointed to the open area south of the house. "Get all the animals out of the way down that way, and I'll see if I figure how to shoot this thing."

Olga pushed the children away from her and toward the small fenced-in area where the shed was, in which the fowl were kept at night to keep them safe from coyotes and weasels. With a whoop the two children began chasing the chickens and the two ducks into their small coop. The running cheered them up and the little one began laughing with pleasure as she sprinted after the rooster who was insisting on keeping his freedom to hunt worms in the manure pile.

With the animals out of the way Christina looked over the ground for a target. The coming and goings of animals and people kept the yard clear of grass, and the roughly plowed ground with its large clods began just a short distance away. Christina thought, "We are changing the land. In just the few years since I came, it is different, but is it really different?" She stood a few moments longer admiring the vast distance to the horizon where the deep blue sky with a touch of cottony clouds began.

A yelp from Ella, who had just gotten the rooster in the coop, broke her reverie, and she refocused on the land immediately in front of her. She settled on a rock about the size of a loaf of bread twenty-five yards away. "I'll shoot at that white rock over yonder."

She picked up the gun to load it, trying to look as if she knew what she was doing, but the gun didn't cooperate. It acted as if it were developing a will of its own. It tipped out of her hands, hit the ground nose first shoving dirt into the barrel. Christina casually dug the dirt out with her little finger. Placing her left hand midway up the barrel and holding the stock on her hip, she brought the gun into a position where she could flip open the trapdoor and insert a bullet. Then she snapped the trap door shut, struggled to pull the heavy hammer back and raised the gun to her shoulder.

Questions bounced around in her head. "Why didn't I get someone to show me how to do this? How tight do I hold it? Will it hurt when it shoots? Why doesn't it hold steady? It keeps moving. I didn't know it was so heavy."

To be safe she kept a light hold on it. She pulled the trigger. Her head jerked back from the shock of the explosion. Smoke vomited from the barrel. Dust billowed up from where the gun hit the ground ten feet away.

Olga rushed over to her. "Christina, Christina, are you all right?" she cried.

Christina looked herself up and down to make sure all of her pieces were still in place. She flexed her arms, shook her hands to bring back feeling. "I think so. It was a bigger bang than I expected." Picking up the gun, she brushed off the dust, flipped open the trapdoor, shook the spent cartridge out. It fell at her feet in the dust.

She took another precious bullet out of her apron pocket and clicked it into the chamber. A part of her apron caught in the mechanism, and it refused to close. Opening the trap door, she ripped the apron bringing an, "Uff dah," from her lips. Finally ready, she cautioned herself, "Tight, remember hold it tight." Following her instructions she pulled the gun tight against her shoulder. Pointing it in the general direction of the rock, she pulled the trigger.

With the explosion a heavy jolt hit her. She was thrown backward, sprawling on the ground. This time it was her bottom and not the gun that raised the cloud of dust.

She sat for a moment, breathless and stunned by the impact. When she found her voice, she shouted at Olga in delight, "This time I held the gun. Now if I can find how to stay on my feet, maybe I'll shoot good."

Still sitting on the ground she took out the spent cartridge and reloaded the chamber. She was developing a new respect for what the gun could do to her but also what it might do to anything that the bullet might hit. Setting her legs apart, holding the gun tight against her shoulder and leaning into the coming shock, she pulled the trigger. This time both she and the gun stayed in place. She had closed her eyes at the noise and the impact against her shoulder and didn't see where the bullet landed. There was elation in her voice when she asked, "Did I hit it?"

Olga shook her head. "No, you missed. It went way off there to the side." She pointed out a spot way to the side and some fifty yards in back of the rock.

"These bullets cost," Christina said, "I'll shoot just two more. I need to keep some for when the Indians come." The last two practice shots fell closer to the rock. She thought, "If I aimed at an Indian, he would have still been standing all in one piece. Well, I can't hit nothing. Maybe the noise and smoke will scare the savages off."

The gunfire reassured Olga that they were now prepared for the Indians. The worry lines in her face disappeared, and for the first time she smiled. "It's hot out here with no shade. Let's go inside, and I'll make us some coffee."

The rest of the day passed uneventfully. Ella and Anna played in the yard, and Olga checked for Indians only three or four times an hour. At bedtime she said, "I think we can sleep good. Meyer told me that Indians won't attack at night. If they are killed in battle, their spirit can't find its way to the happy hunting grounds in the dark."

Olga got up at the first sign of sun and began pacing nervously from one window to another. It was late morning when she suddenly froze in her tracks and cried, "Christina, get the gun—the savages are coming!"

Christina stepped out on the porch, squinted trying to make out the figures. Given the flatness of the land and lack of trees, they were still a fair distance off and neither their sex or race could be made out. "There's only two of them and they're afoot. Maybe they ain't Indians."

"They're probably just the scouts. The others will be right behind." Olga said in a reassuring voice. Christina and the girls were not comforted.

Christina chest became tighter and her breathing more difficult as the two figures approached. They were coming across the grassland from the direction of her farm. No others appeared in back of them. "Christina, they may just be testing us. Watch them carefully."

"Well, they do look like Indians all right, and they are coming right for the house."

Olga wrung her hands and got tears in her eyes. Christina's heart was beating so loudly she was sure Olga could hear it. The sweat on her palms was making it difficult to keep the gun in a ready position. Thoughts fought each other, "They don't look dangerous. You really can't tell. They could be trying to fool us. If I shoot I'll miss. The smoke and noise might scare them away."

Olga pushed the children toward the house. "Girls, go in the house and stay under the bed. Don't come out until I come in to get you. Now scoot." She came back to stand twenty feet behind Christina, lending moral but not physical support. "Maybe you should shoot a warning shot to let them know we got a gun."

"No, the way I shot yesterday I might hit one of them by mistake. Then they'll get really mad. We'll let them come closer. They may not be dangerous."

"Savages are always dangerous. We can't trust them. Please, Christina, shoot at them."

"No."

The Indians stopped twenty yards away. It was a male and a female. They looked at the rifle that Christina held in her arms and showed no fear of it. They seemed to expect white pioneer women to stand around their yards with a gun in their hands. In a loud whisper Olga said, "They're wearing Christian folk's clothes. Maybe they've already killed somebody."

Christina snorted, "If they killed somebody for those clothes, it was some time ago. They're awfully dirty and torn to be recent. That coat he's wearing wouldn't flatter a scarecrow."

Christina could see that the couple were neither old nor young. But she didn't know how fast Indians aged. She would have to ask someone about that. The man was barefoot but the woman had moccasins on her feet. Both of them had hair that was long and black and shiny with grease. The woman had a red band around her head and the man had on an old felt hat. They were, even by the loose standards of the two pioneer women, unbelievably dirty.

The man held his hand up in greeting. There was no sign of a weapon on either of them. The man pointed to his stomach, then moved his hand to his mouth and chewed.

Olga asked, "What's he doing?"

"He's asking for food." Christina stepped closer to the Indians. They looked frail. They were not at all like the vicious bloodthirsty savages she had expected. Reassured by their appearance, she moved within five feet of them and looked into the man's eyes. He stared back passively. There was no fear or hate. Then she looked into the woman's eyes and was surprised by the look of pleading. The woman's large eyes brought back memories of Bossy as she lay dying. These people were hungry. Hunger she could understand. Her nervousness had disappeared, but she still felt a need to be cautious. Not taking her eyes off them, she shouted to Olga, "I think if we give them some food, they will move on."

"No, I will not feed savages," Olga protested.

"Olga, look at them. Look at their eyes. They're harmless, hungry people. Feed them; let them move on. You have extra bread and there's meat. Please, I don't want to see them go on hungry. It will be a long way before they find anyone with food to give them again."

Olga hesitated. Finally she decided that Christina was determined to feed them. She felt a need to keep her contented. After all, if more Indians came, Christina with her gun was her only protection. She gave up her opposition with, "All right, but I don't think it's a good idea."

Olga went into her kitchen and brought out bread and cold meat. She indicated to the Indians that they could not eat near the house. As they ate, she watched them carefully and indicated to Christina by her facial expression her disgust at the way the Indians wolfed down the food using their hands.

Christina watched, thankful that she no longer had to go days without a good meal. She was pleased to be able to help them. For her the message in their eyes had turned them into two hungry people like herself. She no longer saw the two savages that Olga saw. "Olga, just think; they've had their old life taken away by us coming here."

Olga looked at her as if Christina were losing her mind. She was treating these wild people as if they were as good as Christians. She locked her jaw and held back from saying, "I'll be glad when Meyer gets back. He talks sense about Indians."

The next day two more figures moved on the horizon. Christina quickly recognized by their hats that it was Andrew Bakke and his oldest son, Elmer.

After Christina explained about their visitors, Andrew went on, "Well, those weren't the ones you'd been warned about. We heard the story about them on our way home. A week ago a couple of Indians some distance west of here got hold of some firewater and went on a toot. You know liquor makes an Indian crazy. Well, those two stole some cattle and burned down one settler's shack. Wasn't no one home when they did it, so no one got hurt. The sheriff got them back on the reservation by now. I

212

don't know where the Indians you fed might have come from."

After hearing of her adventures with the gun, Andrew said, "If we get more savages visiting us, some might be more than hungry. You've got to learn to shoot the gun better. I will teach you how to hit the rock."

"No, I don't want to know more. Someone else will have to shoot at the Indians."

CHAPTER TWENTY-ONE

SNOWSTORM

The summer was another round of hard work. A dry spell came in July, and Christina had all she could do to carry enough water to keep her potato and bean crop healthy. When the drought finally broke, the moisture came as hail that wiped out her cash crop of wheat. Everyone was cash poor. Even Lars and Petrina couldn't help her since they had put all of their ready money into the lumber for their new house. Without money to buy needed supplies she knew this was going to be a hard winter.

When Christina opened the door and stepped up out of the dank darkness of the sod shanty, the outside air warmed her. She could hardly believe her luck, late September and the weather still friendly. There had been occasional flurries, but the snow that fell soon melted. Taking advantage of the unseasonable warmth, she decided that it would be a good time to lay in more wood before the storms swept in from the northwest.

The prairie, even this close to water, stood nude of trees, but the border of the lake was clad in scant patches of heavy brush. With her ax Christina set to work leveling one of these patches. Early in the day she felt comfortable working in only a sweater. By mid morning she was sweating lightly from the exertion of chopping the scrub wood.

Late in the morning she stopped to catch her breath. Sitting on a pile of small logs, she took a deep drink of water from her water jug. She felt the goose bumps on her arms as the frosty hand of winter brushed over her. Her sweat turned to a clammy iciness. The temperature was dropping. With so much attention directed toward her work she hadn't noticed the change. Across the darkening lake the sky was muddy and unfriendly. Christina shivered. Even the inside of the soddy would be more hospitable. She picked up an armload of wood and returned to the shanty to get a coat.

Cat was waiting for her inside the door. "Looks like it's going to get colder, Cat, maybe even some snow." Cat acknowledged the comment with a "meow."

Christina stored the wood in the wood box, dug out her oldest coat and pulled it on. The first flakes were falling as she left the soddy. Cat followed her out, paused and then meowed to be let back in. "Cat, I'm going to bring more wood in. It looks like we may be in for a cold spell."

An hour later as she was coming back to the soddy with her last load of wood, three inches of snow shrouded the ground. It was a heavy snow, loaded with moisture, which clung to her coat and quickly built a layer on the wood she was carrying. Her tracks from the last trip were already covered, and she could see only a short distance. All markers as to where she was had disappeared.

After a while she knew, she should have seen the soddy's stovepipe. The soddy had disappeared. In a moment of panic she dropped the wood and started to run. A voice in her head said, "Christina, you must stay calm. You'll lose all sense of where you are." She stood still, then turned slowly trying to reorient herself. Nothing. "The house has to be close. You can find it."

She decided to walk in an ever-enlarging circle. Time passed slowly. Her heart continued to beat fast, but she fought the urge to run. Somewhere out there she felt the mackerel was waiting for her. If she didn't stay calm and sensible, it would take her down. A dark shape appeared ahead, and she broke and ran toward it. It was the chicken coop; she was going to be safe. Oriented she moved toward the soddy. The smoke from the stovepipe appeared a short distance ahead. A sigh of relief escaped from her chest as she hurried to the door.

That night the sound of the howling wind woke her. For a moment she confused it with the sea wind that swept over the island. She was comforted by the thought that her Pa and Olaf were in the next room. Then she was jarred by the thought, "That's the past: they're dead. I'm hearing Dakota wind." She went back to sleep secure in the knowledge that the thick dirt walls would keep her warm.

In the morning when she got out of bed, something had changed. The white light, filtered through the blowing snow, gave an eerie quality to the room. It no longer had a familiar, friendly feel.

She tried to open the door to look outside but found it stuck. Wrestling with it, it finally gave. Snow and wind pushed the door back at her. The air outside was a frigid wall of whiteness through which she could see no more than a few feet. Quickly she threw her shoulder against the door battling it closed. In the few seconds the door had been open, a two-inch wedge of snow had blown across the floor.

Christina picked up Cat and sat on the edge of the bed. Petting the purring animal, she said, "We're snowed in, Cat. Looks like it may be awhile before we get out of here." Cat's only answer was to rub her face on Christina's shoulder.

"Cat, I can't go out. I got nothing to read. There's no chores. I don't like this." Christina sat on the edge of the bed looking into the gloomy shadows, broken by only the faintest of light from the hearth. She stroked Cat. "Now all I've got is you, the dark and the cold." There was nothing she could think to do to break the monotony. She was still tired from yesterday's chopping. "Cat, I think I'll go back to bed now." She crawled back into bed and pulled the covers tightly around her. Cat curled up in the hollow of her knees. She slept fitfully, waking only to eat, to feed Cat, and to go to the toilet.

The second day she tried to find something to keep her mind busy. She swept the floor, looked for socks to darn, but she found little to do. Christina was used to spending time alone. When her father and Olaf had been on fishing trips, she had been alone for days. Here on the homestead she went days without seeing or talking to anyone. But she hadn't felt trapped like she did now.

She lost track of time and didn't know if she had been locked in by the storm three days or four. One morning when she awoke and looked around in the dim light, the room seemed smaller to her. Had the weight of the snow pushed the walls and the roof in? Her heart beat faster at the thought that the room was closing in on her?

She tried talking to Cat. But she lost interest and took to sitting and staring at the few pieces of wood she kept burning in the fireplace. Watching the flickering embers, she found her mind returning to Norway. Pictures of her father and Olaf came flipping through her mind: a shot of them in the boat, a quick glimpse of Olaf with Wolfman, her father driving Bossy out to pasture. The memories opened wounds. She wasn't ready for the pain. She forced herself to think of other scenes of the fjords and the ocean.

Time began to lose all meaning. The markers she counted on to organize her day evaded her. Was it morning or noon? Time to eat or had she eaten? She dug a slightly charred potato out of the corner of the hearth and took a bite. She chewed it slowly. No, she must have eaten earlier. A half hour later she was wondering again if it were time to eat. She went to the breadbox and took out a hunk of dark bread and broke off a piece. After swallowing a bite she said to Cat, "I must've eaten, but for the life of me I can't remember."

The next morning when she awoke she felt the presence of someone other than Cat in the room. She peered into the murky darkness of the corners but could see no one. Then she became aware there was something just at the edge of her vision. She turned but whatever it was stayed just out of sight. The presence held itself to her right side and slightly behind her. This time as she spoke to Cat, there was tightness in her voice, "Cat, what's happening? What do you see?"

Cat blinked her amber eyes at Christina. Christina frowned, forcing herself to concentrate on the presence. She now sensed that it wasn't a single object or person but a number of small things.

She forced herself to sit still and wait. They moved in to where she could see them. Her first thought was they were little animals. "Cat, the place is overrun with mice. You haven't been doing your job." A few minutes later a new explanation occurred to her. "Maybe they all came in to get away from the blizzard."

But, would mice be wearing clothes? Each of the little creatures had on a coat with red and blue in it. They couldn't be mice. But what were they? They were moving almost randomly. If they would only stand still for awhile, maybe she would see what had invaded her soddy. "Chirp, chirp, chirp." The sounds were coming from the little figures. The chirps were reedy and high pitched.

Christina looked at Cat who sat passively watching the area around the stove. Something was wrong. Cat's lack of reaction puzzled her. The sounds were loud enough that Cat should be chasing the noisemakers. Excitedly Christina asked, "Cat, what's wrong? Have you lost your ears? Don't you hear the bird noises?" Cat got up and moved away. She sat with her eyes wide open, ears perked staring at Christina.

Christina was becoming frantic. "What's happening? Is this madness? Is there something wrong with my eyes?" She jumped up to pace the room turning her head from side to side as she tried to get a better view of her visitors.

The chirp now became a song. "It's a choir singing. It's like the music that used to come from across the bay on Sunday mornings."

For most of the morning she couldn't get a good focus on the little invaders. She caught only glimpses of them, but around noon they became much clearer. She could see now that they were little people, furry little people dressed in colored suits. They had gotten organized and were marching one after the other in a parade around the room, stopping every now and then to sing an old hymn in Norwegian.

The visitors in the funny colored outfits seemed friendly, and she reached out to touch them. Friendly, but not friendly enough to be touched, they quickly darted back out of reach. Next she rushed at them reaching out to grab them. They disappeared. "Where did you go?" She turned around and saw them on the other side the room. "Oh, there you are. What are you? How can you exist? Are you real? You must be real; I can see you. But can you be real? I can't touch you?"

She found that if she sat still and didn't move, they stayed in front of her and their antics now became entertaining. One in particular seemed to be the leader and was directing the others. She was delighted and laughed out loud for the first time when two little men tossed a woman into the air, and the woman did a double somersault. Her laugh encouraged the leader to have some of the smaller ones do more acrobatics.

Christina leaned forward to examine the leader more closely. He stood still this time allowing her to get close enough to see his face. The small furry man in the red and blue suit was Olaf.

She jumped out her chair and gasped involuntarily. "Oh, my God, it's Olaf! What are you doing here?" He jumped back and with the others darted for the corner of the room. They all disappeared into the dirt walls. Sudden movement scares them, she said to herself. If I want to see them, I'll have to sit still and be quiet. She sat back down in the chair, folded her hands in her lap and waited. Just as she expected they reassembled and went back to giving her a private performance.

Tears of happiness rolled down her cheeks. She whispered, "Olaf, you always did make me laugh. We had such good times together. I'm happy that you've come to visit." Olaf smiled.

She understood what they expected of her and through their actions they let her know that they only wished to entertain her in her isolation. Now that they had her attention, they did some folk dances, acted out a play in pantomime about a bad king and paused every so often to sing a hymn. Hours passed unnoticed as she let herself relax and just enjoy what she saw before her.

She was so caught up with the performance going on she didn't hear the door of the soddy being forced open. The first she knew that someone had entered was when he took her by the shoulder and was shaking her. "Christina, Christina, are you all right?" The little people in the gaily colored clothes vanished.

She turned to the intruder. "You made them go away," she yelled, angry at the interruption. She began sobbing.

Andrew Bakke drew back. "I think you got snow sickness. I come over to see if you're all right. I see you been here alone in the dark too long. You need to be with people. You come with me now back to our place and let Lizzie take care of you for a while."

"But the blizzard...." she protested weakly.

"The blizzard's been gone since two days. We got lots of snow but you can walk in it. Come get your coat on and we'll go to my home now."

Christina moved like a sleepwalker as she got her coat from the peg by the door. Her eyes were staring, and she blinked rapidly at the glare of the snow when they went outside. At the Bakkes she had a hard time answering the questions they asked.

They put her down before the hearth for the night in a collection of old coats and blankets. She slept well. An argument between the two older boys, Elmer and Carl, woke her.

"He poked me first."

"Well, he was in my box of rocks. You said he's got no right to look in it if I don't want him to."

She opened her eyes just as Andrew Bakke slapped each of them across the back of the head. "Behave yourselves, we got company."

Behind Andrew's back they stuck out their tongues at each other. Lizzie Bakke disregarded the argument and continued to bustle in the small space, frying up potatoes for breakfast. The boys moved randomly and unexpectedly, but from long practice she anticipated their actions and maneuvered around them with a ballet dancer's grace.

Christina closed her eyes and shook her head. "Are these people real or is my mind still playing tricks on me." She opened her eyes to see that they were still there. Lizzie saw the confusion on Christina's face and knew that it would be awhile before Christina was able to concentrate and think clearly. Right now she needed attention and a chance to talk with people.

Lizzie didn't mind. Talking with another woman would be a pleasant change from her husband and four boys.

Mid morning, Christina was ready to talk about her plans. "Winter is here, and I don't have the supplies to last me through cold and storms like we just got. I've got as much help as I can get from Lars and Petrina. Now I need to find some way to get cash."

Lizzie looked up from the pair of boy's pants she was redoing. Albert, younger and shorter than Carl, was ready for the pants Carl had just outgrown, but as he was heavier she needed to let out the waist. She was also patching the knees and seat. "You think there would be work for you in Brookings?"

"I don't know. It might be risky going that far if there was nothing. It's a pretty big town, but I don't know where I'd look for work."

Andrew Bakke had been listening to the two women talk. He interrupted. "Old Elofson's been on a trip to Watertown and came back with news. The railroad is expanding. They're hiring men. There'll be work for everyone for a while."

Christina became very attentive. "Do you think there will be work for a woman?"

"Men work, men got to eat. Someone's got to feed them. Bound to be a rooming house for them to live what needs a cook or a servant girl."

Late in the day Christina found herself able to help with the evening meal. Her grit was coming back. That night she woke frequently with questions about her future scratching at her mind.

At the noon meal of sowbelly and beans she was ready to talk about her plans. "I've decided that I can't spend the winter alone in the soddy. If a week alone makes me start seeing the little people, what will happen to me if I get snowed in for weeks. You won't be able to help me by shaking me. I might never get my right mind back. I got to go somewhere else."

Lizzie paused to consider before she said. "You could always stay with us, or maybe go back and live with Petrina."

"No, you're crowded enough here, and Petrina, Lars and I just can't live in the same house." What she held back saying was that instead of putting her away for being crazy, they would put her away for murder. "No, I have to go somewhere else. Andrew's right; with the railroad construction there's bound to be work that I can do. The extra money will help me run the farm."

Andrew put in his bit. "And you'll be around people. Being alone is not good."

"Watertown is a long trip." Lizzie said.

"Ya," he said, "it's over thirty miles and deep snow all the way."

Christina thought for a moment. "Whatever, but as soon as I can find someone with a sled going that way, I'll hitch a ride and find work. Cat can stay with the Finns for the rest of the winter. What chickens I got left, you can have for taking care of me. I'll start a new brood next spring." To herself she figured that the little people could have the soddy to themselves.

CHAPTER TWENTY-TWO

THE SKI TRIP

$\mathcal{T}$he weather was clear but the temperature remained below freezing. Christina was going back to her soddy at night to sleep, but after her experience with the little people feared being alone too much. Even now if she spent the day alone, she would begin to sense their presence at the edge of her vision. The Bakkes didn't seem to mind her spending most of her days at their soddy, and she was happy to accept their hospitality.

Using her skis to travel around to the area homesteads, Christina began looking for someone who was planning to travel the thirty miles to Watertown. She got the same answer from all the men. Bertel Andersen, who was noted for his bravery, said, "Well, I think, I wouldn't risk traveling this time of the year. You just never know when another blizzard might hit, or the weather could suddenly turn colder."

She skied south of the Bakkes to see John Bergerson. He always seemed to have some reason for going to one of the bigger towns to get materials to build up his homestead. "No, now isn't the time to be out on the prairie. This is when we need to repair what we can and rest up for the spring. I don't need nothing so bad I got to go to Watertown this time of the year."

At the same time the men would tell her that there was no way to get there, they would give her information that increased her desire. Elofson said, "Ya, sure they're building railroads in a number of directions from Watertown. Ya, the big companies been coming in."

Efraimson told her. "Watertown? You bet, it's a boom time up there. They're putting up stations every seven or ten miles every which way from Watertown. Seems like they want to be sure that none of us has got to go very far to ship our grain or animals. Yup, they want to be sure they don't miss any of our money."

Andrew Bakke made the six-mile walk to Estelline for supplies and came back to tell her, "I hear there are a heap of men hired to work on the railroad in Watertown. Homesteaders from all around are getting in on the easy money so they can buy seed for next summer."

All this talk about Watertown and the railroad only magnified Christina's longing to get there. She asked Andrew, "Are there jobs for women, then?"

"They say the workers are living and taking their meals in hotels in Watertown. The going rate is four dollars for twenty-one meals. That sounds pretty dang high. It means the pay of railroad workers has got to be darn good."

The Bakkes could see that all the information was only making Christina more uncomfortable. The tension when they were around her was thick enough to saw into pieces. She was becoming frantic in her search for someone who was going north.

One morning two weeks after Andrew first brought her home, Lizzie said, "Christina, maybe you should forget it for now. Later, maybe later would be better."

With a goal in sight and the answer to her need for money about to be met, "maybe later" was no longer possible. Come blizzard, or cold she was going to find some way to get to

Watertown before more of the winter had passed. In her mind's eye she could already see new furniture, more basic tools and seed for next year's crop. The large white frame house had come back into her dreams.

She had another dream. "Lizzie, last night I dreamed about Norway. When we went to Russia, we skied cross-country and pulled our goods on sleds behind us. I think that's what I'll do now. Can Elmer help me build a small sled for some of my stuff?"

A rare look of shock crossed Lizzie's face. "You don't intend to ski all the way to Watertown by yourself?"

"If no one else is going, I'll go by myself."

"No, Christina, we can't let you. You could die out there on the prairie. Andrew's told you why none of the men will go."

"I'm going. My mind is made up. I can't stay here all winter. I must get on with my life. Will Elmer help me?"

"It's against my better judgment, but it will get him out of the house and doing something useful. I can use the space."

The small sled they made only took them an afternoon. It would be pulled with a strap tied around her waist. She intended only to carry clothes and some food for the trip. The large trunk would be left with the Bakkes. Although she was no longer as trusting as she had been before someone had stolen the window out of her soddy before she moved in, she would rely on the honesty of the settlers to protect her household goods and tools.

She set off early on Wednesday morning. "How will you find it? There are so few landmarks," Andrew asked.

"It's north. My Pa taught me to find north at night by the stars or in the day by the direction of the sun. Elofson says I should hit the Big Sioux River about ten miles north. I follow it until I get to the railroad that should be close to Watertown. If I need to, I'll ask at one of the farms."

As Christina disappeared on the horizon, Andrew turned to Lizzie. "Crazy, I think she's still snow crazy. You can't tell a woman like that anything. Could be come summer we find her buried in a snow bank."

Lizzie turned away to go inside their soddy. "No, Andrew, you're wrong. Christina will get where she's going. She's got a head to go with her pluck."

Wolves

Christina had gotten into good shape for skiing during the past two weeks as she tried to find a ride to Watertown. She knew that she could cover the thirty miles by nightfall. The air was crisp and clear. She estimated that it was around zero. If no wind came up, it was a comfortable temperature for cross-country skiing. Her world now consisted of only two colors, white and blue, but mostly white. The surface of the land was featureless, flatter than a calm sea off the coast of the island. She had to concentrate on the position of the sun to hold to the north.

As she glided along, the only signs of life were animal tracks and an occasional strand of smoke rising from a soddy. The smoke was comforting, giving her the feeling that if there was a change in the weather, she would be able to find help.

By mid afternoon she estimated that she had covered twenty miles. She was breathing hard, her heart pumping, but she knew she had reserves left. The additional distance would be no problem. She had tried to control her sweating by taking off and putting on clothes, but despite her best efforts a light coating of sweat covered her body. If she were to stop for long, the sweat would freeze on her body.

She stopped for a breather and scanned the horizon with her hand shielding her eyes from the brightness. In the distance behind her there was movement. Several animals were moving together. "Dogs? No, they were all the same size. Coyotes? They were bigger than coyotes. Oh, my God, wolves!"

Everyone had talked about the dangers of the blizzards and the cold, but no one had mentioned wolves.

There were three of the shadowy gray figures gliding toward her with the fluid looping stride only wolves can do. There were no signs of humans, no smoke anywhere on the horizon. "I've got to get out of here," Christina thought grasping her ski poles and thrusting herself forward. It wouldn't be good to be caught out in the open. Ahead she could see a rise covered with snow. There weren't any trees but perhaps she could get something at her back. Had Wolfman really skied after wolves and killed them with his ski pole?

Although the wolves were moving faster now narrowing the distance, they seemed in no hurry to catch up with her. She labored on. Sweat began to drip from her face and form on her body, An odd thought occurred to her. "Does a sweating person taste any different than a dry one?"

She considered dropping the sled, but couldn't bring herself to leave it behind. Twenty minutes later she reached the rise. It was the shore of a pond and the rise she had seen was snow-covered brush. The wolves were only a hundred yards behind her. Would they attack her? No, she knew the question was, how would they attack? Would they come in a rush, or would one take the lead?

Tears welled up in her eyes. She felt weak and helpless. Her stomach was suddenly the home of two fighting cats. "Christina," she said out loud, "you are not going to let the wolves get you." A charge of anger arched through her renewing her strength. With the snow-covered brush behind her, she placed the sled and her upright skis in front of her to form a barrier. She took her father's fishing knife out of her pack and clutched it in her left hand. She grasped a ski pole in her other hand, and she stood breathing heavily, waiting.

To keep control of her fear she began talking to herself. Both asking and answering her own questions. "Christina, what did Wolfman tell you?"

"That the wolf will jump at you with its mouth open, and you can stick your hand down its throat."

"That's only if you're terribly fast. What if I miss?"

"No, Christina, what if you don't try?" The wolves fanned out, with the largest one in the center, and moved in closer. They had long legs, gaunt bodies and fierce eyes. His broad gray head down, the leader came to within ten feet of her and stared into her eyes. There was a human look in his yellow eyes. The lead wolf looked at her the same way the man on the station platform at Brookings had before he spit at her. The difference was the wolf was handsomer. She stared back meeting his gaze.

The contest went on. Was the wolf testing her? If she broke eye contact, would he leap at her? Out of the corner of her eye she caught the movement of the other two wolves. They had pulled back and were tumbling in the snow like puppies. The large one in front of her continued to hold her stare, his ears pricked to detect any sound from her.

She was holding a conversation of death with the wolf. He was asking questions and listening closely to her answers. If she gave the wrong answers, he would kill her. "But I don't even know the questions," she said to herself.

She was finding her fighting stance tiring; her anger was draining away; in its place fear was coming back. Would the wolf find an answer in her fear? She needed him to act soon while she still had anger left to meet his charge. She began to chant, "Come on, wolf, come on, wolf, come on, wolf." She moved the knife and the pole inviting him to leap. The two others had stopped their game to watch.

The wolf broke his gaze and moved back. He lay down on the snow, placed his head on his paws, never taking his eyes off her. It was not the time to attack. The wolves were gaunt and thin enough she could count their ribs, but they weren't hungry enough to take any undue chances with this peculiar human. She had passed the first conversation of death and bought herself time. They would wait until she fell asleep or was off guard before they came in for the kill.

Later she would learn that she had been right to take a stand with her back to something. If she had continued to run, they could have hamstrung her and, as she fell, slashed her throat with their powerful jaws. An animal or human at bay was more dangerous, and the trio was not desperate enough to chance injury by rushing at something that seemed to be too sure of its ability to fight. They were not cowards but veterans of too many kills to do anything rash.

An hour passed. No action. Then, on the back trail, Christina saw movement. Another five minutes and she could see it was a human but too far away to hear her. The wolves caught the scent of the approaching person and turned to watch.

When he got close enough, Christina, yelled in Norwegian, "Hello, I need help. There are wolves here." The man waved a hand to acknowledge her. The wolves did not appear to be afraid, but stared at each other in a silent conference deciding what to do. They looked at her as if considering whether they still had time to make their kill. Finally, when the man was within a hundred yards, they turned and set off toward the east. It was a fatal mistake.

The man took a rifle off his shoulder, kneeled and as the animals began to pick up speed, fired. A puff of smoke rose from the barrel of the gun. A moment later the sound of the shot arrived. At the same time the wolf twisted into the air and fell back to earth. The animal lay still. The man fired again at the two other wolves that were running at full speed. He missed.

Given her own experience with the rifle at Olga Pearson's house, Christina was amazed that anyone could hit a moving animal at that distance. The tension from her body relaxed suddenly and she dropped to her knees, her whole body shaking with relief.

The man who came up was strangely dressed; his clothes were leather on the outside and fur lined. Colorful beaded designs decorated his coat. On his back he carried a pack from which protruded the fur of at least one other wolf. The man's gray eyes were furious in his ruddy face. As he came up he was speaking English, but she could only make out a few words such as stupid Norsky and dumb ass woman. His angry words lashing out at her called back the tensions to her body.

Her first impulse had been to rush up to him and throw her arms around him, but he showed no pleasure in having saved her life. His mouth dipped down at the corners with a brown stain of tobacco juice leaking out of the right corner. Deeply grooved lines started at the edges of his lips and went up past his nose. This resulted in a most unpleasant expression that he could have developed only after years of practice. The wolf had looked friendlier.

The man went over to the wolf, took out a knife and began to skin it. The way he slashed at the legs showed his hate for the animal.

When he finished skinning the wolf, he motioned her to put on her skis and follow him. Without glancing back to check if she was following, he moved steadily toward the northwest. Night came on and still he didn't pause or look back. The light from the moon reflecting off the snow gave the night a brightness that ordinarily would have made Christina cheerful, but the anger that radiated from the hunter in front of her filled her with apprehension. It was late, perhaps close to midnight before they arrived at the man's house.

His house was two stories high with a large shed attached to the east side. The number of windows and size of the building meant the man had money. He motioned her to take off her skis and set them against the wall. She felt an urge to run. The idea of a night alone in a house with this man frightened her. Just then the door opened and a woman stepped out into the moonlight.

The man spoke to her in his harsh unpleasant voice. Christina caught the words "stupid" and "dumb." Some of the anger seemed to be directed at the woman, some at Christina. The woman came over to her and led her inside the house and offered her some bread and cheese. After Christina had eaten, the women showed her to a cot in a room that had stacks of wolf skins in it. The smell indicated that the skins had not been carefully scraped, and the rotten flesh brought her dinner into her throat. The stench was worse than it had been in the Laplanders' tent in Norway.

Christina's dreams that night were filled with fierce faces: some of them animal, most of them human. Even the wolf took on a human form in her dream. Every time it opened its mouth and jumped for her throat, she would wake up. It was noon the next day before she had enough sleep to feel like even standing up. The emotional strain had exhausted her.

By sign language and slow spoken English she was able to learn from the man's wife, Mona, that his name was Marsh. He made his living as a trapper and a bounty hunter of wolves. The house they were in was only five miles from Watertown. They had plans to go to town the day after tomorrow to drop off a load of early season furs and wolf skins. Mrs. Marsh indicated that Christina would be welcome to stay over a day and to ride along in the sledge with them. Marsh himself made no attempt to tell her anything or even to learn what she was doing out on the snow covered prairie.

At supper that night something about the chicken stew with dumplings displeased him, and he threw the plate across the room smashing it against the wall. Mrs. Marsh was sitting close enough he didn't even have to stand to hit her across the side of her head with a powerful backhand blow that knocked her sideways on the bench. Mrs. Marsh leaped to her feet and hurried to the kitchen. Mr. Marsh sat glaring at Christina who didn't move a muscle, paralyzed with shock at his violent outburst. It seemed an eternity before Mrs. Marsh reappeared carrying a platter with a slab of cold roast beef on it, which she carefully set on the table in front of him.

That night Christina cried herself to sleep, but the wolf dreams were gone. Instead she was a wolf tracking Marsh to kill him.

CHAPTER TWENTY-THREE

WATERTOWN

It was mid morning when the Marshs' sled, pulled by an elderly, dirty white horse arrived in town. The slightly sway-backed beast cringed whenever Marsh touched him. His master had not gone lightly on the whip in training him. Marsh was headed for the general store to trade furs for a load of flour and apples expected to last most of the winter. They dropped Christina with her bag of clothes, skis and small sled in front of the Scandia Hotel.

As Christina dismounted from the sled, the two women's eyes met. Mrs. Marsh's eyes were filled with both hopelessness and pain. She was trapped by Marsh more completely than Christina had been when she was alone in the soddy during the blizzard. Mr. Marsh pointed at the hotel, grunted, flicked the reins and the horse moved off. The presence of evil which had enveloped her at Marsh's place pulled away with the sled.

She sighed deeply and turned to examine her surroundings. Two-year-old Watertown was still growing up out of the prairie. Many buildings were freshly constructed and had the golden tones of new wood. Some were skeletons of frame reaching upward toward the blue sky, snow covered piles of lumber nearby. Here and there she could see dents in the snow left by the holes which would become cellars. It was exciting. For the first time since she got to Dakota, she had something to rest her eyes on besides sky.

The Scandia Hotel was the only building on the south side of the street that did not have a false front. It was a true two-story building, one of very few to be found in town. As she stared at the hotel, it was as though she were standing next to a steep sheer wall of a fjord blocking the open expanse of the prairie.

Thoughts flashed into her mind and arranged themselves into reasons to leave and reasons to stay. It's so big. I need the money. I don't want to be a servant girl. I can't live alone. Maybe no one will speak Norwegian. I can't go back and live with Trina. I don't want people ordering me around.

Christina shook the thoughts out of her head, clenched her fists and braced herself with a short talk. "Swallow your pride, girl. Who do you think you are? It's take orders now or you won't make it on the homestead."

It struck her, "That's just what Pa would have told me." She gripped the cold brass doorknob firmly and swung the heavy ornately carved door open. Gathering the skirts of her brown wool dress around her, she stepped inside. To the left was the dining room with its real factory made wooden furniture. After the sod shanty's dirt walls and cramped space the large room with windows and light was luxurious.

She pulled off her scarf and dabbed at the stray hairs flying loose around her face. A movement startled her, and she was shocked to see her image reflected in a mirror on the wall. She had the same expression she had seen on the immigrants getting off the boat: wide-eyed and scared, clutching her worn heavy overcoat around her. She took off her gloves and tried to dry her sweaty palms on the skirt of her dress. She didn't belong here. It was too fine.

Christina wheeled around to bolt back into the street but froze when she found a neatly dressed woman in a freshly pressed apron blocking her escape. The woman spoke to her in English. Her voice was soft and gentle, but Christina felt as if a weight had been placed on her chest cutting off her breath. She tried to move around the woman to get to the doorknob. Seeing Christina's reaction, the woman smiled, reached out and touched her shoulder, and motioned her to follow.

Taking a final longing look at the door, Christina trailed after her into the dining room through the double doors to the kitchen. Familiar smells reached out to welcome her: onions frying, coffee, a soup kettle boiling on the back of the black iron stove.

One man was cutting pieces off a pig's head, something Christina remembered doing to make headcheese. A woman stood peeling potatoes out of a gunnysack into a large iron kettle. Two others chattered together as they washed dishes. A heavy man was chopping the heads off frozen fish, his knife flashing down with a steady thump.

It reminded her suddenly of Olaf, and tears pricked her eyes. Seeing the familiar scene, Christina started to breathe again. The room was warm and she unbuttoned her heavy coat.

The pretty lady led Christina over to a man who was standing on a stool watching the others work. The woman said something in English to Christina and then to the man. Christina struggled to make out his name. Mr. Harvey Brown. He had the ugliest face that Christina had ever seen, lumpy and brown like a badly shaped potato. He scowled at her as if he were in pain.

There was no change in his pained expression when he spoke to her in broken Swedish. "Well, what can we do for you?"

Christina stepped back, struggling to find her voice. "I need work for the winter," she stammered. "I hear you need women in the kitchen to serve the tables."

Mr. Brown studied her, his eyes searching over her body.

She thought, these old clothes, my awful hair; he can see I'm from the old country. If I had only had some place to get fixed up. After what seemed to her a long time, he finally said, "Ya, we need help. You look strong and healthy." He growled and gave a short unpleasant laugh. "You also look like you'll give us no trouble with the men." Christina blushed, furious at the color rising in her cheeks. Mr. Brown continued, "This is a Christian hotel, and we don't want the women associating with the men that work here."

He turned from her as if the business was finished. Christina didn't know what to do. Shifting uncomfortably from one foot to the other like a ten-year-old being reprimanded by the teacher, she continued to stand and wait. He finally turned back to her and went on as if he had not stopped. "You will help in the kitchen first. When you learn the job, then you can serve the tables. We have a room you will share with three other girls. You can take every other Sunday morning off to go to church, and you will have Thursday afternoons off to take care of any private business."

Christina nodded. He is so ugly, she thought, suppressing a smile. He almost makes me feel pretty. He reminds me of a bulldog the way he's standing there all puffed up, barking at people.

Potato face went on, "The men who live here work with the railroad. Most of them are immigrants from Scandinavia." He stepped down from the stool, and she found herself looking down at the top of his bald head. Now he reminds me of the bantam rooster in Jacob's barnyard, strutting around crowing at the hens.

His expression stayed the same as he said, "Get washed up. You smell from being in the country too long. We expect you to bathe once a week and wear clean clothes. You will find aprons in that cabinet over there." Her hand flew to cover the lower part of her face as it flared red in shame.

The pretty woman, whose name was Abigail, introduced her to the other women in the kitchen and then took her to the room she was to share. The room had two regular beds in it with barely space between them. Clothes were kept in boxes under the bed. There was a commode with a water pitcher and basin and behind its doors a chamber pot. It was almost like being on board the ship again. Her bed mate was named Cora.

Cora, a twenty-year-old Dane, who also spoke English, was even skinnier than Christina. She had sparkling eyes, even features and full lips that men found attractive, but behind the pretty face they found that there was a sharp tongue. The women, on the other hand, found she had a warm heart and a willing ear for listening to their problems.

She had come with her parents from Denmark when she was five. Times had been hard. When the promise of the new world didn't work out and the wolf kept watch at their door, her father took off for parts unknown and left his wife and three daughters to fend for themselves. That had soured her on men, and she swore she wouldn't marry one if he were as rich as the king of Sweden.

Maud and Sarah, who both spoke Swedish, shared the other bed. Maud, tall and dark, from the south of Sweden was also comfortable speaking English.

Now that she was safe, warm and had people around her, the sadness she had been working so hard to hold back enveloped her in a fog. The hard work of surviving, the loss of friends, the loneliness of the soddy had used up all of her energy. When someone talked to her, it was like they were somehow far away, and at times she couldn't sort what they were saying in any way that made sense.

Christina was constantly tired, and whenever got the chance she slept. But sleep held no comfort. Nightmares waited for her when she fell asleep. It was then she ran from the wolves that became mackerel, mackerel that became Mr. Marsh, beasts that were both wolf and fish with men's hands.

Night after night she cried out and woke up drenched with sweat. Cora would put a hand on her and croon to her as if she were a frightened child. "It'll be all right; don't be afraid." When Christina went back to sleep, the dead came back to haunt her. Her father, Olaf, Jacob, and Peter Bjorklund drifted into her dreams, sometimes as themselves and sometimes as one person whose face kept changing.

Christina voluntarily took on difficult and unpleasant tasks that the other women avoided: peeling mountains of potatoes, carrying out the slop pails, washing the linens. Her hands became raw and red from the lye and lard soap they used, but the hard work helped her avoid the painful thoughts that paraded through her mind when she wasn't busy.

One morning Cora stopped her, a worried frown creasing her handsome face. "Don't work so hard, Christina. You're making us feel we aren't doing enough. Brown doesn't appreciate it or pay you any more. Why do you do it?"

Christina dried her chapped hands on her apron, fighting the tears that welled up in response to Cora's kind words. "I think too much of what's past. All the people who've died, the hard times. If I work hard, my brain doesn't run so fast, and if I'm tired I don't have so many bad dreams."

Except for her cynical attitude toward men, Cora was a happy person. Smiles came easily to her. One morning several weeks after Christina had started working at the Scandia, she was setting out the silverware for breakfast. Cora was singing an old hymn, doing variations on the words as she filled the salt shakers. Brown came by, put his potato face close to her and said, "If you sing before breakfast, you'll cry before noon."

Cora closed her mouth, but when he left she made a face at Christina. "I declare, that man's mean enough to curdle milk. No wonder his face looks like a lumpy old cheese."

Christina laughed. Cora arched her eyebrows. "Well, we finally got a response out of you. I was beginning to think that sad look you been carrying around was the natural condition of your face."

Despite Cora's observation, Christina didn't respond to any of the men she served. They were as alike to her as the herring that filled the bottom of Pa's boat. Except for Mr. Brown none of them even had names. Her roommates, however, stood out like candles in a dark room.

The Meeting 1883

One evening a month after the fog had settled over her, Christina was lying in bed exhausted, every muscle twitching, unable to sleep. She had a new blister on her hand from chopping kindling. One of the men had called her a dumb Swede, and Mr. Brown had scolded her in front of the other workers for not moving fast enough. Thoughts plodded through her head. I just can't go on. I'd have been better off if I had frozen to death in a snowbank. Jacob told me it isn't painful, more like just going to sleep.

A sound she hadn't heard before filtered into her thoughts. It was a fiddle. Someone was playing a folk tune that Pa used to play a long time ago in the dark days of Norway's winter. Christina blinked. Her muscles relaxed, and her body began to drift and float. Vivid memories of happy times in Norway began to dance in her head—the midnight midsummer's bonfire, skiing with Olaf, the boat ride to the big island with her father.

The next morning as Christina struggled into her dress to go down to start breakfast, she asked Cora, "Last night before I went to sleep, I heard music. It was so beautiful that it helped put me to sleep. Who was playing?"

Cora opened her eyes, yawned, turned over and covered her

head with her pillow. Christina poked her in the ribs with her elbow. "Cora, you know everything that happens here. Please tell me."

Cora moaned and turned over. "That was one of the Carlson brothers. You've seen them in the dining room. They're two of the Swedes that work on the railroad. They both play music."

Christina frowned, trying to picture them. It was no use. All the faces blurred together.

Cora continued talking. "The older one, Axel, plays the accordion, and Gust plays the fiddle. Usually they're too tired to play, but once a week or so they and a couple men put on a concert for the other workers. You've not been hearing, what with your sleeping so much. They've been doin' it ever since you got here."

"Ladies, cut out the chatter and get your feet on the floor." Maud was, as usual, up earlier than anyone else. Her hair was combed and her apron tied firmly around her slender waist. She was ready to go to work. "Old potato face will scold us all if we don't get moving."

First Cora's humor, next the sound of music, then that same day colors returned to awareness from out of the fog: the red of the fire, the green of Cora's dress, the black of the stove. Outside, the blue of the sky almost took her breath away.

As Christina's spirits continued to improve, she began to ask Cora about her impressions of various of the men who lived at the Scandia. "Cora, that one over there, yes, the one with a checked shirt, what do you think of him?"

"You mean the fat one? Crooked as a barrel of fishhooks. When the railroad finds out how he's using them to feather his own nest, he'll end up in jail."

"What about the handsome one who always wants you to wait on him?"

"Very confused. Watch him when you ask him a question. He doesn't know whether he's afoot or hossback."

Maud was sweet on a big red-faced man with a black beard. She always handed him the serving dish so he could have first choice at the evening meal. In return he always paid her compliments on her looks. Christina overheard Maud ask, "Cora, what do you think of Hank?"

"Ask him a question and see how long it takes to get his tongue in motion. He's so dumb he couldn't row a boat and chew tobacco at the same time."

Maud didn't speak to Cora for the rest of the day.

The kitchen was a comfortable place. It was warm, and the people, except for Mr. Brown, friendly. Best of all was the security of the immense amount of food that passed through there. In the cellar were gunnysacks of potatoes and pecks of dried beans. In the icehouse boxes of frozen fish were stacked high against the walls. Every Friday a whole carcass of a pig or a side of beef would be hung in the attached shed.

Best of all, after the men finished eating, the cooks and waitresses could eat what was left. For the first time in her life Christina was surrounded by all the food she wanted, and now she was developing a hunger which let her take advantage of it.

A week after she had first heard the folk music, it was Christina's turn to set up the dining room for supper. As she entered the dining room, her eyes focused on a man sitting in a corner. His head was down, his shoulders hunched over his task. What was he doing? She stepped closer. He was honing a knife on a whetstone. His head down, he was concentrating on a smooth circular motion that would sharpen the edge evenly. There was something about the way he held the knife. "Olaf!" escaped from her lips. The motion was so like her brother's that she became weak in the knees. She slumped into a chair across from him.

The man lifted his head, and she looked into his robin's egg blue eyes. He had even, handsome features centered around an overgrown pale blond mustache that matched the straw colored hair that fell over his forehead. He returned her gaze with a puzzled look. "Ya, what can I do for you?"

"The knife, you work it just like my brother."

"I need a good edge on the knife; a dull blade could be dangerous." He stroked the knife across the stone again. His cheeks flushed as he glanced at her and returned his eyes to his work. "I see you around. You don't talk much."

Christina smiled at his shy expression. "I think I got the Norwegian winter sickness. "Come spring, I'll be talking again."

"Ya, spring will be good. Winter weather is hard on people. But nights are not so long as in Sweden."

"In Norway, I come from the land of the midnight sun. In deep winter we had only a little light during the day."

Maud bustled into the dining room and set a stack of plates on the table with a thump. "Christina, there's work to be done. You're not paid to entertain the boarders."

Christina blushed, and without saying goodbye to the man, ran into the kitchen.

As her pervasive sadness melted away, other people paid more attention to Christina. Hans Johnson, the cook, commented one evening as they were cleaning up, "You're a good worker, Christina. You never turn up your nose at the hard jobs."

Christina just smiled at him. He went on, "I see you smile now. You sure becoming more cheerful. I think my cooking is good for you."

Cora who was standing behind Hans made a face at Christina. The girls had agreed that Hans could use a lesson or two in how to cook, but nobody dared suggest changes to him. He had made it clear to them that he considered the way the men wolfed down his food proof of his skill.

The next night as the women were cleaning up, Hans called her over, "I like the way you eat; for a skinny woman you sure can put it away." He handed her a plate with fried chicken livers on it. "Here, I saved something special for you. With a little horseradish on it you'll think you're eating like the Queen of Sweden."

Within a month of the violin music and her reentry into the enjoyment of food and the little extras from Hans, her clothes had began to pinch and had to be let out. With the weight gain she slept better. Her dreams were fewer and she no longer felt the need to work so hard. She now knew how to do all of the jobs around the hotel and stopped making embarrassing mistakes.

As she began learning about the railroad workers and learning their names, she noticed that some of them were also watching her. At first she was shy, turning her head away when she saw them looking at her. Then several joked with her in Norwegian or Swedish, and she relaxed and talked with them about the weather, which was mostly cold and windy, and last year's crops which were mostly poor.

Christina began watching for the man with the knife. He always sat with the same man who appeared to be his partner. As far as she could tell neither of them were a bit interested in her.

One evening Christina and Maud were standing at the door to the dining area watching to see which serving plates needed to be refilled. The railroad workers were sitting in their usual position: elbows on the table, forks tightly grasped in one hand, knives in the other. Christina agreed with Cora's observation that they looked like pigs at the feeding trough. Working hard out in the cold raised their hunger to the level where the few social niceties they once had were left at the door.

Maud turned back toward the kitchen to fill another platter with boiled potatoes. "It does my heart good to see men eat so heartily."

Christina nodded, but her mind was elsewhere. When Maud got back and placed the platter on the table, Christina asked her, "Who are the two men sitting together at the window over there? They seem to be partners."

"They're the Carlson brothers. You know, the ones who make the music. I thought you knew who they were. Your head really has been somewhere else, hasn't it?"

"Don't tease. Tell me about them."

"The tall darker one is Axel. He's the older, and I think he bosses the other one around. The shorter one is Gust. He's really the smart one, reads books and the papers and all."

Eager for more information Christina opened herself up for some teasing that night by asking, "Oh, Maud, tell me everything you know about them."

"There was five brothers got starved out of Sweden. They come over here to be lumberjacks up in the Minnesota woods. I think they have only been here in America for two, three years now. Those two got tired of chopping down trees and decided to homestead."

"They're Swedish?" She could see that Maud had caught the disappointment in her voice.

"I know, if only he were Norwegian," Maud grimaced. "We Norse and Swedes, we act like there was some difference between us that means something. What would you think if you met someone really different like an Italian? If I met a good Norwegian, I sure wouldn't turn him away."

Christina couldn't get Gust Carlson off her mind. She found herself thinking about him when she should be doing something else. That evening as Cora brushed Christina's hair, Christina asked, "What do you think of Gust?"

"You got a good eye for a man." Christina was startled. For the first time since Christina had met her, Cora was giving a positive reaction to a man.

"He's smart as a whip and doesn't have a lazy bone in his body. He'll make someone a good husband. You stop worrying about him being a Swede and set your cap for him. You'll get a good man."

Cora continued brushing and after a while continued. "I've been watching you. You're much different now you got your spirits back. Even knowing Carlson's a Swede you been having a hard time keeping your eyes off him. I see how other men try to catch your eye and you just turn away."

Red flared across Christina's cheeks. She hadn't known that she was being so obvious. Cora smiled, "It's all right. I'm the only one who watches that closely. I'm sure no one else is paying attention."

"It's no use," Christina said, frowning. "I can't even get Gust to look at me. Those brothers make me feel like I'm invisible."

The next evening Christina stood staring into the one small mirror in the women's bedroom. Her hair was unbraided, tumbling in loose waves almost to her waist. She studied her face and its imperfections. Her eyes were too deep set, her cheekbones were too prominent, her nose a crag, her jaw would look better on a German soldier. Cora slipped into the room and stood watching. "You look like you'd like to change it," she said.

"Oh, Cora, my ears are like a fishing boat's sails, my nose like a rudder and my teeth—my teeth stick out like an open barn door." She fought back the tears and took another look at herself. "And my hair is even worse. I never can do anything right with my hair. How will I ever attract Gust Carlson's attention?"

"Stop worrying about your face and hair. You've got lots of good bait to catch a man. Besides you're fishing in a sea where there's lots more single men than women. Even you'll do all right."

Christina began putting her hair up in a bun and pinning it in place. "I know. If I paid attention to them and gave them half a chance, there's ones would offer to marry me. I've overheard talk at the tables. Some of the men want a strong wife to work their claim with them. I don't want to marry a man who wants me because I can carry a heavy load. My problem is that the one I want doesn't know I'm alive."

"Gust?"

Christina nodded, misery showing in her face.

"I can't keep my eyes off him. I feel like Cat waiting for a mouse to come out, but I don't have Cat's patience."

Cora flopped down on the bed and stared at the ceiling searching for a solution to Christina's problem. Several minutes later she said, "You put too much faith in beauty. You can't wait around like a pretty flower waitin' to be picked. You're going to have to show him that his life doesn't mean anything without you. Here's what I think you should do."

Next morning before the men left for work, Christina stood at the door to the dining room staring at Gust until he glanced up and caught her eye. She held his gaze briefly, blushed slightly and turned away. A few moments later she caught his eye again, this time she tilted her head slightly and smiled. This time he blushed and turned away. There, that wasn't so hard, she told herself. She didn't know what Gust's response was, but in Christina's mind the cat now had her paw on the tail of the mouse.

A shelf of books had been put in the sitting room. There were more books than Christina had seen since leaving Norway, at least fifty and most of them in Norwegian. Between meals Christina went to return a book and find a new one. Sitting on a stool next to the shelf was Gust Carlson. He put his book down as she entered and said, "Good afternoon. My name's Gust Carlson. I'm one of the men who boards here."

Goodness, Christina thought, does he really believe that I haven't noticed him? Maybe he's not as bright as I thought. She smiled. "I'm Christina Gunnerson." As long as he was making inane comments she decided to make one too. "I work as waitress here."

"Yes, I've noticed you. You have more energy than the other women. You seem to be everywhere at once."

So she wasn't invisible. She struggled for something to say to keep the conversation going. Cora had told her always ask about them. Men can't resist it. She took a deep breath and asked, "You're not working today?"

"I put my back out yesterday. It's hard to stand up straight and I can't lift anything. I hope it doesn't go on too long. I need the money to keep my claim going."

He was as pleasant as she had expected him to be. She remembered Cora's next instruction, "If you like him move closer; look in his eyes." She stepped closer and tilted her head slightly.

He flushed slightly and continued, "My brother Axel and I have claims next to each other south of here twenty miles or so."

Christina frantically searched her memory for Cora's next step. Nothing came. All she could do was nod and say yes. She saw a speck of lint on his shirt and reached over and picked it off. He didn't seem to notice and went on talking about his claim.

Christina was having trouble listening. She was too aware of her heart beating, her shortness of breath. What was wrong with her? Was she coming down with the flu? She forced herself to concentrate on what he was saying and words again became clear. "I miss my brothers. They're still thinking of earning enough money to return to Sweden. Axel and I are going to stay here and make a go of it."

That night Christina jubilantly told Cora, "It worked. Besides talking with me about himself, he asked if I would go walking with him as soon as his back got well."

CHAPTER TWENTY-FOUR

COURTSHIP

Gust took her walking on Thursday. Because Brown had given the girls orders not to get involved with any of the men, they agreed to meet in front of the O.H. Tarbell drug store. Brown knew that some of the men who stayed at the Scandia were sparking some of his help; but as long as he didn't see it, he wouldn't fire a good worker.

As Christina approached the store, she noticed the paint was faded by the sun and in places worn off. Where the boards showed through they were splintered and gray. That gave her a safe topic to comment on. "This doesn't look new like the other buildings in town. It could use a good coat of paint."

She could see Gust welcomed the opening. "Ya, it's been around awhile. They pulled it here from Kampeska City with oxen. That's the old town that was on the lake before the railroad set up Watertown."

The temperature was in the twenties and the sun was shining. They strolled leisurely toward the lake enjoying the mild day. Gust asked, "You came to the job here after the winter had set in?"

"I couldn't live alone in my soddy. I needed to be around people." She went on to tell him about the trip on skis with the wolves following and her encounter with Marsh.

Gust spit. "Marsh. He's got a reputation as an evil man. He may be the best wolf hunter in this part of the country, but he's got a cruel streak."

Christina enjoyed the sound of Gust's voice. It had a musical quality to it that, coupled with his tone of concern about Marsh's cruelty, gave her minnows in her stomach. She encouraged him to go on. "His poor horse cringed just hearing his voice."

"I heard a story that he trapped with a partner years ago. After a bad winter the partner didn't come back. Some say Marsh got short of food and ate him."

"How horrible!" Christina recoiled from the thought and changed the subject. "You came earlier this fall with Axel?"

"We worked part of the summer too. We've been kept on to help with the construction. Axel is a good rough work carpenter, and I got my team to tote supplies. It's a good job. I get to meet all kinds of people, men that work on the rails all the way up to the high ups like conductors and engineers."

The walk had gone well, and Christina's spirits soared with the possibility that Gust really liked her. Then he began acting as if nothing had happened and spoke to her at the hotel the same way he did the other women.

To Christina it was beginning to seem that nothing would ever happen. If Gust was courting her with serious intentions of getting married, he certainly was being awfully slow and proper. He was as bad at advancing the relationship as the worst Norwegian bachelor she had ever heard of. She knew there were rules to follow but this was ridiculous.

A blizzard dumped seventeen inches of snow on Watertown, and nothing could move. Christina was entranced by the fairyland look of Watertown with snow covering all the construction and rutted streets. The men entertained themselves with cards, music and telling stories. The tales Christina overheard were mostly about how awful some of their adventures had been.

"Windies" was what Cora called them. "You notice how the storyteller always makes himself look like a hero. You listen close; and you'll see most of the time if they had any brains, they wouldn't have got into trouble in the first place."

Gust got some of the men together who played instruments, and on the third night the tables were pushed back and they had dancing, both circle and square. Christina could see Gust keeping an eye on her from where he was playing.

He took time off from playing to dance one of the circle dances with her as a partner. Afterwards he said, "You move like a lively young filly. I like to watch you."

Christina blushed. She caught a hint of jealousy when he said, "It looks like lots of the boys want to dance with you." Before she could reassure him that she preferred his company, she was grabbed from behind and pulled into a square.

Gust's team attracted attention wherever he took it. Livestock for pulling wagons were in short supply, so any kind of team that could move a load was taken on; there were teams of oxen, mules and horses. Occasionally there was a team consisting of a mule and a horse harnessed together, but Gust's odd team of a mule and an ox was unique. Still, when Gust showed up looking for work hauling, his team was acceptable to the railroad.

As Gust drove past a crew digging out a section of the switch yard from the blizzard, one of the men stopped and yelled at him, "Hey, Swede, you breed those two what you get, a stubborn cow or a mule with horns?" Gust had gotten used to insults about his odd looking team. He smiled and waved.

An Important Discussion

At lunch Axel and Gust sat next to each other and were eating bread and sausage. Axel spat out some bone that had gotten mixed with the sausage meat, took a drink of cold coffee and gave Gust a solemn look that meant, "We have important business to discuss."

In his best big brother voice he said, "The other men at the Scandia Hotel are talking about you and the Gunnerson woman."

Gust took another bite of bread, chewed and found it difficult to swallow. "Who might they be? The fellows that none of the women want to talk to?"

Axel ignored the question. He waited and when Gust was eating normally again said, "I don't like you getting sweet on that Norwegian girl."

Again a long pause. Finally, Gust answered, "She's a good woman, Axel. I like talking to her. She makes good sense. She'll make some man a fine wife."

"She'll make a bossy wife." Axel's voice had become louder. "She comes on meek as a mouse. But that woman's going to do what she wants, and you won't be the head of your own house."

A puzzled expression crossed Gust's face. He didn't like disagreeing with an older brother who often had been more like a father to him. Gust put down his lunch and turned directly toward Axel. "What makes you say that?"

"I've been talking with Maud. She says your Christina came alone from Norway to live with her sister and her husband. She couldn't get along with them because she was so strong willed. She moved out and got her own claim. That kind of woman got too much will for one person."

"I can handle her." Gust said taking another bit of sausage.

"I see how you handle her. You look like a little boy at school who don't know his lessons. You'll end up doing what she wants. It will get worse, not better, after you marry her."

"Marry her?" Gust was shocked. He hadn't yet said the words, 'I want to marry Christina,' to himself. Axel was making him mighty uncomfortable. He didn't know what to say.

Like a badger going after a gopher Axel kept on. "Besides she's a Norwegian and they're a slow witted people with no imagination. What will you do if your children get too much Norwegian in them?"

Gust was confused. Why was Axel so against Christina? He could only weakly protest, "You don't like Christina much."

"I like her just fine. I just don't think she's a good match for my brother. I think you can do better."

"Look around, Axel. Here I won't do any better. Of the few single women I got to choose from, she's the best. You got me thinking that even if I had more to choose from, she's still the best for me."

Axel cleared his throat, gave Gust a disgusted look and walked away.

Christina Reacts

Back at the hotel Christina was trying to figure out how to get around Axel. One evening after Axel had dragged Gust away from the table before he had a chance to exchange the evening's comments with her, Christina cornered Cora back by the kitchen stove and explained her plight. "Cora, Axel don't like me; he acts like he's my enemy."

"He is. That man don't like any woman with spunk. He wants a woman who'll say, 'yes sir' and 'no sir.' And when he wants something, to drop everything and get it for him."

"What can I do? He gets all stiff when I just come near him. I want him to like me."

The cook yelled at Cora, "You're not paid to stand around and talk. Get these plates out to the late crew before they gets cold and they start blaming me for starving them to death."

It wasn't until after washing up was done that Cora could get back to Christina's problem. "Don't waste your time making friends with Axel. Ignore him. Gust's a big boy; he knows his own mind. If Axel can talk him out of seeing you, you don't want him for a husband anyway."

Meanwhile, Axel's pressure on Gust to stay away from Christina only increased his interest. He lay awake staring at the ceiling lit by the reflection of the moon off the snow seeing Christina's face in the shadows. A hollowness echoed in his chest and his arms ached when he thought of her. "Here I am twenty-eight years old and no wife. If I tell her I think of her all the time, maybe she'll quit seeing me. Does she like me too? There are so many men and so few women, she could have any man she wants."

Gust bit his lip and rolled over. His movement disturbed Axel who muttered and shifted his position. Gust's mind began a replay of his concerns about Christina. How could he get up his nerve to tell her of his interest? Maybe he could ask one of the women that roomed with her. No, that isn't the way a real man would handle it.

When he was a little boy in Sweden, he had heard his father say, "Sometimes I love your ma so much that it's all I can do to keep from telling her." That told him that love must be dangerous. With the powerful yearnings stirring up his stomach and confusing him, he understood that confessing his love could make him a complete slave to Christina. Maybe he should listen more to Axel.

The next day was a beautiful Dakota day. The air was crisp and clear; the snow had a satisfying crunch underfoot. Outside the roundhouse Gust and three other men were moving parts needed for repairing and rebuilding the locomotives. Gust was favoring his back a little, concentrating on lifting the heavy pieces so as not to strain it.

"Hey, Gust," one of the men said, "looks like we got company over there by the office."

Gust looked up to see Christina watching. He had been so involved in moving the equipment that he hadn't noticed her.

He hesitated a moment debating with himself if he wanted the men to know he was interested in her. Finally, he said, "I should see what she wants. Maybe a message from the hotel."

He walked over to her, feeling the eyes of the other men on him. "You're off work today?"

"Yes, this is my day off. I thought I'd come see where you work and what you do." Christina's face reddened slightly when she spoke.

Despite the crispness of the air Gust felt warmth enveloping him and a light sweat break out on his body. "I think maybe I'll tell the foreman I need a break now. I can show you around."

"I'd like to see the inside of the building. Cora says it's dark and smoky and very interesting."

"I don't think they want a woman inside. It would make the men nervous. Besides it's too full of cinders for a lady like you."

Christina tilted her head to one side, held his eyes with hers and smiled. "Please, I really want to see where you work. Couldn't you ask to show me around?"

Gust was torn. On one hand he didn't want to look foolish in front of the other men, but on the other hand Christina looked so attractive in the blue scarf that matched her eyes. Finally he stammered, "I think maybe if you're real careful to stay out of the way, I can show you some of it." The foreman, wise in the way of women and men in love, quickly gave permission saying to Gust, "You're responsible to see that she doesn't get in the way or get hurt. And don't take too long."

Gust held the door open and Christina stepped into Hell.

The noise hit her like a physical force almost pushing her back out the door. Hammers pounding, engines chugging, men shouting and then a screaming burst from a steam whistle stabbed her ears. She took a deep breath and moved into the noise.

The deep breath was a mistake. The room was filled with smoke and steam that burned her throat and set her coughing.

When she regained her composure, she saw Gust's look of concern. She could see that he was thinking, "This is no place for a lady; I've got to take her out of here."

Before he could act she grabbed his hand and pulled him further into the murky gloom of the large room. Narrow strands of light filtered in through grease covered windows. Lanterns hung on the walls casting long shadows in the gloom, and the men working on the locomotives were using kerosene torches to see by.

Glancing down she saw water spilled on the floor stained black with the soot and cinders that covered everything. She dropped Gust's hand and lifted her skirt to avoid the mess. A locomotive was sitting in the center of the building and, as she watched, it began to turn. She leaned close to Gust and shouted, "What are they doing?"

"Come, I'll show you."

He led her over to the engine and told her what was happening by pointing and gesturing. The engine to be repaired was run onto a central turntable. Two men took long wooden handles and inserted them into sockets on each end of the table. They leaned into the handles and pushed, moving the tracks of the turntable in line with another set of tracks that ran into a stall where repairmen were waiting.

Before the locomotive started moving, Gust pulled her by the hand and led her out of the building. "You don't want to be inside when they move the engine," he explained. "It'll throw sparks all over the place and your good dress could get holes burned in it."

Christina was flushed with excitement. Men had such exciting jobs. She thanked Gust for an interesting tour and gave his hand an encouraging squeeze as she said good bye.

As she left she glanced back over her shoulder to see Gust watching her. His look was soft and faraway. Cora was right— the excitement of showing her where he worked had moved him closer to her. Inside she bubbled with delight.

The women were a source of precious information about Gust and his job. Christina was utterly fascinated by everything connected with him. Maud told her about an old boyfriend who had just started work as a brakeman when Watertown was just getting started as a railroad town. He had been momentarily distracted while switching engines, was knocked off the top of the boxcar and crushed under the wheels.

Maud was kneading bread in the kitchen. Christina paused peeling potatoes and asked, "Do you think Gust could get hurt?"

By now Maud accepted the fact that Christina was preoccupied with Gust. "The worst he'll do is to strain his back or drop something on his foot and crush it. The ones who have the dangerous job are the brakemen. You watch and see how many come through here got fingers missing. If they get past the first year alive, there's not much they can't do. Listen to the men talk; you'll hear how much other railroad men respect them."

The other railroad workers allowed as to how the brakemen had the most dangerous job. A man could be injured doing any of the jobs on the railroad, but brakemen had the highest mortality rate. Watching a good brakeman run along the top of the boxcars and twist the wheel that controlled the brake while the cars jerked and shook was as good as seeing a circus performance. Gust would sometimes stop and stand watching with awe at a brakeman's sense of balance in his precarious position.

One morning Gust arrived early to pick up a load of machine parts. He sat on the wagon watching two boxcars being coupled. A young man with hair the color of ripe wheat under a brakeman's cap was running ahead of a car that was headed toward a stationary car. The two cars had almost come together when the moving one hit something on the rail and jumped the track. The brakeman saw it toppling toward him, turned to escape, but tripped and was crushed between the two cars.

Gust heard a sharp crack as the side of the loose car pinned the man against the stationary car. There was a snapping like tree branches being broken. The switchman yelled at the engineer, "Move the locomotive forward."

Gust jumped from his wagon and sprinted to the trapped brakeman. He arrived just as the engine moved forward freeing the man who dropped limply into his arms. His breath was coming in short gasps and blood trickled out of the corner of his mouth. His face was gray under his pale complexion. He reminded Gust of his seventeen-year-old cousin, Johnny, in Sweden. He was still alive but his chest had been crushed.

Other men arrived at the scene. The switchman pointed at Gust and three others and said, "You men carry him to the yardmaster's office. Hans, move. Go get the doc. Tell him we got a man crushed between cars."

The men carrying the brakeman were silent. Accidents were common, and only the youngest weren't aware of how easy it was to get maimed or killed. The switchman broke the silence. "Brady here's a good man. Green but good. If he lives, he'll probably make a good brakeman. Now he knows this can be a deadly business."

The brakeman was still conscious but still unable to speak when the newly hired company doctor arrived carrying a shiny leather bag that looked like it had just been taken off some store shelf. Gust, looking at the doctor, thought, "He's no older than me."

Taking out a knife the doctor cut the man's jacket, shirt and long underwear off and began probing the chest. At certain points the injured man groaned in pain. Finally satisfied he had found the broken places, the doctor straightened up and said,

"Nothing much wrong here. He's got his slats stove in. I'll set' em and wrap him good. A few weeks in bed he'll be all right."

When he was finished, he pointed to Gust's rig. "Load him in that wagon and take him to his boarding house. He's not going to be able to do much for himself for a bit. Somebody will have to look in on him now and then and see he gets fed."

Clarence Brady, the injured brakeman, was only eighteen. His injuries gave Christina and Gust a daily opportunity to see each other. Christina brought Brady his supper just about the time Gust came around to chat with him about the day's doings and help move him around to prevent bedsores. Christina was impressed with how tender Gust could be as he helped Brady move around. She could picture him as a father caring for an injured child.

Within a week Brady, while still disabled, was eager for company to break the boredom of his solitude. During the day he had only occasional visits from some of the women to attend to his needs. While he couldn't talk much yet, he liked to listen to others talk about what was happening.

Attending to Brady gave Christina and Gust plenty of opportunity to talk, but the talk was never of marriage. If Christina nudged it in that direction, Gust only got a blank look on his face. Christina felt that, if something didn't happen soon, she was going to erupt like a whale's spout.

By the time Brady was able to take care of himself, spring was coming on. The railroad workers with homesteads were heading home to get the crops in. Gust still had not played his hand. One morning before the men were to go out on the job, she glanced up from the dishwater and saw him standing at the kitchen door. He motioned to her.

Her heart started pounding, and she was suddenly unable to meet his gaze. Was he finally going to talk about his feelings? He cleared his throat and said, "Christina, I need to stop work to go take care of my plowing and planting."

"Yes, I do, too."

"Will you be back in the fall to work here?"

"If you come back, I will, too." Christina felt he was slipping away. What could she do? She cranked up her courage and said, "I might be able to get up to your farm this summer. Could I drop by and see you?"

The suggestion emboldened him. "No. I think maybe I should come by your place."

As she worked on getting her crops planted, Christina found herself scanning the horizon to the northwest. Occasionally she thought she saw something move and her heart would begin to beat faster. At night in the soddy she missed the sounds of people and the closeness of the women she worked with in Watertown. The loneliness began to eat away at her spirits.

It was a warm spring day two weeks after she had gotten home. Christina was planting corn on land that her neighbor to the south, Bakke, had plowed for her last October. She stopped to rest. Her hair was matted damply to her head, and sweat dripped from her forehead making tracks in the dust on her face. Her dress, soaked with moisture, hung limply from her body.

She checked the horizon to the northwest. She stared and blinked rubbing her eyes to make sure she wasn't seeing things. Was that a man on a horse? Hastily she fought to smooth her hair and mop the sweat from her face with her skirt.

It was Gust on his mule. She dropped her hoe and hurried toward him. "You've come to visit then?" she asked, trying to keep her voice steady. Why did he have to come when she smelled like a cow in heat?

"Hadn't seen this neck of the woods, so I thought I'd come over to see how the planting is going."

"Well, come down off the mule and we'll go in the soddy. I've got a pot of coffee that'll still be warm on the stove."

As they sat at the table drinking, Gust had trouble looking directly at her. She reached out and put her hand over his. He turned his hand over and took hers. Their eyes met and he said, "Christina, I miss you. I can't live on the farm without you. Will you marry me?"

The marriage license said,

> This certifies that Gust Carlson of Hamlin County Dakota Territory and Christina Gunnerson of Hamlin County Dakota Territory were UNITED IN HOLY MATRIMONY according to the Ordinance of GOD and the laws of the Territory of Dakota at Kellerton on the seventeen day of May in the year of Lord One Thousand Eight Hundred and Eighty Four.

CHAPTER TWENTY-FIVE

SHEEN

$\mathfrak{C}$hristina stepped back from the slop pail, took a dipper of water to rinse out her mouth and sat down to catch her breath. The morning sickness was less of a problem this far along. At least now she could sometimes hold down her first breakfast. This wasn't one of those days.

She first became aware that she was pregnant when she found it sometimes took three breakfasts before she could keep one down. She didn't feel particularly sick other than her stomach refused to settle down until midday.

She ate anyway. Given how much work there was to do, she felt she had to eat something to keep her strength up, particularly since she got tired so easily. The bed would pull at her and she would find herself napping in the afternoon. Just for a few minutes she told herself. Before she knew it, two hours had passed, and Gust was clanking pots on the stove heating himself something to eat.

She ran her hands down the whitened wall admiring how Gust had made it look like plaster. Gust was handy with tools, and the sod house he had built was superior to any that Christina had been in before. He had mixed clay with water and put three layers of it over the inside dirt walls. When it dried he covered the clay with several coats of calcimine giving the walls a solid, smooth finish. The opening in the sod wall for the windows had been cut large inside the room and slanted narrow toward the outside glass, allowing the light to spread out into the room.

She heard Gust coming back from the field and felt warmth spread through her arms and shoulders as he came in the door. Gust was an even better husband than she had hoped for. It was a marvel to her that she had found the man who had appeared in her dream in Norway years before.

The sound of his boots on the wood floor delighted her. The broom she had bought years ago as a symbol of what she wanted to have someday could now be used to sweep dirt outside. The floor was made of boards that Gust had patiently hacked out of logs hauled from Lake Marsh.

He took the dipper from the water pail and took a long drink. "Ole Swansen will be coming by for supper today." He sat down on the bed. "I think he's not doing so good. When the hail ruined his crop, it took the sand right out of him."

In June when Christina had met Ole, Gust had warned her, "Ole's wife died this past winter. He was perky last summer, but now he don't move fast and sits a lot just staring."

A tall man, who once had to hunch down to get in the door when he entered the soddy, now didn't even have to take off his hat. His body was shortened by his bowed head and the way he turned his shoulders in and down. Gust had commented to Christina that Ole looked like he was shrinking. There were bags under his eyes and the corners of his mouth drooped as if weights hung from them. Christina thought, so long since those clothes had been washed, he could stand them out in the yard and they wouldn't even need a post to make them into a scarecrow.

"Sit down. Sit down." Christina said to Ole as she hurried to finish frying the chicken killed "special" for the day. "You look like you could use some food. Are you eating all right?"

Ole's voice was soft and his speech halting. Each word was squeezed out with effort. "Sorry to put you to so much trouble,

Mrs. Carlson. I ain't much for eating since the diphtheria carried away my Missus. Seems I don't need much to keep going."

Christina kept up chatter throughout the meal trying to stay away from the ordeals pioneers faced. She had to work hard for topics since everything that could go wrong had gone wrong on his farm. Ole only picked at what she put before him.

As they finished his favorite rice pudding, Gust turned the conversation back to hard times. He looked at Ole and said, "You came here the same year Axel and me did. We sure didn't know what Dakota held for us."

"If I had knowed, I'd a stayed in Norway. Lost most of my crop to prairie fire that first year. Cattle died next winter. Now my corn and wheat that was doing good was beaten into the ground by hail. God doesn't intend for me to stay here in America."

"Not stay? What else would you do?" Gust asked.

Ole sat a long time. Christina and Gust eyes met over his bowed head. The silent question passed between them. "Did he hear us?"

Finally, he started to speak, his voice now somewhat more forceful. "I came here with more than any of you. Lilly had money from a dowry, crops ruined, my babies got stillborn, my Missus dies. God has forsaken me."

He put his head in his hands and leaned forward. They waited, unsure if he would continue. "I think I'll go back to Norway. I'll sell the two cattle I've got left cheap. My horses get boils on their shoulders and can't pull. They ain't worth much even to a crooked horse trader. I figure the house'll bring something. If I sell everything, it ought to give me enough for passage back to Bergen. Might even leave me a little extra to buy a small place there."

"What will you do in Bergen?" Christina asked.

"I won't have the prairie fire to wipe me out or the hail come and hit my crops. It won't be worse because it can't get worse than it is here. No, I have to go home."

The light breeze sent waves across the field of grain made golden by the morning sun. Albert Sheen was having a good year selling his wares to the settlers. Hopes were running high that the crops would be good this year, and the homesteaders were willing to dig into their secret places for money. His business would be better if he took trade, but he had no way to carry chickens, pigs and potatoes in his buggy.

Albert knew he was close to the Carlson farm. He hoped that Gust's new wife was more friendly than Axel's. Mahilda Carlson seldom bought anything without consulting with her husband and often as not he told her, "You don't need that. We have better uses for our money than to buy junk that peddlers carry."

Axel spoke to his wife in Swedish thinking that Albert wouldn't understand. He hadn't bothered to find out, or maybe didn't care that, as a peddler working in a Scandinavian settlement, Albert had picked up enough Swedish to carry on trade conversations and a little bit more.

All his life Albert had put up with rude people who distrusted him because he was one of the hated Jews. He was tempted to tell Axel that besides speaking English and understanding some Swedish, he spoke Polish, German, Yiddish and understood Russian. But he held his tongue. Holding your tongue was one way to stay alive in a dangerous world, and Albert, even after the years in America, was not totally convinced that this was a safe place for a Jew.

This year business was so good that he decided to pass up Axel Carlson's farm. Besides, Axel's wife didn't set that good a table.

Albert had emigrated from Poland to escape poverty and prejudice. Arriving in 1874, he tried to make a living in New York, but there was too much competition. Besides the city was overcrowded and full of strange illnesses and, unlike his fellow immigrants, he wanted space to move around. So he went west.

First, he worked the farms in Wisconsin with a pack on his back with small items like needles and knives. Then, on to Minnesota where he got ahead enough to buy a horse and small cart. He could have stayed as the community grew and bought a small store, but he was used to moving around and meeting people. With Dakota Territory taking on new settlers and few stores, he moved on.

Sheen respected the fact that peddlers like him were the pioneer women's news service. They carried month old news from the big cities and week old news about what was happening around the area. A good peddler was a bit of a gossip, and Albert was a very good peddler. Until they could get a newspaper in the county, the settlers best bet for information were men like Albert.

His horse broke into a trot. She smelled water and knew that rest from the hot sun was at hand. Gust Carlson's soddy came into sight. The woman who had been hoeing in the garden beside the soddy wiped her hands on her apron and came forward to meet him. She was tall with strong arms and shoulders. As he got closer, Albert felt a nervous tension in his chest and a cold chill run down his back.

It took a moment for Albert to recognize that with her high cheekbones this woman reminded him of a Cossack. He hated the Cossacks who were used by the Russians to control his part of Poland. He had seen them ride into a group of protesting Poles, slashing with their sabers and whips leaving bloody screaming people in their wake.

The woman pushed at her hair moving wisps out of her eyes. When she smiled and said, "Good morning," the image of a Cossack vanished, and he again saw a countrywoman struggling for existence in a land filled with hazards.

He spoke to her in broken Swedish. "My name's Albert Sheen. I have some beautiful and useful things to show you today, if you have time."

She smiled, then as if embarrassed held her hand in front of her mouth. She's ashamed of her large front teeth he thought.

"I'm Christina Gunnerson." Again she paused and reddened slightly. "No, I mean I'm Christina Carlson. Gust's my husband. I was hoping you might be around. I've got coffee on the stove and some molasses cookies. Come set a while, and then I'll look to see if you have what I need."

Albert felt an inner tension relax. This woman didn't react like someone who wouldn't trust him simply because he was Jewish. "I'll need to water my horse first. Then I'll join you."

He had expected her to ask about the crops around the county or what the more distant neighbors were up to. Instead she said, "You talk like you come over on the boat too. When was that?"

The question was not a usual one and caught him off guard. "I came over from the old country in 1874." He paused, not sure of what else to say.

"Oh," Christina said, "You came over on a sailing vessel. That must have been very slow and very hard."

"It was a hard time. It took us six weeks. We were all terribly seasick and that weakened us. Seven people were buried at sea. We hadn't been warned about the medical examination; and when we came into Boston, the American doctors found some of the passengers had diseases and were sent back to Europe."

They began comparing notes on the trip over and the problems of adjusting to American ways. Christina was so interested in him and his adventures that he felt warmth toward her that was unusual for him. She even became much better looking than the tired farm woman who had met him out in the field.

When she said, "I have my own homestead over on the other side of Lake Poinsett," he became curious and encouraged her to say more.

"I put in a crop of wheat and corn right before I got married. Now I'm thinking of selling it, so we can buy more land nearby. If I can get enough, we can finally build a real house to live in, instead of this old soddy."

Sheen expected his customers to be hardy, but he knew few women who had set up their own farms much less remained long enough to own them. In his experience only about one out of four survived through the ordeals to permanent ownership. He picked up another molasses cookie and took a bite. He didn't really like them, but so many of the Norwegian women made them that he had adapted to the taste.

He chewed thoughtfully and began, "The new immigrants are pouring into the territory now. Good land is hard to get, with a ready supply of water even harder. If it were my land, I would do everything I could to hold it another year. Next summer prices should be up, and you will have the money you need to buy more land here and enough left over for lumber to build your house."

"But, the land we want is for sale now. We'll never be able to buy land any cheaper than what we can get this piece for."

"Borrow, or beg or do what you must to buy it now. But hold your farm until next year. I go to Brookings for supplies. I hear things. Maybe I'll hear of a buyer."

He paused. Careful of his next offer. He knew that Scandinavians were careful with their money and that some did not understand how money could get money. "Mrs. Carlson, let me be honest with you. In a year land prices will be up. I'm sure I will be able to find a buyer who'll give you more than you'll be able to get from anyone else. To be fair to me I'll take a small finder's fee from the buyer for finding your land for him."

Christina had to think about that for a few minutes. Money was a bit of mystery, but she sensed she could trust this man. His air of knowing what he was doing convinced her that she would make a profit if she allowed him some also.

"The law says I have six months after I leave my farm to sell it. I'll harvest the crop in September. That means I'll need to clear up my business before March."

As Gust and his team of mules came over the rise to the north of the farm, he saw a handsome well fed roan tied to the water trough. From the brooms and churns sticking out of the cart standing next to the house he recognized it as belonging to Albert Sheen. He had bought a few things from the peddler in the past and enjoyed passing the time with him.

Gust stopped by the cart and looked its contents over. There were kerchiefs, bonnets, boxes of finger rings and earrings, combs, brushes and assorted pots and pans. Christina looked up as Gust came in the door. She and Albert were standing by the table examining assorted ribbons, tapes, pieces of lace, needles and spools of thread. Sheen was slightly shorter than Christina and very slender. His hands were weasel quick, the buttons and thimbles he was showing Christina appearing and disappearing as if bewitched. The scene reminded Gust of a magician he saw one time in Minneapolis who could make objects appear out of thin air.

Sheen wore a black suit, white shirt and black bow tie. A small beard, pointed at the end, a prominent nose and intelligent eyes that took in everything added to the illusion that he was a middleman for the hidden people. But it was the eyes that made Gust nervous. Was it possible that the man could actually read what was on your mind?

"Ah, Mr. Carlson, your lovely new wife is just picking out a few pretties that she can use to make beautiful new clothes for your new arrival."

The comment about Christina's pregnancy embarrassed Gust who ignored it. "You have a good looking horse outside. Business must be good."

"Yes. Lots of newcomers in the county and more arriving every day. One day I'll have to settle down and start a regular store. For now I do well enough. A bad year for crops will be a bad year for Albert Sheen."

Christina placed a package of needles, some ribbons and buttons to one side and stood staring at a set of combs to hold her hair in place.

"Take them," Gust said. "We have little enough that's fancy here."

Gust saw a flicker of a smile race across Sheen's lips.

After a dinner of fried chicken and boiled potatoes Gust went out to help Sheen hook the horse up to the cart. As Sheen adjusted the collar he said, "Children coming. Now you're going to need clothes for them. Nice woman like your Christina shouldn't have to do it all with a needle. Why don't you do like the Americans hereabout when they're expecting their first baby and buy your wife one of those new machines that does the job? I can get a good one in Brookings and make you a good price."

Gust felt his mind being read again. In his last sentence Sheen had spoken of two things that were important to him. He wanted to learn and adjust to American ways, and he was fascinated with the new. Especially if it made work easier and led to a better life. They discussed price and delivery details.

As he drove away from the farm Sheen thought, "A good marriage between pleasant people. How is it that one brother can be so different from the other? One tied to old ways, one facing toward the new. I think maybe I'll throw a bit of luck their way. It would sure make Axel mad if his younger brother did better than him."

And so the land was bought from Swansen. Swansen's small wooden house was moved on a sled the half-mile to Gust's place. Only two rooms and a shed, it was sturdy and would provide lumber for the new house when Christina's land was sold.

Six months later Albert Sheen brought news of a buyer for Christina's claim. The profit as he had foretold was enough to pay off the debt for Swansen's claim and to buy lumber from Watertown for the new house.

Elmer Bakke came up and helped them build a real wooden house of four rooms which eventually became ten.

And the babies came. Eight of them.

CPSIA information can be obtained
at www.ICGtesting.com
Printed in the USA
FFHW02n0116200918
48368354-52206FF